The Pursuit of Mary McBride

Bruce Cooke

BALBOA.PRESS
A DIVISION OF HAY HOUSE

Balboa Press books may be ordered through booksellers or by contacting:

Balboa Press
A Division of Hay House
1663 Liberty Drive
Bloomington, IN 47403
www.balboapress.com.au
AU TFN: 1 800 844 925 (Toll Free inside Australia)
AU Local: 0283 107 086 (+61 2 8310 7086 from outside Australia)

Print information available on the last page.

ISBN: 978-1-9822-9018-4 (sc)
ISBN: 978-1-9822-9019-1 (e)

Balboa Press rev. date: 04/05/2021

CONTENTS

Acknowledgements xiii

Chapter One 1
Chapter Two 12
Chapter Three 27
Chapter Four 45
Chapter Five 62
Chapter Six 76
Chapter Seven 85
Chapter Eight 93
Chapter Nine 104
Chapter Ten 114
Chapter Eleven 120
Chapter Twelve 128
Chapter Thirteen 145
Chapter Fourteen 153
Chapter Fifteen 163
Chapter Sixteen 174
Chapter Seventeen 182
Chapter Eighteen 189
Chapter Nineteen 195
Chapter Twenty 208
Chapter Twenty-One 216
Chapter Twenty-Two 222

About Bruce Cooke 233

Also by Bruce Cooke

The Irish Retribution

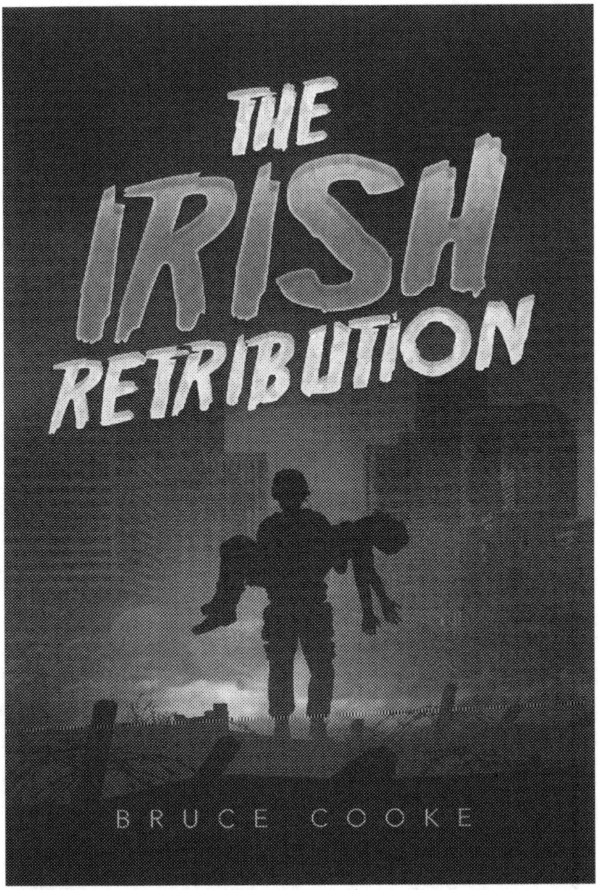

Acknowledgements

To Jess Corbet who worked tirelessly to eliminate my mistakes and point out my errors. She made me aware of simple mistakes that I would have ignored, and thanks to her I hope it is a very readable book.

To my darling wife, Nancy, who succumbed to a terrible disease and left me heartbroken in 2007. She was my inspiration and will remain in my memory forever. Her confidence in me enabled me to continue writing even when I was having no success.

Chapter One

London 1832

The three bodies hanging on the scaffold brought little comfort for their well-being. They were still suspended by their necks, moving slowly in the breeze, their arms still tied behind them, their legs three feet above the ground where they had undoubtedly kicked until they slowly strangled to death. Crows sat on the scaffold waiting to feast on any other morsel available seeing their eyes had gone. They had been there for over a week and left to rot as an example to others not to break the laws of society, even though their crimes may have been minor. Rebecca Smith noted one was a woman of perhaps thirty, her face turning black, her breasts visible for all to see, and she wondered what her crime had been.

The prisoners were taken to the court, but Rebecca's confidence in the outcome of her trial wasn't shaken. She fidgeted uncomfortably as she sat on the hard wooden bench in the bowels of the old Bailey, waiting with eight other women for her trial to begin. A depressing room, she thought, solely designed to make the defendants feel intimidated before they even faced the court. The cold grey building had seen many a prisoner brought before the bench to face English justice, with unfortunate results.

She watched apprehensively as a large cockroach scampered over the floor, only to be crushed under the boot of the grinning guard. The smirk on his face gave her the feeling she might be next.

Three times in six months they had been brought before Sir George Cavendish. It seemed to be a regular appearance, and as usual she expected the result to be the mandatory five pounds fine. After all, wasn't Sir George one of her best customers as were most of London's gentry? The bordello was well known to the gentry, and those who could afford the prices usually went away well satisfied.

Just a chance to get away from their prudish wives was enough to draw their custom. Where else could the delights of naked young flesh be so readily available with the added bonus of the excitement provided by these young nymphs?

The disgrace of a Lord or Magistrate pursuing the kitchen maid for carnal delights would bring gossip all over London Town. So the temptation of the high-class courtesans, all indeed beautiful and who lavished the attention men sought but never received from their middle and upper class wives, was reward in itself.

It mattered not if their stomachs hung over their trousers, or their heads resembled a baby's bottom, they were each treated as royalty, making most more than willing to pay dearly for the pleasure.

London was not the ideal place to live in 1832. Only those well versed with society and with sufficient funds to warrant the position enjoyed life. For the majority of the population it was a matter of living on one's wits, something Rebecca had learned from the moment nine years before when she had been deserted by her father at the tender age of ten.

* * * * *

When her mother had died suddenly, her father wasn't prepared to hinder his way of life by being saddled with a sniveling child and just never returned to the rat infested room they had called home. She quickly learned that to survive one had to steal and deal with all sorts of unsavory characters in streets filled with orphans, thieves, pickpockets, footpads, and murderers.

After starving on the street week in and week out, she found the one act of kindness that actually saved her life. Scavenging through refuse thrown in the lane at the back of a brothel one cold winter's day, she felt the cold hand of the madam grab her by the collar. The other urchins with her ran off, but Rebecca slipped on an icy patch, turned her ankle and fell to the ground directly under the baleful stare of the woman. A light snow fell gently. The woman scowled as she brought her to her feet.

"And who might you be, girl?" she said with arms folded, towering over the frightened child.

"Rebecca Smith, lady. I weren't doin' no harm."

The appalling accent made the woman turn up her nose.

"And just what is it you were trying to steal?"

"I weren't tryin' to steal nuthin. I'm just hungry."

"How old are you, girl?" The woman looked frightening with her hands now on her hips looking down at the trembling child. Rebecca gulped quickly, expecting the wrath of the woman.

"Twelve I think, lady."

"And where do you live?"

"I don't live nowhere. I just sleeps where I can find a spot."

"In the gutter by the smell of you. I gather you're an orphan."

Rebecca watched the women exaggerate the motion of extracting some foul smell with her nose.

"Me mum died a couple of years back. Me dad ran orf an' left me."

Rebecca heard an audible sigh. She had little idea of the woman's background. A whore she might be, but she herself had been in much the same position when she was twelve, and her heart went out to the children in the same circumstances.

"I think you had better come in and have something to eat, and perhaps a good wash," she said, averting her nose.

Rebecca jumped at the offer and followed the woman into the house. Her eyes opened wide when a bowl of hot broth was placed in front of her with a slice of fresh bread. She gripped the bowl tightly and shoveled the hot broth into her mouth as though afraid this pleasure would be taken from her.

The woman carefully studied her features as Rebecca ate. A thin undernourished body supported the clothes she wore which were nothing more than rags. A pretty child with long, unkempt dark hair, and big, bright brown eyes. However, even at twelve it was obvious to Claire, someone who had a talent for such observations, that Rebecca was going to be a very attractive woman, that is, if she ever reached adult hood.

"Do you know what this place is, Rebecca?" She stood with her arms folded but had a soft look as she spoke to the child.

Rebecca in turn appeared to study her, as well. Claire took in the young girl's eyes taking in her fine clothes. She gave the little one a smile to reassure her she meant her no harm.

"It's a men's club, isn't it?" Rebecca paused only for a second in her assault on the bowl of broth, her fingers turning white and grasping the spoon tightly.

The woman laughed heartily at Rebecca's innocence.

"You could call it that for it's the name upon the door. The London Club for Gentleman is a place where men come for pleasure, a pleasure that only women can give them."

Rebecca paused from her assault on the broth. "You mean you serves them drinks and food."

"Drinks and food? And a little more than that," she said, laughing at the innocent comment.

"What else then?" Rebecca continued to eat, speaking between mouthfuls.

"Why for the warmth of a woman's body. Of course, they are willing to pay for such comfort. Do you understand what I mean?" She waited for a reply, not knowing if the child really did understand.

Rebecca nodded understanding perfectly. "I've seen the whores in the streets. Some say they get three pence for doing it."

Claire laughed loudly. "I dare say they do, my dear, but this is a class establishment, and we only entertain the very best of society."

"You mean you get more than three pence?"

The woman tightened her lips in an amused smile. "Considerably more. How would you like to work for me?"

"Doin' what?" asked Rebecca. She raised one eyebrow as she stared at the woman.

"Cleaning the rooms and helping in the kitchen. I will pay you two shillings a week and feed you."

"Cor!" gasped Rebecca. "Can I have somewhere to sleep, as well?"

"There's a cellar. You can sleep there on a bunk. However, you must follow certain conditions."

"Such as?"

Claire took on a stern approach. "There must be no stealing, and you must never mention any gentleman's name away from this establishment.

To do so would mean you would be back on the street at once. I will provide you with more presentable clothes, and you must bathe at least once a week."

"Can I sleep here tonight?"

"Of course. I'll arrange for your bath and get you some clothes. The sooner we get rid of those rags the better, and you can start work at once."

Rebecca hesitated. "What does I call you, lady?"

"You call me Miss Thomas. We'll see how things work out."

* * * * *

Later Rebecca lay back naked in the tub enjoying the warmth of the water. Pleased to be off the streets fighting to stay alive with the rest of the urchins, she was comforted by the fact that she at least had a roof over her head and food to eat.

* * * * *

For four years she worked at the brothel, doing her chores diligently, making sure to finish her chores exactly the way Claire Thomas expected. She watched the girls come and go with great envy and longed to wear some of the clothes they displayed.

"How much do the girls get for each customer, Claire?" she asked one day. Claire allowed Rebecca to address her by her first name now since Rebecca had become a favorite of the establishment.

"The gentlemen pay one sovereign and I get half, Rebecca. Why do you ask?"

"I wouldn't mind having some money like that to buy some dresses like the girls have."

She watched as Claire studied her critically. Rebecca was actually a year older than Claire had been when she had begun the profession.

"Sit down, child while we talk. Whoring is an honorable trade, Rebecca, providing it is done in an establishment such as The Gentleman's Club. When it is done on the streets with the scum of London, it's very dangerous. You're very pretty and could be an asset to my establishment, but you need guidance I am willing to offer you along with the other girls here. I want none of you caught with a bun in the oven."

"I'll do whatever you tell me, Claire," Rebecca enthused. The thought of making big money was tempting.

"I suppose it's ridiculous to ask if you can read or write."

Rebecca looked down, her head bowed, and her cheeks felt flushed.

"Then you will have to learn. I want no illiterate girls working for me."

"I'd like to learn, Ma'am."

Some of the girls had told her they made over eight sovereigns a week. She really wanted to get into that sort of money.

"Very well. First you must make the men think that you consider them to be the most wonderful lovers, no matter how bad they might be. Some of them will be over fifty, maybe older, but you must learn to ignore their age and their appearance."

"I've seen some of them. Sometimes they can hardly get up the stairs."

"Men like to look upon a naked female body and to touch your breasts. At all times you must smile and always tell them how magnificent their manhood is, even if they are as small as a terrier's stumpy tail. Encourage them to take some wine and engage them in conversation as best you can, always agreeing with them."

"And when they are finished?"

"You stay with them until they're ready to go or until they fall asleep. You never, never steal from them. Is that understood?"

"Yes, Ma'am," nodded Rebecca.

Claire touched her chin with her finger. "Have you been with a man, or with one of those street urchins?"

"No, Ma'am, not yet."

"Good. Then it is time for you to learn a trick or two the proper way." Claire disappeared into the pantry returning with a fresh carrot, which she handed to Rebecca. "I will use this to demonstrate some skills you will find very useful if you are to succeed in this business."

What Clare could do with a carrot astonished Rebecca, and so her lessons began. She learned how to please a man with both her body and her mouth as well as how to flatter and admire and appear interested in him alone. At first she was clumsy, but Claire guided her in the right direction, and she became most skillful in the art of exciting and satisfying a male client of the subtler arts. She spent three days a week learning how to read and write, and engage in sensible conversation.

During breakfast, current affairs were discussed with the other girls to enable them to converse with the customers on their own level. Until then she had known nothing of the affairs of France and its relationship with England, the discovery of the new country by Captain James Cook, and of the transportation of English prisoners to the Colony.

Three months later saw her ready for her initiation into the working side of the brothel, and her first customer was a seventy-year-old man of some influence among the gentry. Although the action was somewhat brief, her conversation and friendly attitude delighted the man, and he praised her talents both to Claire and to other likely customers.

Word soon spread about the new girl at the London Club, and she became much sought after, entertaining some of the most respected men of the community, including Sir George Cavendish. Claire made sure she kept up her lessons in reading and writing, a task she Rebecca relished.

* * * * *

When she reached nineteen, she was the toast of the town, and all the gentry craved to have this beautiful courtesan. However, a change in government brought a more severe view of the moral fiber of the London community. Orders issued meant to keep the salons in check, much to the chagrin of some of the clubs' patrons. Twice the Gentleman's Club had been raided, with most of the girls arrested. The fine in each case had been five pounds; a sum easily earned back over two nights by each of the girls. It became a standing joke with bets taken as to when the next raid would be held just to make the law appear to be working.

The latest raid had occurred near midnight, and the chief constable came in red faced when he had to face Claire.

"Sorry, Miss Claire, my orders are to make an arrest."

"I understand, Patrick," she said smiling. "I expect to see you here tomorrow night."

"Wouldn't miss it for the world. This time I have to arrest all the girls."

"What? The whole eight of them?" Claire was appalled.

"Yeah, don't worry. The case will be held tomorrow, and they'll be back working by tomorrow night."

Claire sighed. "This is really an inconvenience, Patrick. I have several men from the legal fraternity coming tomorrow."

"I'm sure it will just be the usual fine, and then they'll be free to leave."

Next morning, the group sat patiently waiting for their case to come before the bench.

A fine was but a small irritation when one considered that the penalty for stealing by a member of the lower class was to be shipped off to Van Dieman's land in the New World.

The girls sat talking as they waited for their call, each laughing and telling of the men they had and of the nonsense some of them spoke about. None appeared worried. Rebecca's instincts told her something was not quite right. Earlier, she had been confident as to the outcome, but a doubt crept into her mind. The atmosphere in the courtroom was subdued whereas other times it had been more jovial.

"It's a wonder Sir George can keep a straight face when 'e fines us," one said. "He had me twice last week."

"Time to go, girls," called the guard, and they entered the dock as a group. When Rebecca saw who was sitting on the bench her heart began to race. "Oh Gawd, its Puritan Perc," she gasped. "Where's Sir George?" she whispered to the man who led them in.

"He's in bed sick. Has been for a couple of days. Sir Percival Tait has been taking 'is cases. Been real nasty to the prisoners he 'as, too."

Rebecca gripped the railing of the dock, a feeling of doom overtaking her.

Sir Percival Tait, or Puritan Perc as he was known, was renowned for his stern discipline and drastic punishment of unfortunate prisoners found guilty of any crime. His nickname came about because of his deep study of the Bible and the harsh line he took with those he considered to have broken God's law. He considered it his duty to protect the God fearing members of society from the evil clutches of those wretched temptresses.

Rebecca watched him as he listened to the evidence; his grey wig not moving, his face masked with a blank expression as he stared at the eight girls clustered in the dock. Rebecca saw his eyes fall on her. I wish he had attended the club, she thought. Maybe he would have had a smile on his face to give us some comfort and hope for a light sentence.

Perc looked at the sheet placed in front of him and read it slowly. "Apart from whoring, Bailiff, is there any other crime of which these women are accused?"

"Yes, M' Lord. One of their customers has complained that ten sovereigns were stolen from his purse while attending the establishment."

Rebecca gasped. This couldn't be right. She sucked in a breath with a feeling of dismay. This was the first she had heard of a theft in the bordello. To steal always meant instant dismissal. Claire had made that very clear from the beginning

"And is the gentleman present to give evidence?" asked Sir Percy.

"Yes, M'lord, he is."

The girls all looked to see the accuser. A short, stout man entered the witness box and took the oath. Rebecca recognized him from two nights before. While she had not served the man, she was aware of his bad temper and his abuse of the girl who had. Claire had asked him to leave and not return. Rebecca remembered him leaving red faced from the laughter of some of the other customers.

"And what have you to say, sir?" asked Sir Percy.

"First, before I testify, I would like to keep my name suppressed to save embarrassment for other people, M' lord."

The judge cleared his throat and looked around red faced. To show favoritism would be frowned upon. "Very well. We will call you Mister. Brown for the sake of the court. Now your evidence please?"

"Two nights ago I attended the London's Gentleman's Club and was entertained by one of the accused."

"Could you point her out?'

The man pointed his finger at the girl next to Rebecca, and she paled visibly.

"While she was entertaining me, my purse was taken and ten sovereigns removed. I didn't notice the theft until I returned home. It's obvious the money was shared by all of them as they were most anxious for me to leave the premises."

"That's a lie," said Rebecca, jumping to her feet and slamming her fist on the front of the dock. "He was thrown out for abuse."

A murmur of disapproval ran over the people watching. One didn't shout at the judge.

"Be quiet, woman. Are you suggesting that someone as honorable as Mister. Brown would commit perjury?"

Rebecca became a little subdued. "Yes, M' lord. No one has ever had anything stolen from the Gentleman's Club since I have been there. I suggest the gentleman is mistaken."

"The word of a whore carries little credibility in this court. I find you all guilty. Have you anything to say?" he addressed the girls, who had now abandoned their frivolity.

All were stunned by the verdict. They looked at each other with blank expressions before answering.

"No, M'lord," each answered as they braced themselves for his verdict.

"I find you each guilty of offences against the common decency of the citizens of London and the Crown. This crime of selling sexual favors must be stamped out, and I intend to come down heavily against those found guilty of such crimes. It matters not to me whether you are sluts of the street or courtesans serving a higher clientele; you must be taught that this sort of profession will not be tolerated. Are there any previous convictions?" he asked the clerk.

"Yes, M'lord."

"Please read them so that all may hear."

"Patricia Stock, four previous convictions, Rebecca Smith, two convictions, Madeleine Fishwick, one conviction, Elizabeth Baker two convictions, Marybelle Burly, four convictions. Alice Green, Charlotte Spriggs, Vivien Allsop and Eileen Murphy have no recorded convictions, Milord."

"Very well. It appears you have all ignored the warnings set by previous court appearances, warnings that you should have heeded. Sadly, your sexual profession is not a transportable offence, however stealing is and this, added to your poor record, leaves me no alternative.

Alice Green, Charlotte Spriggs, Vivien Allsop and Eileen Murphy, you are sentenced to six months in Newgate prison and twenty lashes each to be carried out on arrival. Patricia Stock, Rebecca Smith, Madeline Fishwick and Elizabeth Baker, you are each sentenced to seven years imprisonment at his Majesty's Penal Colony in New South Wales. At the completion of your sentence you will not be permitted to return to England for a period of fourteen years, giving you a total of twenty one years, which will give you ample time to consider your sins against God's law and the law of the realm."

He slammed his gavel hard on the bench and shouted. "Next case."

Each girl felt stunned by the verdict. Rebecca sat silently, taking in the sentence imposed. She gave a shudder at the thought of transportation to the other side of the world. There would be no comforts there. For a second she thought it was some sort of a stupid joke, the judge didn't mean it, he couldn't have? He said whoring was not a transportable offence but stealing was. She became aware of the chatter of the crowd after the sentence. Why wasn't Claire there to speak for them? Of course, she expected the usual mandatory fine.

Bile came to Rebecca's throat, and she wanted to vomit. Seven years was a life sentence as far as she was concerned. Her life of luxury was now over.

Outside, the prison wagon waited. It was as if the sentence had been expected. The jailers grinned as the shocked young women were herded into the cage of the wagon.

"Get in ladies. A nice cell awaits you. No warm beds but we can be very accommodating."

Rebecca noted how they stared at the women's bosoms and one slapped her on the backside as she entered. It was obvious they expected favors once the women were inside the prison.

The girls were led away to begin their sentences. The four sentenced to a flogging had tears streaming down their cheeks, but those sentenced to New South Wales were too stunned to cry. Silently they filed into the prison wagon to Newgate to await their departure, knowing the comfortable life they had led was now at an end.

One burst into tears, and Rebecca put her arm around her to comfort her. It didn't help as the girl continued sobbing.

CHAPTER TWO

The hellhole of Newgate prison shocked them. Cells originally designed to hold twenty women now had fifty unfortunate prisoners packed inside. They entered, the steel doors clanging shut behind them.. Rebecca shivered when she saw the cold stares from the other prisoners. None were dressed as the girls from the club were. Most wore rags, their faces dirty, unwashed hair hanging to their shoulders. Some were missing teeth while others wore scars from beatings inflicted in their former life. One or two were no more than fourteen years old while others bore the hagard look of years of poverty.

It seemed the dregs of humanity occupied the stone cell. Women of all ages, shapes and sizes looked at the new arrivals some shouted mocking jibes. All were in the same position, and none expected sympathy from the others. The stench of unwashed bodies, urine and feces lying in open buckets was enough to make one or two vomit. Rebecca held a handkerchief to her nose to try and hold out the smell, but to no avail. Some of the girls looked at her with eyes wide open as they thought about the hopelessness of what stood ahead. A large tub of evil looking water stood in one corner, along side the brimming buckets of urine and feces. There was absolutely no privacy for anyone. Rebecca quickly averted her eyes as she saw one woman squatting over one of the buckets trying to relieve herself.

The four sentenced to a flogging were dragged out into a courtyard by guards. Each cried and struggled as they tried to dig their feet into the bluestone floor. It proved useless. Several minutes later their screams echoed through the prison. Some girls shook violently as if they were the ones being flogged, but the other prisoners gave it little interest. They had heard the sounds before. Many placed their fingers in their ears to try and block out the screams.

None returned to the cells and Rebecca wondered what happened to them.

"Are they going to flog us, Rebecca?" one asked with a fearful tone in her voice.

"We were sentenced to transportation, not flogging," she said unconvincingly.

"Why are they doing this to us? We haven't done them any harm."

"Because Puritan Perc is a religious bastard who thinks we should all act his way."

"I've never seen him at the club," said another.

Another sneered. "He probably takes himself in hand and has never been with a woman, mores the pity."

Rebecca gave the idea a little thought. "It's an easy option to clear women like us from the prison. He obviously has decided that women in our line of business are the scum of the earth."

* * * * *

Soon a strange kind of hierarchy took over. With little floor space for the prisoners to sleep they struggled to find a suitable place to sit.

One tough looking woman pushed one of the girls aside. "Find somewhere else to lie down, bitch," she said savagely.

Rebecca stood up and stared the woman in the eyes. "If you fight one of us, you fight us all. Can you handle that?"

The woman stared at Rebecca who had her fists clenched and her head held high. Then she looked at the others who gathered around Rebecca.

"Just make room for the rest of us," she said, as she backed down and then moved away.

The girls, still dressed in their finery, but now soiled and disheveled, were prime targets of the other women who had no such luxuries to display. Rebecca noted how the women from the club cowered on stinking straw in the corner of the stone cell. They huddled together for protection and shelter from the taunts of the street whores and thieves who hurled abuse at them.

"Whores," some shouted but Rebecca knew most of them were in the same occupation. None would have qualified for the Gentleman's Club.

"Where did you get the fancy clothes?" said one, laughing. "How many times did you lay on your back for them? I bet you've had it in you more times than the King has had dinners."

"What's going to happen to us, Rebecca," asked one of the frightened girls.

An obscene cackle came from the lips of one of the other prisoners, a woman of about forty with several teeth missing from the front of her mouth giving her a grotesque appearance. Her hair hung down like dirty string.

"Don't ya know, luvie? There are thousands of men sent to the new land and only a small number of women. We's bein' sent there to serve 'em. All those men are goin' crazy without wives or women. The only purpose is to satisfy their cravin' for you know what. You'll have to deliver the goods without the rewards."

Rebecca stared at her in disbelief. "You mean we'll be sex slaves to the men of the new colony?"

"Not sex slaves, dearie, just convicts. Of course you'll have a choice, you can produce the goods or live like pigs. The option will be yours."

Rebecca frowned as she took in the woman's words. "She's right, that's why they're picking on the whores. We all know what men without women are like."

Terrified, Patricia turned toward Rebecca for comfort and advice. "Then what can we do?"

"There's only one thing we can do. Make the best of our talents to see that we survive."

"Class don't mean nuthin' out there, luv," said the crone. "You'll 'ave to take what you get."

Rebecca nodded. "We'll be reduced to the same clientele as the street whores. It means we'll be on our own and have to make our own decisions."

"I've never had to do that before," wailed Elizabeth. "Claire always did the arranging."

"Then you had better do some thinking on the trip out. Life's going to be hard from now on."

They sat silently as they took in Rebecca's words, each knowing those soft beds and perfumed clothes had come to a sudden and inglorious end.

Each of them were remarkably beautiful in face and body, the very reason why Claire had selected them, and each knew that they would be among the first choice of the males in the new colony. How the society of Sydney town would treat these "working women" of London was unknown. They would learn soon enough as they had seven years to serve before their release came about.

What would each look like in seven years time and would they be accepted by settlers or be at the mercy of the convicts? One thing was certain; Rebecca was going to make the most of any opportunity that presented itself.

One of the guards rapped the bars of the cell with his baton. Two of his yellow teeth were broken, his hair long and hanging down under his hat and the four day growth of beard on his face repelled Rebecca. She wondered when he had last bathed. To get attention he rattled his baton against the bars again until the chatter stopped.

"Ladies," he said, grinning. "Is there anyone here who would like a slice of rich pork and half a loaf of fresh crusty bread for supper?"

Some nodded, but he looked at the new arrivals. "How about you, love?" he said leering at Rebecca.

"No thanks," she said turning her back.

"No? Is there anyone else who might be interested?"

Some of the other prisoners held up their hands and rushed to the bars.

"I would," said one of the younger women who had already been there when Rebecca and the girls arrived.

"Me too," said another, trying to elbow the other out of the way.

"Any others?" called the guard, and two others pushed forward.

"Of course there will be the usual fee," he said as another guard ambled up. The man winked at his mate who sported an equally sadistic grin.

The women looked at each other and nodded.

"Okay, you four lift your skirts, we want to see what you've got."

Quickly they did as ordered, and each guard reached through the bars and fondled each woman in turn.

"What do you reckon, Charlie?" he said, turning to his mate.

"I'll take the young blonde one, you have the other."

"Sounds fair. I like dark ones. They can be very amiable."

He unlocked the door and let the two girls out, quickly locking it behind them, then led them away.

"Take me, take me," some shouted, anxious to have something decent to eat.

"Maybe tomorrow," said Charlie, laughing as he led the girls away.

Half an hour later the girls were escorted back, each chewing on half a loaf of bread, anxious to finish it before they returned to the cells.

Neither looked embarrassed at having to pay the fee for the luxuries. Rebecca sighed knowing worse was to come.

"That's what is ahead of us," she said sadly.

"But they're horrible," said one of the girls. "I couldn't do it with them."

"I don't think I could either, but when we get really hungry, who knows what we will do."

* * * * *

A month in Newgate was enough for them all. Some paid the fee for fresh food while others didn't. As always, the strongest used their power for whatever comfort they could muster, but all remained wary of Rebecca as most were very aware she was not someone to cross.

At four in the morning, a month after being put in the hell hole, the doors clanged open. Five guards entered carrying several sacks of clothing.

"Right my lovelies, everyone strip."

Rebecca rubbed her eyes and glared at Charlie, who seemed to be in charge.

A murmur went around the women, and some seemed reluctant to obey the order.

"You heard," roared Charlie. "Get those dresses off and strip down to the nitty."

He brought his hand down across the face of the nearest prisoner, and immediately she began to strip. The others quickly followed suit.

Rebecca and the other Gentlemen's Club girls were the last to comply. Charlie moved towards Rebecca and stood with his hands on his hips grinning evilly at her. "You, too, Miss Fancy Pants, and the rest of your Queens of the gutter"

Rebecca stood almost as tall as Charlie's five foot six and gave him a steely glare, then slowly began to peel off her clothes.

"Just as you say little man".

The insult hit home and she received a deep scowl.

The others complied as well. Soon the entire cell filled with naked women. The guards began to make crude comments about some of the prisoners.

"I've seen better bones on my old nag," said one, grinning at some of the unfortunate women."

"Yeah," said another. "They'd be lucky to get three pence on the street."

Charlie leered at Rebecca who now stood naked. Rebecca knew exactly what he would like to do with her.

Rebecca had been naked in front of men before so she looked at Charlie insolently. The other guards fell silent when they looked at Rebecca. Long legs, perfect breasts, dark hair around her shoulders and steely brown eyes that showed her contempt for them. She held her head high and looked like a lady, even though she was naked. Charlie reached out to place his hand on Rebecca's breast, but she smacked it away in a defiant gesture. He became wary of her action then sneered at her and the other girls.

"Throw your clothes in the corner with the others and put on this prison garb. Anything that doesn't fit, swap with someone else."

One guard emptied the sack onto the cell floor displaying clean, drab cotton dresses and the women rushed to find something to wear.

Now dressed, one of the girls whispered to Rebecca, "Why are they doing this? I was happy with my clothes."

"I think they are going to move us," she said, shaking her head.

Charlie nodded to one of the other guards who wheeled in a barrow filled with leg irons. Rebecca's thoughts were confirmed as they immediately began fixing them to the legs of the prisoners.

Fear and apprehension appeared on all the girls' faces. They staggered side to side as they struggled to walk in their confined condition. Each expected a flick of the lash held in one of the guard's hands.

"Why are we wearing these?" asked Rebecca.

"Because you're all going on a little holiday," Charlie said, smirking. "We should have some new talent to try out in a few days. Now all of you out."

They were escorted out into the cold morning air to several wagons waiting. Once locked in with the girls, the wagons began their journey to the estuary to board the waiting ships.

The women jealously protected the few possessions each had, afraid they would be stolen by one of their companions. By the time they reached the Thames, the first streaks of light began to fill the eastern sky. Rebecca shivered repeatedly from the bone chilling cold.

"Hurry up," shouted one of the crew as he hustled the women onto the ship. One fell, pulling others with her as she shuffled in the leg irons.

"The tide turns in two hours."

Rebecca glanced up at the huge masts holding the still rolled up sails as the crew bundled the prisoners together on a very crowded deck. The captain waited for the noise to subside before he spoke. Three other ships stood nearby with crews preparing the ships to sail.

"My name is Captain James Bartholomew, and I am in command of his Majesty's convict ship, The White Swan."

"Looks more like the dirty duck," whispered Rebecca to which the nearby convicts laughed.

"Who said that?" bellowed a stern faced officer standing nearby.

No one spoke and utter silence reigned until the Captain intervened.

"Lieutenant Crawford, what appears to be the trouble?"

"One of the convicts has insulted the ship, sir, and nobody will own up."

"Then select ten from the group and give them twenty lashes each. Maybe we will learn who the culprit is, and the rest will learn orders must be obeyed."

This horrified Rebecca. They were going to punish ten innocent women for her folly. She stepped forward. "It was me, sir." Rebecca spoke quickly. "The others weren't to blame."

"Your name, convict?"

"Rebecca Smith, sir."

"Then you will receive twenty lashes once we are at sea, Convict Smith. Now, as I was saying, the trip to New South Wales will be long and uncomfortable. To prevent the respectable women of the colony from being offended, you will be unloaded at Botany Bay and taken to the female factory in a place called Parramatta. There will be no complaints from any convict, and you will obey orders at all times. To disobey will result in harsh punishment. Any inquiries concerning the journey will be done through a spokesperson, who will be selected by you and who will report to me each day. Orders given by any member of my crew are to be treated as though I issued them personally. We are waiting for the last of the convicts to arrive from Birmingham, and we should be under sail within the hour."

Captain Bartholomew nodded to the crew who proceeded to march the women below to their quarters. The first thing they noticed was the smell, not unlike Newgate. Sweaty bodies and the odor of urine tingled their nostrils, but a dampness was more noticeable. The floor was covered in straw pallets that reeked from the spilled urine from the buckets placed around the floor. Rebecca shuddered at the look of despair on the faces of the prisoners already there. She was surprised to see at least forty other women held in the hold. Most sat forlornly against the hull of the ship. One rubbed her leg where her leg iron had been removed.

"How long have you been here?" she asked one of them.

"Some of us 'ave been 'ere for two months, luv. We'll be glad to get to the new land after bein' held in 'ere."

Rebecca groaned when she saw the conditions they had to endure. Although cold outside, the interior of the ship was warm and stifling. She shuddered to think what it would be like in hot weather. The new arrivals leg irons were removed, and the bosun stepped back and addressed them.

"The Captain said to select a spokesperson so you had better make that your first job. Once we're under sail you will be permitted to go on deck in groups of no more than twenty unless you are detailed to do specific jobs. I'm the one who allots the jobs so if anyone wants an easy one 'ad better look after my interests," he said, leering. "If you know what I mean."

The bargaining was beginning even before they left port. From the midst of the crowd came a voice with a Yorkshire accent.

"Well, girls, we 'ave to elect someone to see the Captain each day. It better be someone who can talk well."

They looked toward a woman of forty who stood with her hands on her hips. The woman stared straight at Rebecca.

"You mean someone with a big mouth," was the reply that brought a laugh.

"How about Miss Fancy Pants? She earned herself twenty lashes before we even got under way," another yelled.

"Yeah, at least she owned up and saved the rest of us from a floggin'. How about it, Smith?"

Rebecca saw it as a chance to maybe help make the journey a tolerable one. "All right, I'll do it if no one else wants the job."

No one else spoke so it was agreed. The remaining prisoners arrived and within the hour they were sailing down the Thames out into the estuary in calm weather, followed by the other ships.

Once they were heading out toward open sea, a woman who held a Yorkshire accent gathered some of the new arrivals around her. "If you want an easy job like working in the galley or making the officers' bunks then you'll have to fuck some of the crew. The big fat slob who is the bosun's mate is one to avoid. He wacks anyone who he thinks is not up to standard. Some of the officers like it, too, but most are not violent."

"What about the others?" asked one of the club girls.

"Most are okay though not all, but they all need a bath. The bosun likes a blow job, If you're good at it you can get him off quickly before he sticks it into you. If you don't want to do any of that then you'll probably starve for the entire journey."

Rebecca sighed. This was going to be a terrible trip.

"What about your punishment, Rebecca?" said one of her friends.

"It ain't goin' to be pleasant," said one of the experienced prisoners. "I got flogged in prison for not putting out."

Some nodded in agreement. If they hadn't been lashed they had seen it happen in their past experiences.

By late afternoon, land was nowhere in sight, and the air in the bowels of the ship became intolerable. Rebecca sat and thought about the punishment that was promised. Maybe they had forgotten it. Nothing had happened for a few hours. Her hopes were dashed when the doors were thrown open, and the bosun entered and blew a whistle.

"Everyone on deck to witness punishment," he yelled, and they hurried out to at least get some fresh air even though they knew it was a side benefit. The crew, all armed with muskets and other weaponry, greeted them. Rebecca's hands shook as she knew what was coming.

"Convict Smith, come forward," a voice yelled, and Rebecca stepped forward to see a seaman stripped to his trousers, holding a lash.

The Captain nodded and quickly two sailors dragged her to the rigging. One produced some cord and began tying her until her hands were securely tied and her legs spread-eagled. The cord cut into her flesh and began to burn.

"I apologize." Rebecca thought it might get her a little respite but really didn't hold much hope.

"Too late now, deary," said the man who had stripped down. She could see him from the corner of her eye, and his biceps looked huge and powerful. He gave a grin and by his attitude, she knew he had done this before.

"Convict Smith has earned herself twenty lashes for insulting his Majesty's ship," said the Captain standing above them with his hands clasped behind his back. "Let this be a warning to all of you that disgraceful behavior will not go unpunished. No insulting words will be heard on this ship, and any breach of discipline will not be ignored. Carry on, bosun."

The bosun nodded to the seaman who stepped up to Rebecca and ripped her dress from her back, exposing her pale flesh for all to see. He spat on his hand, grinned, and took a position. He brought the lash down with all the strength in his arms. The convicts cringed as the cracking sound reached their ears a split second before Rebecca's piercing scream. Immediately, a deep red welt appeared on her soft white back, and the shock ran through her body, diving deep into her brain. Her body heaved, but she was unable to move away from the painful onslaught of the lashing. All the air in her lungs seemed to have vanished.

The seaman waited until the bosun called the count before he took his stance once again.

"One" came the cry, then he brought his arm back again to deliver the next blow. Again the lash came down, and again the sickening crack brought another scream from Rebecca, and other red welts appeared. If the first blow was a shock, the second almost made her faint.

"Two" was the shout, and she waited for the next savage blow to rain down. The ends of the lash this time flicked under her back catching the lower part of her breast. Ribbons of blood appeared as the flesh parted. The convicts were horrified, and some began to cry while others turned their heads to avoid watching the spectacle before them. The Captain, noticing that some had looked away, stopped the proceedings.

"Everyone will witness this punishment. If you look away then you will be the next to feel the bosun's lash. Re-commence, bosun."

Again the cruel blow landed, and again Rebecca felt the white-hot agony race through her body, with the boson's shouts ringing in her ears. Mercifully, Rebecca began to lose consciousness, and the horizon took on a dark mode as each blow brought more pain and anguish. She slumped forward now in a faint as the sailor lifted her head.

"She's fainted, sir," he barked in a rough voice.

The Captain stood with his arms behind his back, his peaked hat shading him from the sun. "It matters not. Continue the punishment."

The sailor continued his strokes until at last it was over. Rebecca felt nothing after the tenth blow.

The prisoners watching maintained a vigilant silence after the captain's warning.

"Take her below," ordered the Captain, and willing hands gently lifted her body, her back now bleeding from the lash with the blood seeping down across her breasts. A replacement dress was fetched, and her body placed face down on a straw pallet, her back bathed in salt water before she regained consciousness.

When at last she opened her eyes, the waves of pain washed over her, and she was unable to move without feeling intense discomfort. Each movement was agony as her flesh had opened up, exposing bloody tissue. Some of the women stayed with her, bathing her open wounds until they began to heal. Slowly, she was able to sit up and a bowl of watery soup was fed to her. She felt grateful for the attention given by the other prisoners.

It took three days before she could stand comfortably, and on the fourth day she was allowed to go on deck.

The wind now blew with force, and Rebecca wondered if the pain was any worse than the seasickness that hit her. She wasn't alone as many of the other women suffered with her. Most were unable to keep anything down, and Rebecca gritted her teeth to the sound of vomiting heard all night. Her stomach heaved as she stumbled and then leaned over the already filled bucket. The sight and smell of the vomit started a five-minute episode of heaving her stomach contents out. She was aware of another prisoner, a slight woman trying to move her aside in a desperate attempt to reach the bucket, but it was too late. She vomited all over one of the straw pallets and down her dress.

It seemed when one started then the rest of the women followed. The sound of heaving stomachs was the trigger for many others to try to reach the buckets. Rebecca felt as though her stomach had lifted to her throat. When nothing else came up she began to gag. If the ship had sunk at that moment, she wouldn't have cared. Nothing could be worse than this, and if it was going to continue for the long trip then she and the others didn't know if they would survive. When all the buckets were full, the vomit still ran like a tap turned on.

"I'll never go on a ship again," said Ada, the Yorkshire woman she had met on the first day, as she vomited into a bucket.

"How can these men put up with it, day after day?" said another.

"It's what they call sea legs. It doesn't seem to worry the sailors at all." Rebecca heard some of the men walking across the deck without a worry.

"They say the journey will take months. We'll all be dead by then," one groaned as she vomited again, bringing up a colorless bile.

"One of the sailors said you get used to it after a week or so. I'll never survive until then."

"We have to," said Rebecca, determinedly.

When the bosun entered the hold he grinned at the distress of the women. "Anyone care to go up to the deck and scrub it down. I want some volunteers."

He was almost knocked over in the rush to get some fresh air and escape the sickening smell below. Some gasped for fresh air and enjoyed the fresh breeze in their faces. Sick or not, it felt good to escape the stench of the hold.

Two days later the nauseating feeling left her. It was like a miracle. Others began to overcome the seasickness as well, and some semblance of order prevailed. As her first duty upon recovering enough to walk, Rebecca gently knocked on the Captain's door. The wind had dropped remarkably. The sun had begun to set, and at that time, between day and night, it gave a breathtaking quality to the ocean. It looked like an orange ball as it sank toward the horizon sending a golden shimmering glow across the water. For a girl who had lived in the city all her life this was a spectacular scene.

"Yes," she heard him call loudly.

She opened the door and entered to see him sitting at his desk with a quill in his hand, writing in a journal. His attention immediately went to Rebecca's face, and Rebecca smiled to herself as she had seen that look before on many a customer.

"What is it?" he said with a scowl.

Rebecca was readily aware of his gaze going up and down her body. "I'm the spokeswoman for the prisoners, sir," she said, smiling at him.

"Oh, yes. You're that convict we had to flog, aren't you?"

"Yes, sir, Rebecca Smith. I apologize for my words and humbly ask for your forgiveness."

He cleared his throat a little, but kept his gaze on her body. "You realize, Convict Smith, that we had to punish you. Otherwise there would be no discipline at all on the journey."

"Yes, sir." Rebecca studied him as he sat without his hat. He was around forty-five, with a slight potbelly and a balding head, but his face was pleasant as was his manner.

Immediately she thought about the bargaining going on between the crew and the convicts. While she had no wish to cohabit with the scum of a crew, she considered the Captain himself might offer some comfort for the journey. After all, she had entertained worse than him in the Gentlemen's Club back in London. Rebecca undid the top button of her dress and feigned heat as she fanned herself with her hand. The swell of her breast became more visible, and the Captain gave a little cough as he stared at them.

"Perhaps you can sit, Convict Smith," he said, offering her a chair. She smiled and leaned forward, revealing a little more of her cleavage as she sat.

"And is your back healing well?" he asked, totally surprising her.

"Nicely, thank you, sir," she said and smiled sweetly.

"I hope you learned your lesson, Smith. I want no more of this poor behavior on this long journey."

"I understand, sir, of course you are correct, and I deserved it." She certainly had been trained to always agree with the customer.

He cleared his throat again trying to give the impression he had a sore throat, but she knew it was her presence that made him uncomfortable.

"You know, of course, that I can make the journey very unpleasant for anyone who misbehaves, even for you."

"Of course, sir, but if I may be so bold, I can, in my way, make the journey more enjoyable for anyone, especially you, sir.".

She could almost see his mind turning over. He coughed, lifting his hand to his mouth in a gesture to hide his embarrassment.

"I must say you are one of the most attractive convicts on the ship. What crime did you commit to warrant your sentence?"

Rebecca smiled. "I was an employee of the London Club for Gentlemen. It was my job to see that gentlemen like you were suitably entertained—and pleasured," she added looking up in her most seductive manner.

She could see beads of sweat forming on his brow. "You mean you were a whore?"

"I would be preferred to be called a courtesan, for I was never a harlot of the street, sir."

"Is there a difference?"

"A harlot of the street would give her services in a dirty lane for three pence to any man who would pay. My services were only for gentlemen such as you in the best of establishments. Nobody ever went away dissatisfied. Did you ever attend the club, sir?"

"No, I did not. I have mostly been at sea for the last five years and not had the chance. Would you like a small wine, my dear?"

Rebecca smiled slightly. She had never heard of a Captain offering a convict a glass of wine in his cabin. "Why thank you, sir. That is most generous."

She watched as he poured the wine, then took the glass smiling graciously. She mentioned the concerns of the other convicts about poor food and living conditions as she drank, but he dismissed them without consideration.

"This boldness of yours about making the journey more pleasant for me, Convict Smith, just in what way could things be improved?"

Rebecca stood up, smiling like a schoolgirl. "Why, in the way of my profession, sir." She loosened the tie at the top of her dress letting it fall to the floor and suddenly stood naked in front of him. He stared, open mouthed as her luscious breasts hovered just inches from his face.

His tight navy issue breeches did nothing to hide his increasing arousal.. She reached her small hand toward his trouser buttons.

"Sir, I'm sure I can help pass some of the long tedious hours of the voyage."

She smiled to herself and knew the long days ahead would not be as torturous for her as for many of her fellow convicts.

She hurried with his trouser buttons.

"Shall I slip the bolt on the door, sir?"

Chapter Three

The journey to Botany Bay resulted in the most humiliating and degrading episode in the lives of most of the convicts. Two weeks out, the second floggings took place when two women fought over a scrap of stale bread. Both were tied to the rigging, as Rebecca had been, and both received the mandatory twenty lashes. The experienced whores used their trade to gain extra food from the crew, while those women who were not serving their sentences for that particular crime soon learned the benefits and began to adapt to that way of life. With so many females available, the crew became selective in their choices, and the girls from the Gentleman's Club were first picks, ~~just~~ as Rebecca had predicted. Rebecca was left alone, as the crew knew she was the Captain's private property; however, she lacked no offers for extra rations. Several times Rebecca used her influence to gain better conditions for the convicts, but even she had to be wary of the Captain's temper.

Once when she thought she had his confidence she took it on~~to~~ herself to question his orders. "Sir, don't you think cutting back on rations was a little harsh?"

He brought his hand back and struck her on the face. It sat her on her backside, and her hand flew to her ~~face~~ bruised cheek.

His brow creased, and his face flushed as he looked at her still sitting on the floor. "Never question my orders, Smith, or it might be another flogging."

Rebecca rose and showed a face full of remorse. "I'm sorry, sir. I apologize. Perhaps I can make amends."

She came to him and undid the buttons of his breeches. The response was automatic as he pulled down her dress to her ankles and thrust her onto his desk. Rebecca lay back thanking her stars for her quick thinking.

Of the one hundred convicts on board, fifteen died and were buried at sea with hardly a Christian word spoken. Many of them were in poor health even before they joined the ship, and the lack of good food and medical attention was a prime cause of their demise. All but three were over forty years of age and convicted of petty theft for just trying to keep their families alive.

Upon crossing the equator, with little fresh air, the quarters below became like an oven and most nights not even a breeze stirred the fetid air. Boredom became their greatest enemy with only twenty allowed on deck at a time, and they learned the hard way by more floggings that any dissension meant harsh punishment.

Rebecca continued to serve the Captain at least three times a week. It was not a task she enjoyed, but it was certainly better than serving some of the crew. Occasionally, she received one or two luxuries like a glass of wine or cake especially made for the captain. It was easy to make her mind go blank when she was asked to perform, a skill she had learned long ago from Claire, but when necessary she was also capable of a performance that would do any actress proud. It was on these occasions that she had some power over the captain.

* * * * *

When the captain summoned her to his quarters, Rebecca wondered if she was in trouble or he just wanted more sexual "favors". "Sit down, Smith, I have some news for your ears only. I don't wish the rest of the prisoners to know this yet. Is that clear?"

"Of course, sir." She wondered what the news would be after six months isolated on this terrible ship.

"Tomorrow we will arrive at Botany Bay. This will be the last time you will see me. I must congratulate you on the way you have behaved since you've been on the ship. Some of the prisoners have been troublemakers, but not you. I have been informed that twenty two women have become pregnant, and I hope you haven't fallen into that condition."

"I have not, sir," she said, nodding her head. "Mistress Claire showed us all how to avoid that condition."

"Good. You will be transported to the Female Factory on the other side of Sydney Town as soon as you all arrive."

"And what will happen to us then, sir?" she said, happy to get off the stinking ship.

"You will serve your full sentence in the prison unless you are lucky enough to get domestic work. I don't really think you would qualify because of your past occupation. I understand part of your sentence was that once you have served your time you will be unable to return to England for fourteen more years."

"Yes, sir. That was made clear. I will probably never get back so I will have to make a life here."

He hesitated for a few seconds. "I guess that is all, Smith—-unless you…"

"Of course, sir. Seeing we will never meet again then I will give you my best effort. Shall I lock the door?"

He smiled and nodded. Rebecca smirked to herself, then turned the snib.

Next morning, the ship arrived and once anchored, the prisoners had leg irons fixed once again and were unloaded. She turned towards the ship to see the captain standing on the deck with his hands behind his back looking down. He gave her a nod and turned away. She noticed a few of the sailors didn't look too happy as their supply of sex was about to disappear.

It was a different attitude from the prisoners, some who cheered just to touch solid ground. Most were glad to see the last of the sailors

Most of the girls suspected that life over here would be no better. There were guards in the prison who would expect similar favors to those at Newgate.

Once herded into the wagons, Rebecca felt like a caged animal as the slow moving prison cart made its way through the new colony, bringing looks of disgust from the citizens of Sydney Town. The journey was rough as potholes seemed to be every three feet on the road, and the wagons swayed side to side. Respectable well-dressed couples paused in their journey to watch the prison cart go past. Others, mainly young settlers, cried out derogatory comments.

"I've got a penny if you have the time," one laughed.

Children skipped behind the cart laughing and pointing to the women who sat behind the bars holding on tight from the rocky trip.

Men stared and smiled until the wives pulled on their arms in an endeavor to get away from this trash. Even one horseman rode alongside inspecting the girls.

"What are you lookin' at," one of the girls yelled. "I wouldn't fuck you for even a pound."

He turned away and galloped off.

Once the prison gates clanged shut behind them their shackles were removed, and they were made to form a group and sit on the ground as Colonel William Collins, the prison Governor laid out the rules.

"I am the governor of this prison, and I expect all orders to be obeyed. Various tasks will be allotted, and you will do them without question. We have a garden at the back of the prison, and some will be selected to grow our food. Others will be given duties of looking after the prison offices, cooking meals, and chopping wood. If you disobey orders you will be flogged. I hope it doesn't come to that, but it will if you do not comply. Each of you will share a cell with five others. I want no squabbling as to blankets or bedding. If you do your duties as asked then you will have reasonable comfort during your time here. There are no female prison guards here, only men who know how to treat bad prisoners."

He turned and left the guards to take them to their cells. Rebecca's was cold and had walls built from bluestone. The window was high and out of reach. The embedded bars did not contain any glass or other protection to keep out the wind or rain. Rebecca saw the other girls from the ship, but none of them were from the Gentleman's Club. What happened to them she didn't know.

The days dragged on. Work began at five am. Rebecca mended clothing or sometimes worked in the kitchen as part of her duties. Except for the tasks, one day was no different to the rest. Boredom set in. They usually finished at six and fell exhausted into their cells. The food was not the best, and again bargaining began as the guards offered better food for favors. Some accepted, but Rebecca knew that to return to that life was not an option. She rejected offers and was left alone to serve her sentence.

* * * * *

Two guards entered the cells, one standing with his hands on his hips as they surveyed the women.

"We have a request for three inmates to act as domestics. No pay, only board and lodgings. Anyone interested?"

Many rushed forward ~~all~~ trying to reach the front for a quick selection.

The guard ordered them to line up and walked along the line inspecting each girl. When he came to Rebecca he lifted her chin with a baton and leered at her with a sadistic smile. "Get back, Smith. They don't want whores. You already know that."

"I'm not a whore now," she said defiantly. He put his hands on his hips, still holding the baton in his right hand. "I've noticed. Things would be more comfortable for you if you were."

She sucked in a breath. "Then why aren't I eligible?" She stood with her head held high, unlike some of the others who stood with heads bowed.

He laughed. "Because the lady of the house wouldn't trust her husband to keep his hands off you. The last thing she wants is to find him with the likes of you." Sadly she stepped back knowing there was no way to escape this hell hole. It seemed she was going to rot in here until her sentence was up.

She'd heard from some guards that most settlers used them just as slave labor while a few fortunate ones found a little kindness providing they willingly accepted their place on the lowest level of the society of the colony. She would have been grateful to find one of those. Others found they had to perform or lose their new found privileges.

Rebecca found that what Governor Collins had told them about whores was right. The wives of the settlers did not look upon whores with favor, and so most of them were used to attend gardens and more degrading tasks inside the prison such as cleaning out the sewer drains under the watchful eyes of the guards. There was no pleasure in serving men like the captain for a living. This was a new country, and maybe in the future she would have a life, perhaps even a husband who would love her. Maybe kids. No man would marry her if it was known she had been a woman of the street. Once she left this place then she would keep herself chaste, move away from Sydney Town and look for something better than laying on her back for some man. For three years she served her sentence without trouble or interference and learned skills she had not known before. Being one of a few who could read and write made her popular with the other prisoners, and she conducted lessons for those seeking to learn and improve their lot. Then abruptly her life changed once again.

"Convict Rebecca Smith," a guard yelled, and Rebecca frowned at his manner. He didn't sound friendly.

"Here," she said, wondering what he wanted.

"You will accompany me and no talking." His tone was as disturbing as his manner as he pushed her in front of him, almost causing her to stumble. He prodded her with his baton every second step she took and Rebecca was afraid of where he was taking her.

She was escorted from her work in the garden to Governor Collins' office. She wondered what she had done or what trouble she was in. At least she was put not in leg irons, as was the usual practice for women taken from the prison walls.

"This is the Governor's office," she said, her eyes opening wider in wonderment. "No one is brought here unless they have killed someone and then only in chains. What have I done?" "Shut up. Wipe your face and make yourself look tidy." The guard handed her a dirty rag he produced from his pocket. Once she wiped her face the guard ushered her in and shut the door behind her.

Collins had a head of grey hair and showed no traces of baldness. He was clean-shaven and looked smart in his red uniform. Gold braid on his shoulders indicated his rank, and he stood at least five foot ten inches tall. Rebecca thought he looked rather elegant and remarkably fit in appearance. He looked to be maybe fifty years old but it was hard to tell. His voice showed the authority he held.

He sat at his desk and waved his hand at her inviting her to approach. She stood patiently waiting for him to speak. The Governor took no more notice of her as he continued to write his reports of the day until finally he put down his quill and stared at her. He then stood and walked around her as if he were choosing a mare.

"Convict Smith, you have been here now…"

"Three years, sir," she finished for him. She felt nervous as she stood in front of him

Collins placed his hands behind his back like the captain of the ship. He picked up a sheet of paper and read it. "Yes, three years, and I see that you have caused no trouble. There has been no cause to reprimand you once since your arrival."

"I was flogged on the ship on the journey out, sir. It's something I can never forget. All I wish to do is serve my sentence and begin a new life."

He again looked at the report and rubbed his chin. "I see you were convicted for the crime of whoring and theft, is that correct?'

"Yes, sir."

He raised an eyebrow and looked sharply at her. "You were a common street harlot?"

Rebecca felt insulted and frowned. "No, sir, I worked in The London Club for Gentlemen."

"Ah, yes I've heard of it. Many years ago I even had the opportunity to attend there myself. I trust Mistress Thomas was well when last you saw her."

Rebecca gave a smile. "She was, sir. I hope she still is. She was a true friend to me. She took me off the streets when I was a child."

He resumed his seat and tapped his fingers together. "From what I know of Mistress Thomas, she taught you the skills well, no doubt."

"I never had complaints from any gentlemen, sir."

He looked at her again. "Do you intend to resume your profession once you are released?"

Rebecca shook her head vigorously. "No, sir, that part of my life is behind me."

He again tapped the tips of his fingers together as he studied her. It was at least thirty seconds before he spoke again.

"What would you think about having your sentence reduced by one year, Convict Smith?"

A glint flew to her eyes. "I would like it very much, sir."

"Of course there will be an obligation to perform to deserve such leniency."

Rebecca sighed knowing what he was going to say. "You wish me to visit you regularly, sir, so I may obtain this reward?"

The governor laughed loudly as he threw his head back. "What a delicious thought to have someone as pretty as you to regularly visit me with your skills, but I'm afraid my wife would not approve at all."

"I'm sorry, sir, I thought..."

"Well your thoughts were not exactly off the track. Perhaps I'd better explain."

"Yes, sir."

"Next month there will be a company of officers and troops arriving to relieve some of my men at the garrison. Among the officers there will be a gentleman who has rather close attachments with the crown. While he is not of royal blood, he is a very close friend. His role is only to inspect and report back to Westminster on the efficiency of the colony."

"I don't understand, sir," said Rebecca puzzled.

Collins gave her a smile before continuing. "This gentleman has a reputation as a ladies man, and I believe he has broken a heart or two in London. I've been told he has bedded more women than I care to recall, and no doubt he will be looking for more fresh faces. At such short notice it is difficult to find willing partners in the colony with sufficient skills to please him. Most of the suitable women are married, and I'm quite sure their husbands would not approve."

Rebecca listened closely as he continued.

"This particular gentleman would never consider whores as they are well below his social class. He only has to snap his fingers to get a woman. However, someone such as yourself…" He paused then continued. "Well schooled in the needs of such gentlemen, well versed in the art of conversation, pretty to the eye and fairly capable of playing the part of a lady might just get away with it."

"You want me to serve him?" Rebecca was astounded.

"I must say you certainly would not pass any test dressed as you are, but you do carry the beauty and poise needed, and you can read and write. As I have already stated, your conversation is adequate, even quite impressive. If you were dressed in the finest clothes then I'm sure we could pass you off as a lady quite successfully. If he raises any questions we could say it is just the lifestyle out here."

"But you said he wouldn't entertain whores."

Collins opened his hands in a gesture. "Why, Convict Smith, he won't know ~~you're a whore,~~ will he? There is a ball to be held in Sydney Town next month to welcome him. If he went away with a favorable impression of my administration, then there may be a knighthood in it for me. Yes,

Sir William Collins is very pleasing to the ear, and my dear wife would be a great asset as Lady Collins."

Rebecca looked doubtful. "Sir, won't the Governor of the Colony, Sir Richard Bourke, and other distinguished persons be in attendance? They would be horrified if they found out that I was present, and their wives would refuse to be in the same room as me."

He nodded. "I admit that is a risk, but you have been here for three years and have never been to Sydney Town. No one will know you, and I think you have the skill to carry it off. Do this for me, and I will see that you are released a year early."

"And if I don't?'

"Then I can promise you a very unpleasant time for the next four years."

Rebecca sighed, what choice did she have? A night or two with some snooty officer would be little trouble for a chance to escape this hell hole one year early.

"Very well, sir, I would be pleased to do your bidding if you let me see you mark my papers so that I know you keep your end of the bargain."

"Good. My dear wife is privy to my plan so we will begin immediately. The week this officer is in Sydney you will be accommodated in one of the best establishments in Sydney, at my expense. Until then I will have you assigned to my quarters under the guise of my wife's maid, which will enable you a chance to learn the latest dances and to polish up on your manners. There will be a selection of dresses to be made, and we will have to do something with your hair. I'm sure you know what's needed."

Rebecca was taken to the Collins home to meet Collin's wife. Rebecca stood nervously as Mrs. Collins approached her. "You are Rebecca Smith, are you not?" she said tersely.

"Yes, ma'am," she answered dutifully.

"Turn around girl and let me inspect you."

Rebecca did as ordered. "Hmm. You are a very pretty girl and should fill the bill adequately. You were a whore in England?"

"A courtesan," said Rebecca, making sure she distinguished the difference.

"Whore, courtesan, it still means you lay with men for money. Let me make this quite clear. If you lay with my husband, you will be sent straight back to where you came from. And if you fail at this task, my husband and I will be very angry." She folded her arms in front of her and stamped her foot.

"I can assure you, ma'am, that Colonel Collins, himself, made that quite clear."

"Good You will call me Mrs. Collins. Now, there is much to do before the gentleman arrives from England. First I will show you your room. It will be more comfortable than what you have been accustomed to. I expect you to keep it neat and tidy at all times. Follow me."

She led Rebecca to a bedroom at the back of the building. Rebecca gasped when she saw it. The bed had a colorful embroidered satin quilt on a canopied bed. There was a large wardrobe and a delicately carved wooden desk. There was a lovely crystal lamp on the table and lace curtains covered the window. It was far more than she expected.

"It is almost lunch time so settle in and come to the dining room in half an hour. The servants must not know what you are doing here. There is a dress in the wardrobe. I want you to put it on until we get more suitable clothes. Change now."

She closed the door and left Rebecca alone. She sat on the bed and bounced up and down. She had seen nothing like this since the Gentlemen's Club, and she was going to enjoy sleeping in it. Much better than a thin mattress on a cold stone floor.

The dress fitted reasonably well, and Rebecca found her way to the dinning room. The high ceiling offered plenty of light, and the walls were decorated with fine looking oil landscapes.

The servants were introduced and accepted that Rebecca was a visitor from England and a close friend of the Collins.

Roast lamb was served for lunch with roast potatoes and carrots. Green fresh peas gave it an attractive look, and a delicious gravy sat in a fine china vessel. Rebecca waited for Mrs. Collins to begin before lifting her fork. She tried not to look like a starving woman, but every mouthful of it was the best she could ever remembering having.

Over the next few weeks, the dinning room was closed off from the servants, while a well-dressed middle-aged gentleman was brought in to teach her the latest dances. She was a keen pupil and learned quickly.

Next was table etiquette where she was shown the best cutlery and how to use each piece. "Always begin from the outside, Rebecca," Mrs. Collins said, watching her closely. This was followed by explicit instructions on how to pour wine and delicately taste it. By the end of three weeks she was performing splendidly.

Mrs. Collins brought in an array of new dresses and touched her chin with her finger as if in deep thought when viewing each one. Rebecca walked around the room, turning as instructed, and Mrs. Collins smiled, happy with the result. She now looked every bit a lady, and Colonel Collins invited her to dine with him.

"You are doing well, Rebecca, but the time is close, and we must put you through a test."

"I don't think I'm ready, sir." Rebecca was terrified.

"Nonsense. There will be a member of the garrison coming here to talk about Sir Robert's security this morning. If you can convince Colonel Whitby then we can proceed with our plan."

"When will this gentleman, Colonel Whitby, be arriving, sir?" Rebecca was shaking, unable to keep her hands still so she thrust them behind her back.

"At eleven. You will dress in your best clothes and be having tea with me as he arrives. After meeting him, you will excuse yourself and retire to your room until he leaves. Is that understood?"

She nodded, understanding exactly. "Yes, sir,"

As she went to prepare herself, she wished she was as confident as Governor Collins seemed to be.

At precisely eleven, Whitby arrived to find Rebecca sitting with the Governor, an empty cup in front of her. He stopped when he saw her.

"Colonel Whitby, how nice to see you again." Collins smiled, getting to his feet and thrusting his hand out to the visitor. "I'd like you to meet Miss Rebecca Courtney. Miss Courtney is here to investigate a business proposition for her family and will be returning to England quite soon."

Rebecca smiled and offered her hand. Colonel Whitby raised it to his lips and kissed it. It was clear he was impressed. He put one hand behind his back and bowed while smiling. "It's a pleasure to meet you, Miss Courtney. I hope you are having a pleasant time in the colony."

Rebecca raised her hand and waved it. "I am indeed, Colonel. Mrs. Collins has seen to it that I have met many of the ladies and been almost everywhere. I have attended parties and dances, and I shall be attending the Governor's ball shortly."

He raised his eyebrows. "How fortunate you are. I myself will not be attending, but I do hope you enjoy yourself, my dear. I'm sure you will be the most attractive lady there."

"Why thank you, Colonel, how nice of you to say. A girl doesn't get such compliments out here in the colony."

"I find that hard to believe." His eyes never left hers, totally captivated by her beauty.

Rebecca offered her hand. "Well, I must be going, Colonel Whitby. I'm sure you gentlemen have business to discuss."

"Of course, Miss Courtney. It's been a pleasure to meet you."

Governor Collins ushered her to the door, leaving the two men alone. Whitby smiled at his companion.

"By jove, Collins. Where did you find her? She's smashing!"

"Her Father, Sir James Courtney, who died years ago, was a friend of mine and while visiting the colony she just dropped in to pay her respects."

"I'd like to pay her more than respect," Whitby grinned. "Pity I can't go to the ball."

When Whitby had completed his business and left, Collins summoned Rebecca to his office.

"Well, Smith, you passed with flying colors. I think we're ready to proceed."

The big day dawned, and a carriage arrived to take her into Sydney to prepare. Governor Collins introduced her to a junior officer who was in charge of seeing her safely into Sydney Town. Collins took her aside before she entered the carriage.

"Remember, Rebecca, do this well, and you will be amply rewarded. When the event is over you will be returned to the prison and will say nothing of this little episode to any other prisoners. To do so would cancel our bargain, and you will receive twenty lashes. Lieutenant Yardley will bring you back when your rendezvous is completed. He knows nothing of the situation and certainly not that you are a convict. If you need anything you have only to ask him. Do you understand?"

"Yes, sir." She kept her head low as she entered the carriage.

"Good luck."

The carriage pulled away, and the journey began. Lieutenant Yardley said little on the journey. His gaze hardly left her face, clearly in awe of the poised young lady seated opposite him, and Rebecca felt her confidence rising with such admiration.

She glanced out of the carriage window and admired the green gum trees of the area. There was nothing like this in England. "You have been in the Colony a long time, Lieutenant?" she asked, trying to make conversation.

"Nearly a year, Miss Courtney."

She smiled to herself at the way he was looking at her. "And are you enjoying it?"

"I must admit, I come from a family of meager means back home, but this colony offers opportunity that I didn't know existed. The Government wants the colony to develop and is offering land for such a cause, and I might take up the offer." Yardley cleared his throat before continuing. "If I may be so bold, Miss Courtney, that beautiful blue dress matches your eyes perfectly."

"Thank you, Lieutenant." Rebecca understood it was the latest fashion in the colony. Narrow waists were in but fitted higher. There were less frills and lace, but she liked the colors and the puffed sleeves. "What do you think, Lieutenant? Do I look nice?"

He looked a little embarrassed. "I think you are one of the most beautiful women I have ever seen. My orders are to take care of any request you make, and I am a willing servant."

She smiled and touched his hand. "That's so nice of you. I'm sure I am going to enjoy the ball."

Rebecca found that a room had been reserved for her at a fine looking Inn. It overlooked the harbor and had a veranda on the first floor that enabled the guests to step from their rooms and take in the view. From her room she could see many sailing ships anchored in the blue waters. Small boats moved on various journeys, and the sun shone on the water giving a sparkling effect. Her thoughts flew to the long trip she'd had to endure to get here, but these didn't appear to be convict ships. They were more like ships bringing valuable cargo to the colony.

She thought it was the most beautiful sights she had ever seen. Trees grew to the water's edge and a series of little bays wove in and out of the major part of the harbor. Some houses had been built on the upper hills, and it must have been wonderful to see such a sight first thing in the morning.

The size of the town exceeded her expectations. Her vision of Sydney Town had been a small hamlet with dirt tracks and run down shacks. Some of the streets had bluestone pavers falling to the middle of the road where rainwater gushed down the hilly streets and into the harbor.

Many houses and shops had been built, some of them in brick, with similar architecture to the mansions in England. She was certain that any of the gentry would be proud to live in such establishments. The streets seemed alive with people and troopers who always seemed in control. It was vastly different from the rain and fog of London. The bright red of the troopers coats and the colors of the women's clothing all reflected the brilliance of the Sydney sunshine and gave her a feeling of freedom for the first time since arriving in the colony.

"My word, this place is big!" she said to Yardley. "I had no idea."

"As I mentioned before, the country is opening up. Settlers are moving both north and south, and there is now quite a large town in the colony of Port Phillip. It's a vast country inhabited mainly by savages, but it's growing quickly. There is opportunity here. I'm tempted to leave the army and claim some of the land being offered."

"Land is being given away?" Rebecca was incredulous.

Yardley gave her more information. "Respectable people may apply to the Governor."

"You mean no convicts are eligible?" Rebecca listened with interest. Yardley had a look of superiority on his face like a schoolteacher instructing a pupil. "Maybe some of the men, but women convicts are here for one purpose only, to help populate the place. I'll leave you to get ready for the ball, Miss. I'll return for you at eight o'clock." He handed her the invitation that would admit them to the ball.

Rebecca's eyes opened wider in surprise. "Why this is in the Governor's own house."

He gave a little smirk. "Of course, Miss. You don't think a friend of the crown would be entertained in some inn?"

"Who is the gentleman that the ball is in honor of?'

"Major General Sir Robert Northcote, once in charge of the Kent

Grenadiers and now an attaché of Sir George Mortimer of the Surrey Regiment. It is whispered he is a close friend of the King himself."

"Then he's quite old?"

"I believe about thirty-four. He got his position early through his father's attachment to the right people."

"Like the King?"

"So I've heard," said Yardley stiffly.

"You have met him?"

Yardley shook his head. He gave a sigh indicating he was not privy to such meetings, certainly not as a Lieutenant. "No. I haven't had the pleasure."

"Then we had better start getting ready, Lieutenant," she said sweetly.

When left alone Rebecca surveyed her room. The bed seemed rather high, but the mattress felt comfortable. The walls held impressive wallpaper similar to what she had seen in the club. A small bedside table was made of polished oak and a large mirror was fitted in front of a dressing table. It was a single room but much larger than some of the Inns in England. It was obviously designed to attract guests who had money.

Yardley had carried a case into her room before departing, and Rebecca unpacked the clothes and cosmetics that Mrs. Collins had supplied. She stripped down to the two layers of underclothing and sat in front of the mirror studying herself. Being free made her think of escape, but escape to where? It was a wilderness away from Sydney, and blacks inhabited the bush. She didn't know much about them, but they might be cannibals. Not a good option.

She washed her face from the bowl of water supplied and began to apply some of the cosmetics. Then she put them down. Her natural beauty needed no such additions. She gave attention to her dark hair, combed it until it shone and lifted it up holding it in place with a large clip. She chose a pale yellow dress with a matching ribbon around her throat. When her dressing was completed, she studied herself once more in the long mirror and felt satisfied at what she saw. She would know as soon as Yardley returned. His eyes would tell her everything.

He arrived at eight in the carriage that brought them to Sydney. When he knocked on her door, she noted his mouth drop open when he saw her. His eyes widened, and he cleared his throat before speaking.

"I must say, you look absolutely beautiful, Miss Courtney. Like a Greek Goddess."

Their carriage arrived at the house at eight thirty. All the important people of the Colony were present with their wives; judges, garrison officers, magistrates, politicians, businessmen, all showing off their best clothes.

When she entered with Yardley, more than one head turned her way. She was exquisite in her dress that she would never have been able to afford, even with the money she had earned at The Gentleman's Club.

The residence had a high ceiling and a large ballroom. Tables had been set up, and Rebecca thought there must have been close to one hundred and fifty people in attendance. A man dressed in an officer's red uniform stood at the entrance announcing each guest as they arrived.

"Miss Rebecca Courtney and Lieutenant Yardley," he called. A murmur went up as the men all looked at her and then enviously at Yardley.

She was introduced to Governor Bourke as Rebecca Courtney, the niece of the late Sir James Courtney. Miss Courtney was in the Colony on an extended holiday and to investigate business propositions and would be returning to England quite soon.

"It's unusual for a young lady like yourself to be involved in business, my dear," said the Governor.

Rebecca curtsied respectfully, smiled, and offered her hand as Mrs. Collins had instructed. "My family thought a woman would be better at judging the needs of other women in the colony, sir. After all, dresses and other garments are strictly a woman's territory."

"Of course, my dear, I quite understand, and the dress you are wearing bears truth to your statement," said the Governor, but Rebecca could see he had no interest in her business requirements, only her face, figure, and ample breasts.

His eyes never left her bosom. Yardley intervened and asked her to dance, making her glad of the chance to settle her nerves before General Northcote arrived. She was surprised that several other men asked her to dance, and she noticed Yardley couldn't keep his eyes from her.

Yardley stood stiffly with his head held high as he whirled her around at every second dance trying to give the impression he was her husband. Some of the other men smiled and chatted with her, but she held back as much information as she was able. Some were elderly, some were fairly young, and some had wives who glared at Rebecca as she danced past.

One of the men had a stomach that kept him well away from her. His walrus moustache kept wobbling up and down as he spoke, and his heavy beard hid most of his face.

"I'm very pleased to meet you, Miss Courtney. I am Percival Hainsworth, one of the magistrates in Sydney. You certainly are a bright light to the colony. How long have you been here?"

"Only a short time, sir," she said trying to avoid probing questions.

"And what ship did you arrive on?" he asked.

Rebecca gulped. He obviously knew which ships had arrived lately, and she didn't have a clue.

"Oh dear, I keep forgetting the name of it. I do know the captain was such a nice man. We had several dinners together in his cabin. He was very knowledgeable about the world and its politics. I'm afraid they hold little interest to me."

"Of course, my dear. I understand perfectly. And how long are you staying? Perhaps we can meet, and I can show you the sights of Sydney Town."

"Thank you for the offer, Mister Hainsworth, but Governor Collins has already offered me such kindness. He and his dear wife have been most kind since I arrived. He knew my father quite well before he passed on"

The look of disappointment was written all over his face. "Then I hope your stay is very pleasant, my dear."

She was glad when Yardley rescued her for the next dance.

The music stopped, and a cavern opened up in the middle of the ballroom as all the guests moved to each side of the great hall. Yardley tucked her arm into his as he pulled her to the corner. She looked at him inquiringly, and he nodded towards the entrance of the hall.

Then a fan fare sounded as Governor Bourke led a group of men down the center of the hall. Rebecca's eyes opened wide when she saw Sir Robert Northcote. He was by far the most handsome man she had ever seen in her life, and she felt her heart beat faster. He was tall, close to six foot, his hair was blond like yellow corn, and his deep blue eyes took in everything around him. His red uniform stood out like a beacon. It was spotless and held a gold sash around his waist to go with the gold pips of his rank on his shoulders. He walked like a king surveying his subjects. On his hip he wore a ceremonial sword that had a gold ribbon hanging down. Rebecca watched Governor Bourke greet him. They shook hands, and others were introduced. Once this was done, the music began again, and dancers resumed their places.

Maybe this wasn't going to be as bad as she thought it would be.

Chapter Four

Sir Robert Northcote cast his eyes around the room, ignoring the men but noticing every woman in the hall. At first his gaze swept past Rebecca, but hurriedly returned and stayed transfixed. Rebecca saw him whisper something to his aide before giving his attention to Governor Bourke. The aide in turn spoke to another officer who left his position and walked away.

The music started, a bright polka, people began to dance again, and Lieutenant Yardley took her arm to lead her back to the dance floor. *And just how am I supposed to meet Sir Robert?* wondered Rebecca. As if by magic her question was answered when a man tapped Yardley on the shoulder, a captain dressed in the same mode as General Northcote, but a little younger. He wore a thin moustache that stretched when he smiled.

"Excuse me, Lieutenant, I would be honored if you would allow me to dance with the most beautiful lady in attendance here tonight. My name is Captain Alfred Cutter."

Yardley frowned but stood aside.

Rebecca curtsied and smiled. "Rebecca Courtney, sir, and you have been here too short a time to make such judgments."

He took her hand and bowed curiously. "I need no further inspection to make such a judgment, madam, for you are indeed breathtaking."

"I thank you for your compliment, Captain, but we have only just met, and you embarrass me."

His smile was disarming. He seemed quite accustomed to talking to beautiful women. "I had no such intention in mind, and I apologize. Am I forgiven?"

"You are, sir." She laughed and took his arm as he led her to the dance floor, passing Sir Robert Northcote who was in conversation with the Governor. Rebecca noted his gaze never left her face as they passed. As they danced, Captain Cutter questioned her on her background.

"Do you live permanently here in the colony, Miss Courtney?"

She smiled. "Oh no. I'm from Cornwell. My father died recently, and I'm here on business to open up a market for some of the ladies in the town. New gowns, that sort of thing."

"I must say it is unusual for a lady like yourself to be interested in business." He slipped his hand around her waist as they danced.

"As I said, my father died, and I seem to be the only one who can make an income for my dear mother. I enjoy the challenge." Rebecca held her stare in a convincing look and was sure Cutter believed her.

"Please accept my condolences, Miss Courtney."

"Thank you. You are part of Sir Robert's company?" asked Rebecca, smiling guilelessly.

He squeezed her hand gently and continued to whirl her around. "I am, and I must confess, I have been sent to complete an important mission."

"A mission?" Rebecca gave him a look of surprise.

"Yes, Sir Robert Northcote has asked to be introduced to you. He is most anxious to meet you."

"Really? How exciting! He seems to be a very elegant man."

Cutter broke away and bowed to her. "He is indeed, madam. May I be so bold as to escort you to him to complete the introduction?"

"You may indeed, Captain Cutter." Rebecca took his offered arm as they walked towards Sir Robert, who turned as they approached.

"Sir Robert, I would like you to meet Miss Rebecca Courtney. She is here on holiday after completing some business. The late Sir James Courtney was her father."

His eyes began to sparkle as he looked deeply into hers. "My pleasure, Miss Courtney. I'm afraid I never had the privilege of meeting Sir James." He clasped her hand gently and kissed her fingers tips as she curtsied while smiling up at him. She noted his hand held calluses from hours of sword practice. His fingers were lean and long. When he bent down his eyes fell to her breasts. His lips were dry, but he had a gentle touch, a touch she hoped to explore if the opportunity arose.

"I'm very pleased to meet you, Sir Robert. Are you visiting the colony for an extended time?'

"Unfortunately, only a couple of weeks or so. I am to inspect the prison and the garrison and report back to London soon."

"The prison! That's run by Colonel William Collins, a delightful man. I had the pleasure of meeting him last week. He does a wonderful job." Rebecca said.

"I have heard that is correct. From all reports he does seem to carry out his duties in the proper manner. I have an appointment to see him later in the week. You say you have met him?"

"Yes, I spent a few days in his home. Mrs. Collins is also a delightful lady. They are both dear friends of my parents and knew my father very well some years ago. I just had to catch up."

"Then it is good to meet up with old friends."

"Yes it is. He seems genuinely concerned for the women prisoners. Of course, I didn't enter the walls, but from all accounts he's doing a wonderful job."

Northcote stood with one hand behind his back. "It's unusual to see an unescorted lady here in the colony. It's hardly a place for a holiday. Are you here for business?" he said raising an eyebrow.

"Yes. I hope to bring the latest fashion to the women of the colony next year."

"Then I wish you success. I, too, am here on business. I have many things to do while I am here," he said still holding his stare.

"Then you have little time for pleasure while you are here."

"I think perhaps I might make time, Miss Courtney." He smiled, looking deeply into her eyes.

"I admit, I haven't had the chance to see the sights of Sydney yet. I have been busy paying visits."

His face broke out into a huge smile. "Then maybe I can be your escort, Miss Courtney, perhaps tomorrow?'

"That is very kind of you, sir." She held his stare.

He took her hand again. "I wonder perhaps if I may have the pleasure of the next dance."

She curtsied graciously. "Of course, Sir Robert."

"You must call me Robert," he said as he swept her expertly toward the dance floor.

"And I'm Rebecca."

"I'm beginning to like this colony already, Rebecca." She saw Lieutenant Yardley watching intently as they danced past, his expression bland. Rebecca suspected he was jealous.

"I must say, Rebecca, I never expected to meet such a beautiful lady like yourself when I arrived. I want to claim all the remaining dances with you."

"I'd be honored, Robert. You are such a wonderful dancer. You handle the waltz so well. I feel like I'm floating on air."

He grinned at her. "Angels are supposed to float on air."

She gave a little giggle. This was going well. Rebecca was very aware of the scowls from the other women as they waltzed past. She knew quite a few of them expected Robert to dance with them, but he showed interest only in her.

He escorted her to the refreshment table, and they stood talking as they ate and drank an elegant red wine.

Although Rebecca's knowledge of the politics of France and England was somewhat out of date, she did manage to gain his interest. Claire had certainly done her job well in keeping the girls up to date with foreign affairs.

At last the evening came to an end when Robert's handlers prompted him. "Its time to leave, Sir Robert Etiquette dictates that the other guests depart any time after you."

Robert nodded to him then took Rebecca's hand and kissed it. "Which inn are you staying at, my dear?" he asked.

"It's called the Rose Manor. It's on the waterfront and has a beautiful view of the harbor."

He kissed her hand again and held it as he continued talking. "Then I shall pick you up at eleven tomorrow, if that suits you?"

"It will indeed, Robert. I look forward to meeting you again."

She gave him an alluring smile. Yardley approached her to take her back to the inn.

Once in the carriage she smiled at Yardley. "It has been a wonderful night, Lieutenant."

"Sir Robert seemed very interested in you, Miss Courtney."

"Yes, he's a charming man, and I won't need your services in the next few days as Sir Robert is personally going to show me around Sydney."

"I see," Yardley said quietly.

The next morning at eleven a knock on her door attracted her attention. A clerk bowed to her and spoke excitedly.

"Miss, there is a gentleman waiting below in a small carriage."

"Thank you," she said, closing her door behind her. She had been up since seven preparing herself Her eyes opened wide when she saw the small carriage devoid of guards.

"Why, Robert, you are by yourself."

He leapt down and took her hand, helping her into the open carriage. "I didn't want others intruding on our rendezvous," he replied, smiling into her eyes.

She noted he still held her hand.

"Rendezvous? I thought you were going to show me Sydney town."

"Just a play on words, my dear. I'm sure I can give you an exciting day. I have some lunch and drinks packed, and the weather is excellent. I think a picnic is in order."

She looked at him coyly. "Then I am ready," she said. He gave the horse a flick of the reins, and she settled back to enjoy the excellent day ahead of her. Rebecca clearly understood how he had left behind so many broken hearts; his handsome looks and charm would have attracted many women. If she had been some innocent young girl, she could easily have fallen into such a trap as he looked so regal in his red and gold uniform. He gave the impression everyone was expected to obey his orders. She liked men of power.

Robert took her on a tour of the local sights. Their first stop was at the Harbor, where he stopped the carriage in a spot overlooking the water. Several ships were in sight.

"That's my ship," he said, pointing to one of the larger vessels. "She's a fine lady who carries me safely."

"What is her name?" asked Rebecca softly, taking in the large vessel. After her trip out here she had no ambition to board any ship again.

"The Royal Princess. A worthy name."

They continued on, and she smiled at the wonder about her. "Robert, see those beautiful gardens. They remind me a little of home."

"Look," he said, pointing to some red and blue Rosella parrots tasting the succulent buds of the tree they had landed on. "Look how they almost turn upside down to get the buds."

Rebecca almost jumped out of the carriage when a huge flock of white sulphur crested cockatoos gave an ear-piercing screech as they took off in panic, spooked by the carriage.

"Noisy aren't they?" said Robert, laughing at her antics.

"Goodness. There must be over two hundred of them. They are quite large, aren't they?"

Again he laughed. "They are indeed and loud to go with it."

As they continued through the bush, Robert grabbed her arm.

"What is it, Robert?" she asked startled.

"There, ahead of us. I think it is called a kangaroo."

"What a strange looking creature. Will it harm us?"

"I don't think so. I'm told the natives eat them. Those long legs carry them over great distances very quickly." He flicked the reins and continued on.

"It is a strange country this Australia."

The tour went on, and they passed many fine homes. "One wouldn't expect such fine homes to be built so quickly in the colony," she said, admiring the white brick mansions.

"Really, Rebecca? The place has grown considerably since the first fleet arrived in 1786. I would expect nothing less."

Eventually he stopped the horses in the shade of a clump of large trees. He spread the tartan blanket over the native ground cover and produced a basket of chicken and wine.

"Why, Robert, how clever of you. You really did bring lunch."

"A lady like you deserves better, but under the circumstances it's the best I can offer."

"You're such a gentleman," she said, watching him preen.

Once he had the blanket spread out Rebecca continued her conversation. She wanted to know as much about him as she could.

"I presume you have had much experience in the army," she asked.

He grinned at her. "Of course. My father is a friend of the King, and I was given a commission at an early age."

"My God, the King?" she said feigning surprise. "Have you actually met the King?"

"Oh yes. Quite often as a matter of fact. I spent quite a while at Buckingham palace. The invitation was always open to our family."

"But to know the royal family? That's incredible."

"It is certainly no barrier to my career."

"Is it true what they say about the King, that he's a little-" she raised her eyebrows.

"I can tell you a few tales that would make your hair stand on end."

"Really?" she said. "Please do."

"It might make you blush," he said, grinning.

"I'm sure I can handle it." She picked up a piece of chicken and offered it to him. He took it and poured a glass of wine.

He eased back and grinned. "One evening after a ceremonial dinner in the barracks, a few of the officers, myself included, entertained the King. We were very drunk, and his Majesty suggested we go to his club for entertainment. We were all very merry and more than surprised to see his club was a bordello."

Rebecca couldn't help but gasp.

"Well the place was filled with many beautiful women. At least I think they were for I was as drunk as the rest. When the King took one of the girls upstairs we knew instantly what sort of a club it was. Seeing we were there we all decided to try the talents. A stunning looking girl took me up to her room and taught me tricks I had never heard of before."

"What did you say the name of the club was?" she asked as if surprised.

"The London Gentleman's Club. I heard a judge tried to close it down, but he died before that could happen. Just as well," he said smiling.

"Really?" So Puritan Perc is no longer with us, she thought with some satisfaction.

"Yes. I must say the Madam was most appreciative of our business. She made us very welcome."

"The Madam? Is that a woman who operates such a place?" she asked, deliberately appearing naive.

"Yes. She was a delightful lady although she didn't entertain. I think her name was Claire someone. Can't remember the rest."

"Did this happen long ago?" asked Rebecca.

"About three years ago now. The mistress said she had to get a new batch of girls in as the others had left in mysterious circumstances."

"I see. And you haven't been back?" she asked. This was the first news she'd had of Claire since she'd left London. So Claire was alive and well. She had always been grateful to her for pulling her from the slums when she was a child.

"No. I never had to. I have met so many beautiful girls in the last three years that I've lost count. I have to admit, none of them were prettier than you."

"You're too kind, Robert. You make me blush."

"Nonsense, I tell the truth. Now tell me a bit more about yourself. Where in England did you grow up?"

Rebecca drew in a deep breath. Now she had to be careful for he might be familiar with whatever she told him.

"Well, do you know much about Cornwell?" she asked smiling.

"Not really. I spent most of my youth at my father's estate in the north country."

She let out a sigh under her breath as if reminiscing her past.

"And where is your father's estate?" asked Robert, interested in learning what he could about this beautiful woman.

"It's in Cornwell. Have you ever been there?" She crossed her fingers in case he asked where in Cornwell.

"Never had the pleasure," he said, enthralled by her eyes. "And you were well educated?"

"Oh yes. I went to a private school. You see, I am an only child, and, I must confess, thoroughly spoiled by my father."

"I can understand that," he said grinning. "It must have been hard to take when he died."

"That's when all my trouble started. The estate flourished until he died. Then taxes had to be paid and our income depleted."

"So that's when you decided to do something about it. I admire your courage, Rebecca."

"Thank you. It was that or starve, and I'm not one to sit around and do that."

He patted her hand. "I can see you are a courageous and headstrong woman. I wish you well in your business prospects."

She took a quick glance, relieved to see he believed her. "I understand this place is going to grow in the future, and the women deserve to be able to buy the latest fashion. Once I've established business contacts, I will return home and open a factory to make the garments, then ship them out here. I have much work to do."

"You sound as though you know what you are doing. I wish you success."

"Thank you, Robert. It's kind of you to say so."

She constantly kept her attention on him, always agreeing with him as Claire had taught her long ago. Although on a mission, she could feel herself falling under his spell, and she enjoyed the first contented moment she had experienced since her internment.

Their meal completed, Robert moved closer, taking her hand She lifted her head delicately, and he brought his lips down to hers, taking her breath away. She returned his kiss with passion, something she didn't have to fake. She had pretended to like many in her profession. The captain, the customers at the club, all part of the act, but this was the first time she had actually enjoyed such a kiss. He slipped his hand to her breast, and she quickly removed it in mock innocence.

"Robert!" She hoped to sound suitably shocked.

"I'm so sorry, Rebecca, but you are so beautiful I just forgot myself. Please forgive me."

She sat up just far enough for the front of her dress to gape slightly, affording him a glimpse of her white milky breasts. Not wanting to scare him into celibacy, she lowered her eyelids and murmured.

"You scared me. I didn't think you were like that."

"We had better return you to your accommodation," he said stiffly, clearly not used to rejection. Rebecca thought quickly.

"It's so public here, Robert, my reputation would be in tatters if we were discovered. If we were alone..."

His eyes lit up.

"I assure you your reputation will be well protected, Rebecca."

"A woman's reputation is everything. You are a very handsome man, but I must be careful in what I do. Maybe in privacy things might be different. I could not face the embarrassment back home if my friends found out," she added.

"Be sure not a word of it will pass my lips. Shall we go?" He eagerly offered her his hand.

The journey back to the inn was quiet as Rebecca pondered in her mind all the possible ways to entice him a little more. Show resistance to giving in? She wasn't sure. This man expected women to fall at his feet. She moved a little closer to him, and he glanced at her when her thigh pressed against his. She smiled coyly and noticed a grin beginning to crease his mouth.

When they reached the inn he surprised her by pulling her close and kissing her gently on the lips. She tried to look flustered, glanced up and down the street and then smiled at him.

"This has been such a lovely day, Robert."

"I have a special request," he said holding her hand.

"And that is?" she said raising an eyebrow.

"Would you do me the honor of dining with me in my quarters at Government House tonight?"

It took all of Rebecca's willpower not to smile. A former courtesan being invited to dine at the Governor's mansion? How Claire would laugh. She forced a little gasp of surprise. "Oh, Robert, that would be lovely."

With the arrangement settled she returned to her room to rest and sort out her thoughts. How could she seduce him and make it seem like it was his idea? She spent the remainder of the afternoon napping and bathing, and then selected a dress of emerald green that she knew complimented her dark hair and eyes perfectly. The bodice was fastened with a row of small pearl buttons finishing at her tiny waist, which was swathed with a long sash falling almost to the floor. She arranged her hair, tying it loosely at the nape of her neck with a green satin ribbon to match the dress.

Standing back, she surveyed the finished result in the mirror, pleased with her reflection. She felt sure he would melt like snow in her hands.

The carriage arrived for her at the appointed time, and she journeyed to the Government house to dine with Robert. The look on his face when he saw her delighted her and gave her more confidence.

"My God, you're beautiful!" he managed to gasp.

"Thank you, Robert. You know how to compliment a lady."

"Let me show you to my quarters," he said after taking her wrap. He led her into another room where a large desk stood away from the wall. A thick carpet decorated the floor and tapestries hung from the walls.

"This is very nice," she said, inspecting the room.

"This has been made available for me to write my reports on the condition of the colony."

"And what's behind that door?" she asked, having a fair idea what his reply would be.

"My bedroom. I'm sure you don't need to see that."

"But I do. I haven't been in such a grand house for a long time." She showed enthusiasm that gained his attention.

"Very well, my dear, if you insist." He opened the door and stood back as she entered.

Rebecca stood and took in the decor.

A large bed lay against the middle of a wall. A lovely fur rug lay on the floor and a polished wardrobe that held a large mirror adorned the opposite wall. A large well padded couch with a tasteful covering was at the end of the bed. Several lovely murals adorned the walls. A warm fire was burning in the fireplace.

"Robert, this is magnificent."

"Well one would expect Government House to be well decorated. The Governor himself is away at the moment so we have the place to ourselves-except for the servants, of course." He took her hand. "You must be starved, shall we dine?"

He led her to another room where a small table had been set with a white tablecloth and gold cutlery. A small vase of red roses was placed in the center and was accompanied by two candles in a small but elegant candelabra. A servant appeared almost from nowhere and held her chair out for her.

"I think white wine would go best with dinner?" said Robert, sitting opposite her.

"Thank you."

The servant poured a little into his glass for him to taste. When satisfied he nodded, and the man filled both glasses.

Rebecca had never dined like this before, and she meant to savor every moment.

The first course was a cream soup that tasted delicious. Rebecca gently dabbed her mouth with the napkin, and the man took away her empty plate.

Roast vegetables were taken from a silver dish that sparkled with brilliance.

Rebecca wondered how much time it took to get it to this sheen. Next, a large turkey was placed on the side table where a man began carving delicious morsels of the meat onto each plate.

"I hope you find this satisfactory, Rebecca," Robert said sipping his wine.

"This is wonderful, Robert. Thank you for inviting me."

The meal continued until sweets were served, a hot steaming pudding covered with rich custard.

Over the meal they discussed the politics i nn Europe, although she knew little about them.

"We are still having problems with the French, my dear. I fear they want to conquer the world."

"But of course they won't overcome our powerful navy, will they?" She hoped this would impress him.

"No. And of course our army is much superior to theirs. I have no fear for England when I see our magnificent fighting men."

"I must admit, Robert, as a mere woman I have little knowledge of the ways of politics."

He lifted his glass. "And that is the way things should be. Women have other things to fill their minds instead of constant bickering between nations."

"Do you think the colony will be a valuable source of trade for us, Robert?"

"Not yet, but I do see there will be room for expansion. Wool is the likely source of wealth. Already some of the settlers are raising sheep, Merinos I've heard."

Sheep didn't interest Rebecca. She took a sip of her wine. "As I mentioned last evening, I was most impressed with the way Governor Collins is running the prison for women. I had afternoon tea with him recently, a delightful and efficient man."

"I have a meeting with him in a few days. I'll keep my impressions until then." He sat back staring into her eyes, and she knew she certainly had his attention. It appeared Collins had little interest to him.

Rebecca had never enjoyed the company of a man so much, and she had moments where she totally forgot she was there to do a job, a job only her special talents could fulfill and one that would earn her a twelve month reduction on her sentence.

"Perhaps we could take a brandy in the drawing room," he said as another servant pulled her chair out to allow her to stand. Once in the drawing room, a glass of brandy was handed to her, and Robert dismissed the servants for the evening.

"I hope you don't feel embarrassed by having dinner alone with me. It's not really done in England, but we do give some freedom here in the colony."

"Of course not," she said looking up at him. "It's as you say, we are a long way from home, and we should enjoy ourselves."

Rebecca sat on the sofa when Robert came to stand behind her. He bent toward her, removed the glass from her hand and placed it on a small table. She felt his hands run gently across her neck and exposed shoulders.

She gave a little shudder of excitement. This certainly hadn't happened before. When he found no protest he bent lower and kissed her neck. Rebecca turned and looked upwards into his eyes. He dropped to his knees, kissing her gently on the lips. He then rose, took her hand and guided her into his bedroom where he pulled her closer and gave her a kiss with more passion than the first.

"My God, Rebecca, he whispered breathlessly You are the most beautiful woman I have seen in years."

He kissed her again taking her in his arms. His hands went to her bodice as he fumbled with her buttons, but she placed her hand on his making him pause.

"Are we alone?" she said as if scared someone would intrude.

"Absolutely. I've dismissed the servants for the night. We will not be interrupted."

"You understand I don't normally do this," she said as he continued to undo buttons.

"This will be a secret between the two of us." He smiled as her bodice flopped open. The sight of her breasts spurred him on.

She stared into his eyes as she undid his coat and helped_him slip out of it. Her fingers slowly unbuttoned his shirt, and when his naked chest was exposed, she ran her hands over his flesh. His skin was taunt and as smooth as silk. Hairless, unlike some of the men from the club, but she liked that. She ran her hands over his flesh and noted the muscles of his chest. He seemed to keep himself in top condition. No sign of fat, just smooth firm flesh.

"You're such a handsome man," she said, smiling at him.

He pulled down her dress to reveal several layers of underclothing and slowly he removed them one by one until she remained in nothing but her chemise. With false modesty she looked down, but he lifted her face and kissed her once again. When he pressed his face into her breasts she closed her eyes and-he swept her in his arms and carried her to the bed.

As he slipped down her last item of clothing a shudder ran through her. It was a shudder of pleasure and a totally new experience for her.

He leaned back and stared at her. "My God, you're beautiful,"' he said taking in her shape. Her figure was perfect, her breasts pert, and his eyes fell to the silky hair between her legs. "I must have you. I'm a desperate man in seeing such beauty. I can't help myself." He placed both hands on her shoulders and stared into her eyes with a passion she had never seen before.

"Please, you will be gentle," she said like a frightened schoolgirl.

He pulled her close and kissed her passionately, then dropped his lips to her breast. Rebecca threw her head back, taking in the pleasure. Then he tore off his own clothes until both were naked.

Slowly she reached out and touched him, then grasped him in her hand. He gave a groan of pleasure.

He murmured and closed his eyes as she stroked him. He pulled her hand away quickly and rested for a few seconds, then dropped his lips to her throat, her breasts, and her belly.

He was eager and eased her legs apart as he dropped between her thighs. When he slipped inside her, he made her gasp with delight. She had done this many times before, but never had she felt this crescendo building inside her She sensed he, too, was reaching that point, as his thrusts became more urgent. She could hear someone moaning and gasping, and then realized it was herself as her pleasure began to peak.

A wonderful flood washed over them both, and she wrapped her legs around him tightly, unwilling to let him go.

He touched her face gently with his hand. She threw her arms around his neck and kissed him again. He nuzzled her neck and whispered, "I think I'll extend my stay. Tell me my, love, you'll see me again."

"You needn't ask, my darling" said Rebecca as she allowed her hand to fall to his groin. She immediately felt him begin to stir again.

Over the next week, Robert visited her every night, and his desire was met by her own as they made love in a wild frenzy of passion. They could never get their clothes off quickly enough, and their lovemaking was the most passionate Rebecca had ever experienced. It was no customer client relationship, this had true feelings she found hard to control.

After one erotic bout of lovemaking, they lay back on her bed and stared at the ceiling.

"I have to tell you I am leaving very soon to go back to England. I have finished my inspection, and the ship must leave in the next day or two."

A wave of disappointment swept over her. He was ready to leave, and she wanted him to stay longer. This was living. A nice inn, comfortable surroundings, great food and a lover she never thought she would have. Soon it would be back to the prison cell to serve out the rest of her sentence. She prayed Collins would keep his word and release her a year earlier. At least she would have the memory of Robert and their lovemaking. It would seem as though he had died, and the pain of loss would hurt her considerably.

"I shall miss you terribly, Robert. I'm so glad I came to the colony."

"I'm glad, too, my darling."

Did you ever visit the prison, Robert? She asked trying to pull information from him.

"Yes, my love, I visited the prison as I said I would."

"And you saw Colonel Collins?" she asked hopefully.

"Yes. The man was as you said he was. I'll recommend him for a knighthood when I return. I think that will please him."

And me too, thought Rebecca. She just hoped Collins would be satisfied with her effort.

He took her in his arms once again and kissed her forehead. "You must give me your address in London. I'm going to make sure we meet once again."

She thought quickly. "Oh Robert, at this time I am without residence as my home was sold before I came to the Colony. Perhaps you can give me a contact address for when I return to London, I will find you so we can meet again."

"I'll look forward to it, my dearest love. I'll be counting the days until I hear from you." he said, smiling as he reached for his coat, produced a notebook and scribbled out his address with a pencil.

She went with him to the dock to see him leave. Before he boarded the ship he took her in his arms and kissed her passionately. She returned the kiss and soldiers turned away, embarrassed by the passion between them.

"Goodbye, my love," he said sadly. "Until we meet once again in England. Hopefully within the year."

"I look forward to it. Thank you for the most wonderful three weeks of my entire life."

He swept her into his arms for one last lingering embrace and then turned and boarded the ship. Rebecca waited until the large sails were lowered, and the ship pulled away from the dock and towards the open sea.

Tears gathered in her eyes. She felt a love like she had never experienced before but knew it was over as she would never see him again.

She heard the sound of horse's hooves and turned to see Lieutenant Yardley beside the carriage in which they had traveled to Sydney Town.

"Governor Collins sends a message saying we must return at once, Miss."

Keeping her head turned so he couldn't see her tears, she nodded and stepped into the carriage to return to a life that could never be the same, now that she had tasted freedom, luxury, and true excitement and perhaps the love of her life.

As the carriage made its way back to Parramatta, Yardley smiled at her. "I hope you had a very pleasant holiday in Sydney, Miss."

"Very pleasant, Lieutenant. The General saw that I missed nothing."

"He's a handsome man, isn't he?" he said with a slightly jealous tone in his voice.

"He is indeed, Lieutenant. I have fond memories of his company."

Nothing more was said as Rebecca stared out of the window at the passing countryside and gave her thoughts to Robert and their passionate encounter. What lay ahead for her once she was back behind the prison doors she didn't want to think about.

She watched Collins smile and rub his hands together. "You have done well, Rebecca," he said gleefully. "Sir Robert said he would recommend a knighthood on his return. I shall keep my bargain and grant you an early release."

"Thank you, sir."

"Now get out of those clothes and return them to Mrs. Collins. She holds a new prison dress for you, and once you are changed, a guard will escort you back to the prison."

Rebecca sighed. She had somehow hoped Collins would see to it that her comfort was better considering the favor she had shown to him.

Sadly, she removed the dress and soft underclothes and picked up the new prison dress under the supervision of Mrs. Collins. The depression of returning to the prison hit her. Life could never be this good again.

Mrs. Collins patted her hand. "As my husband said, Rebecca, you have done well. Remember, do not say anything about this episode."

Rebecca nodded and watched as she signaled a guard. He jerked his thumb at her, and she followed him back to the prison.

"Well look who's back," said one of the women. "Where the hell have you been for the last month?"

"I did some domestic work for Colonel Collins. It didn't work out."

The woman laughed. "He wanted more than domestic work, did he?"

"Not exactly, but Mrs. Collins thought he did. She sent me back here."

The woman laughed again. "Are you sure he didn't stick it into you. He's a man, remember."

"No, he didn't. Looks like I'm back here for good."

"Like the rest of us, luv, like the rest of us."

Chapter Five

Rebecca was eating her morning meal when suddenly she felt nauseated. She ran to the nearest toilet bucket and vomited into it.

"I know the food is crook," said Beverly Ryan, one of the women with whom she shared the cell, "but it hasn't made us sick."

"I'll be okay in a minute," she said as she rested.

"Seeing you're sick then you won't be wanting that." Beverly reached across and grabbed her metal plate. Rebecca didn't mind as food was the last thing she thought about. Next morning it happened again. Beverly frowned at her.

"Has one of the guards been sticking his dick into you?"

"Why do you say that?" she said, but the first suspicions began to form.

"Bein' sick in the morning is a sign you might be pregnant."

Rebecca gave thought to when she had her last period. It was utter shock when the realization hit home.

"My God. I think I am." She stared at Beverly as the consequence became obvious.

"Oh shit," said Beverly. "Babies can't survive in here. Already they had to take out four to bury in the last month."

She hadn't given precautions a thought during the passionate weeks she had spent with Robert. It had been two months since she had returned to the prison, two months in which she thought constantly about the delicious body that held her so dearly and of the weeks' lovemaking she had enjoyed so much.

This was a disaster. She had seen over twenty babies born in the three years of her imprisonment and only four survived to the age of two. The horrendous mortality rate left her in no doubt her baby would suffer a similar fate.

The prison authorities had little sympathy for women who fell pregnant. It only confirmed the fact they were harlots who continued to practice their trade in their detainment, a crime most had been found guilty of in England. There were no facilities to raise children in the confines of the prison, however, some were fortunate enough to be adopted by settlers' wives, even though children of such people were considered inferior. No thought was given to the fact that the women were forced into giving themselves just to achieve some comfort in life.

She asked to see the Governor, a request she didn't expect to be granted, but surprisingly it was. She assumed he still had concerns that she would break the secret they shared.

"What is it, Smith? I am a very busy man and can't spare you much time."

"I am in trouble, sir, and need your help."

"Trouble? What sort of trouble?"

"I am carrying a child."

He fell down into his chair and poured himself a brandy before speaking. "I suppose you expect me to believe that Sir Robert is the father of this child?" he said, his face taut. "How do I know that this is not the child of one of the guards?"

"I have been with no man since he left, sir," she said, lowering her head.

"Suppose I believe you. You want me to do something about it?"

"Yes, sir. I'm asking if you will allow me to seek employment as a domestic to enable the baby to survive."

He slammed his fist onto the table. "Absolutely not," he roared. "If this gets out then I will never be knighted."

"But, sir, it was your request that I sleep with Sir Robert. You must help me."

A dark scowl covered his face. "May I remind you that you are a convict here found guilty of selling sexual favors. I don't have to do anything. No one would believe such a tale." Then he paused as he turned the news over in his mind. "However, it could cause some embarrassment or gossip. I remind you never to speak of this with anyone, especially the guards. I will give it some thought. Now leave."

Rebecca returned to her cell and broke down in tears. A touch on her shoulder disturbed her.

"You got trouble, luv?" an elderly woman asked kindly.

"I'm pregnant," said Rebecca as she wiped her eyes.

"Got a bundle of arms and legs in your belly have ya? It happens all the time. Which guard did it?"

"Does it matter?" Rebecca asked sadly.

"I suppose not. I can help ya you know."

"How?"

"I can do wonders with a bit of wire. Have ya right in no time."

Rebecca was horrified at the thought. She had seen others die in agony after some such person had helped.

She almost spat at the woman who stepped back quickly. The sharpness of her tone made the woman wary. "No thank you. I'll solve the problem some other way." But she really didn't know how.

The woman shrugged her shoulders. "Suit yourself, but if ya change ya mind come and see me. I was only trying to help."

"Thank you, I will," she said, anxious for the woman to leave.

For another two weeks she worried as to the chances of her baby surviving for she could not bear the thought of killing it. Then she was summoned to the Governor's office once again.

Nervously she knocked on his door. *Perhaps he was going to relent and let me out into domestic work. Perhaps he had made enquiries and found out I had not been with a man since Robert left. Perhaps he was going to dash all my hopes and make me suffer for getting pregnant.*

"Enter," she heard him call. She stepped inside the office to see him seated at his desk.

"You wish to see me, sir," she said boldly. If it was bad news then she would not give him the pleasure of seeing her cower. He snapped his book shut and stared at her. "Convict Smith, I may have a solution to your problem. However, you will only have one chance and one chance only. If you turn it down then you will only have yourself to blame."

"What chance is that, sir?"

"Tomorrow the women will be assembled in the yard of the prison. Those with light sentences will be displayed to some of the settlers of the area. I admit that some of these men are what I would call undesirables, but they are needed to develop the country."

"What are you saying, sir?"

"There has been a request for single men to obtain wives so that they may develop the land and populate. They will be given a chance to select wives from the women prisoners, who will find their sentences suspended if they wed these men. Any woman who turns down a settler will be escorted back to her cell to finish her term."

"You mean we will have to marry them and live with them as man and wife?"

"It shouldn't be such a hardship for you; after all, you're used to submitting to such men. Think it as a way out." He looked at her as if she were scum.

"But not to the likes of that class. Only to gentlemen."

He smirked. "Really, Convict Smith, you know and I know that most men are interested in only one thing, and it doesn't matter if they are of the noble class or the lower class. They want what a woman can give them, and if they are lucky enough to gain a domestic servant at the same time, then all to the better." He sat tapping his fingers together to give her time to consider the offer.

Rebecca looked dismayed. "But they could be anyone, old, cruel, mean, violent, anything."

He gave a snigger as if it didn't matter. "That is the chance you will have to take. If you turn them down there will be no second chance."

Rebecca drew in a breath as she considered the offer. "What if he learns that I am already with child?"

"I would suggest you do not tell him until later. Some of them are so stupid they may think it will be theirs."

Rebecca shook her head. The Governor certainly underestimated the intelligence of men. She had a serious decision to make, marry one and possibly save the life of her child or remain in prison to serve out her years and see the baby die.

She knew that whoever the man would be, he certainly wasn't going to care one way or another about her well-being. He would only want a woman to serve him in any way he wished. She had seen this sort in the streets of London and clearly knew of the character of such men. It was unlikely that they would be of good stock, for who would come to such a far away place willingly? Most were convicts who had regained their freedom and had little money. Only the gentry who saw opportunity to great wealth in the new land were people of substance, and they would not be seeking women from the prison.

She sighed and looked at him. There was not much choice-agree or rot in prison. "Very well, sir, I agree to offer myself as a wife, but I feel I must inform the man of my condition. Would that be considered turning down the man's offer?"

Collins shook his head in the negative. "No. It would be he who turned you down. There may be several offers forthcoming, but you will have to take the first to accept you."

Her shoulders slumped as she thought of who might pick her.

"I understand, sir," she said reluctantly and prayed that it would be a good man who selected her. For the sake of her unborn child she would put up with whatever he was.

When she returned to the cells she noted that the message had already reached the other women via the guards.

"Have ya heard?" said Beverly when she stepped into the cell. "We all got a chance to get out of here."

"I heard," Rebecca said quietly.

"Ya don't look too happy about it," said another, obviously pleased with the news.

"The man could be anything. He may knock us around. The chances of getting a good man is slim."

One gave a laugh. "The bloody guards stick it to us at their whim. What's the difference in letting a settler do it? I can lay on my back and pretend I enjoy it if it gets me out of here."

"Yeah," said another. "Old, young or ugly, they all have cocks, and they all feel the same. Once we are out we might be able to piss off and find someone nice."

"And how will you do that?" asked Rebecca raising an eyebrow. "You won't have any money and probably neither will the settler."

"If I have to do it for free, then I can do it for money. I've been a whore before."

"But life is different here." Rebecca shook her head. She knew that life as a whore was not going to get them anywhere.

"Anyone got a comb? I gotta look my best when they put us on show. The man can feel my tits, touch anywhere he likes. I'll smile and tell him I can offer him a lot more than that."

Others agreed, and they spent the rest of the day trying to make themselves look presentable.

The women were lined up about two yards apart. Some made last minute alterations to their hair, licking their fingers and brushing strands back in place. Others loosened their tops to reveal as much breast as they could. All stood nervously waiting for the show to begin. Then the gates opened. Twenty-five men walked in, and the women knew there would be fierce competition as fifty of them were going to miss out.

Rebecca groaned when she saw them, for they were just as she expected: grubby, in soiled clothes, many of them bearded and a few young, with most over thirty-five. Some of the women smiled broadly at them, throwing out their breasts inviting closer inspection. Rebecca was by far the prettiest girl there, and she got close attention from several of the men although she stood straight, never making eye contact but looking ahead with a tense expression on her face.

One of the younger men, perhaps no older than she was, stood in front of her, chewing briskly on tobacco. His face had a bad case of acne, and his nose had been broken. She noticed he had two teeth missing from his upper jaw. He spat on the ground and circled her twice, then held her by the mouth.

"Open your gob," he said curtly and waited for her to comply. She did so, and he looked into her mouth as if he were inspecting a horse or other livestock. Her skin crept as he moved his face close to hers.

"You're not bad lookin'; bet you're good in bed, too. Got any diseases?"

"Not that I know of," replied Rebecca. "However, there is one problem."

"And what might that be?" he said frowning.

"I'm with child."

"Shit, you've got a brat on the way. I ain't looking after anyone else's brat. Are you a whore?"

"Yes," said Rebecca. "I've had thousands of men."

"Well I won't be one of them, slut," he said moving away much to Rebecca's relief.

A second man approached and gave a similar inspection, looking into her mouth. He was about forty and wore a soiled shirt, a dark ill-fitting coat and a large hat. He smelled as though he hadn't had a wash in weeks. He ran his hands over her shoulders and then held her breast.

"Not bad, not bad at all," he said giving his seal of approval. "You're quite a looker. What's ya name?' The man had a slight Irish brogue and looked at her insolently.

"Rebecca Smith."

"I'm Irish, and I don't like the English much, but I could take to you. Me name's Michael McBride and I'm lookin' for a woman. Do ya know how to cook and sew?"

"Doesn't everyone?" said Rebecca insolently.

"Yeah, well that's the second most important thing I need in a woman." He expected Rebecca to ask what was the most important, but she remained silent.

"I need some comfort at night, too," he added as though he expected her to be enthusiastic at his suggestion.

"I can recommend a warm blanket."

"Smart bitch," he snarled. "But then I like a woman with a bit of spirit. I can soon knock any rough spots off you."

Rebecca again inwardly groaned. He was even worse than the first. She thought he would be put off in the same way as the first concerning her pregnancy.

"I'm afraid you will have two to worry about. I'm going to have a baby."

She was further dismayed as he rubbed his chin as though deep in thought.

"That proves you know what's expected, and if it's a boy then he will come in handy on my land. If it's a girl then you'll 'ave someone to give ya a hand cookin' and lookin' after me. I'll take this one," he shouted to the guard, and Rebecca was pushed forward to join others already selected. An hour later, all twenty-five men had selected a woman and the others were herded back to their cells, some bitterly disappointed.

Rebecca looked across at the Governor, who stood with his hands behind his back and stared at her from the balcony of the prison, then looked away.

"The marriages will be held immediately, and you can all be on your way with the necessary paper work," he called and then nodded to a minister who stood patiently with a book in his hand. The groups were lined up to hear his words.

"You will all answer yes to the following question. Do the following people consent to marriage with their partners, Ralph Wallis and Victoria Green?"

"Yes," both answered.

"Michael McBride and Rebecca Smith?"

"Yes," they answered, Rebecca's reply was barely audible.

The minister went right along the entire group naming each person and waited to receive the reply. When he reached the final couple he closed his book. "I now pronounce you all husbands and wives. May God bless your union."

A marriage certificate was handed to each and release papers from the prison signifying that each prisoner was now a free woman.

"Let's go," said McBride, and led her to a wagon waiting outside the limits of the prison.

"Where to?" asked Rebecca, now resigned to her fate.

"I have land here in Parramatta, and a cottage built by the convicts. It's not much, but it's a roof over our heads. It'll be your job to fix it up—and me." He grinned, ogling her body. She shuddered at the thought, but knew she now had no choice.

After a slow trip they reached his property. The cottage was much better than Rebecca had imagined. It was small, no denying that, but it had a wooden floor and a stove fitted in the kitchen. There were two bedrooms. One was quite tiny with a living room that held sparse furniture and a pot-bellied stove. The place was filthy with dust and grime.

"It needs a bit of cleanin' up," said McBride. "You can start on that tomorrow."

"It will take me a week," said Rebecca defiantly.

"Whatever. Your brat can sleep in here after it's born," he said, pointing to the second bedroom. "I'll make some sort of a bed when it gets close. When's it due?"

"In about six month's time," said Rebecca totally disillusioned.

"Right, into the bedroom and get your clothes off. I want to see if the trouble was worth it."

She looked at the bed with its cast iron head and base. The mattress felt reasonably soft so she removed her clothes under the watchful eye of McBride as she carefully folded and placed them on a chair.

He grinned as he ogled her, then dropped his trousers but left his shirt on. He stepped out of his boots and pushed his erect penis in front of her.

"You know what to do," he said and grabbed her hair, forcing her head down. As much as it horrified her, she did his bidding until he pushed her back onto the bed. "Now open ya legs, I want to see, what ya got." he said, waiting for her to comply.

He rolled on top of her. Rebecca lay there gritting her teeth. Mercifully, it was over quickly.

"Not bad, but you'll get better," smiled McBride as he buttoned up his trousers.

That's what you think, thought Rebecca.

"Now we'll see if you can cook. Get the stove goin' and make me a meal. I'm partial to mushrooms and bacon."

* * * * *

Two years earlier.

It was with great regret that Michael McBride stood on the deck of the ship taking him to Sydney on his release from Norfolk Island. Not that he was unhappy to be getting away from that hell hole, but the whole episode of him being there in the first place was the cause of his regret.

Drink and women, a combination mixed with greed ~~that~~ was nearly always fatal. Life in Ireland was hard for everyone, except of course for the English. To survive one had to see an opportunity and grasp it, before it was whisked from one's hand, and Michael McBride was never one to let opportunity slip by. He had a simple philosophy. If it was there then think about how you could steal it. If it was English then definitely steal it, and so he made his way through life by taking advantage of anyone gullible enough to believe what he told them.

As a boy, he had seen his father thrown off his land by their English landlord, even though he had tried his best to pay his debts. His father had been as honest as anyone could be in those hard times, but where did that get him? The English had no sympathy for honest, hard working Irishmen, and when Patrick McBride had died of sheer exhaustion years before his time, Michael resolved to make his money anyway he could.

While he had never been called handsome, he did have the Irish skill of blarney and could talk most honest people into anything. More than once he had offered to work for women living alone for the price of a meal.

On more than one occasion he brought a smile and color to their cheeks with his complimentary words. He would flatter them by telling them that such attractive women should not be doing menial tasks. When they fed him, he would tell them he felt strong and would chop wood or clean up the yard.

Then he would just walk off when they left him to the task. Anything he could take with him was sold to provide drinking money at the local pub. It amazed him how these lonely women would succumb to his charm and lead him to their beds. It was the first time with a man for some, and when he'd had his fill he would leave and look for new victims.

He preyed on lonely people without conscience and became a user in the worst sense of the word. His troubles started when he came to the house of Kathleen McMillan.

Kathleen lived alone in a comfortable house in the village of Galen when McBride wandered in. His offer to work for the price of a meal was accepted, but surprised when Kathleen made him a counter offer. Sleep in the attic for a week and tend to the many chores on a list she produced, and she would pay him four pounds and meals.

Tired of wandering around the country, the offer gave him a chance to have a rest for a change, as his funds were just about exhausted. A week's work would provide him with money for grog and perhaps to pay one of the local girls for his pleasure.

Kathleen, a spinster of thirty, surprised McBride, as she was friendly and not unattractive. He decided to try his luck with her after three days instead of wasting good money on street women.

A true virgin, Kathleen thought her chances of finding a husband were gone. When McBride began to flatter her with his blarney, she felt like a schoolgirl again and began to fall for his charms.

The week turned into a fortnight as Kathleen began to find all sorts of jobs to keep McBride from leaving. When he took her to his room the first time, she gave no resistance, and McBride could see all sorts of possibilities arising. It seemed Kathleen had a small income from a deceased parent and owned her own home.

Free room and board, a woman to take care of the pleasures of life and money to spend in the pub. What more could a man ask for? Things were going along sweetly for over two months until Kathleen broke the news that she was pregnant.

"Oh, Michael," she sobbed. "You'll have to marry me. I won't be able to show my face in the village again."

Like hell, thought McBride and made plans to move on. Late at night he gathered up any goods he thought he might be able to sell and left before first light with the sack over his shoulder. He had gone no more than a few miles when a rider approached. He was shocked to see it was a police constable who pointed a pistol at his head.

"Michael McBride no doubt," the man said grinning. "Open the sack."

McBride emptied the sack under the threat of the pistol and stiffened as the constable slipped a pair of manacles around his wrists.

"Why are you arresting me?" he asked, mystified that Kathleen could call in the police so quickly. It had only been three hours since he had left.

"Because you have the property of Kathleen McMillan. This little lot will get you ten years in prison."

"I don't know any Kathleen McMillan," he said, defiantly.

"Now that's strange, she knows you quite well. Enough so she says you made her pregnant."

"Now that's a lie." McBride smiled. He knew any respectable woman wouldn't confess she was pregnant to a police constable she had never seen before.

"Are you telling me you haven't been living in her attic for over two months and that you haven't been having a little fun with her?"

"Absolutely not," said McBride, trying to sound convincing.

"Then perhaps we had better go back to Galen and sort out the matter."

Shit. At least he knew he could talk Kathleen out of bringing charges against him. Ten years in prison was not something to look forward to.

When they arrived back at Kathleen's home, the constable roughly pushed him into the house.

"Kathleen, my darlin'," said McBride. "This has all been a terrible mistake. Tell this man to release me, and we'll talk about the matter when he has gone."

"Please take off the manacles, Ryan," she said to the constable.

"Ryan?" McBride said. Kathleen seemed to know this man intimately.

"This is Ryan McMillan, Michael. He's my brother and has only just returned from a trial in Belfast."

"And it looks like I'll be returning for another," said Ryan, scowling at McBride.

McBride's face paled noticeably. She had not told him about having a policeman in the family.

"Did you say brother?" Christ, no wonder he knew about her being pregnant.

"Yes. It seems we have a problem here, Michael," said Ryan pleasantly. "You have a choice. Spend ten years in prison or marry Kathleen and be a good father to her child."

"Why, Kathleen darlin'. I was only taking the goods to sell them so I could buy you a wedding ring. I had every intention of coming back."

"Of course, Michael. We both know that, don't we, Ryan?"

"Of course. I think I can arrange the wedding to take place next Saturday. When I explain the circumstances to Father Clooney I'm sure he'll hurry things up a bit. Will that be satisfactory, Michael?" He grinned at McBride's discomfort.

"That will be fine," said McBride, knowing he was beaten.

The wedding was a quiet affair, and Ryan left the two newlyweds to return to his small farm where he ran a few chickens to supplement his income. McBride felt trapped; especially when Ryan told him his duty was to see that Kathleen was taken care of. He let him know loud and clear that if he harmed Kathleen in any way then he would answer to Ryan.

McBride brooded during the months of the pregnancy. He stayed in the pub every night until thrown out at closing time and staggered home drunk to fall under the biting tongue of his wife. The only pleasure he got from the marriage was the sex that Kathleen expected, even though she was pregnant, but sometimes he even regretted that because it was the cause of his entrapment.

Ryan came around every second day only to hear about Kathleen's complaints. McBride kept well out of his way. He knew he would suffer the consequences if he hurt Kathleen in any way, no matter how much he wanted to bash her head in.

The night her labor started, McBride looked at her with contempt. Now he'd have a brat to look after as well as his wife. He had never thought about being a father.

"I think it's starting, Michael. Will you fetch the doctor?"

"It's too early yet," he said. "Wait a while longer. Then I'll go."

Kathleen groaned as another spasm hit her and lay back in the bed. She held on until the pains were ten minutes apart and then pleaded with McBride to fetch the doctor.

"All right, keep your shirt on," he said reluctantly, putting on his coat and stepping out into the cold air. As he walked past the pub the music caught his attention, and he hesitated in mid stride. Perhaps just a quick one, he thought and turned into the bar.

"Michael, me lad," someone called. "Come and have a pint with us."

McBride looked toward a group of men he had known from drinking there every night. He ordered a drink and then sat down to enjoy the company. Anything was better than putting up with his nagging wife.

The pint turned into a second pint and then a third. By the time the pub shut he was rather drunk.

"Better see if the bitch has had the kid yet," he muttered to himself

He staggered home just as he had done most nights and then remembered he hadn't seen the doctor yet. He sobered up very quickly when he saw her lying dead on the bed, a still born baby at her feet and blood everywhere.

Fear gripped him when he thought of what Ryan would do to him, and he knew he had to get away. He needed some cash in a hurry, but where? Kathleen had only two pounds in her drawer so he quickly put that into his pocket. Nothing of much value to steal, he thought, and then he remembered Ryan had a few chickens he sold. If he made a midnight trip to his farm, wrung the necks of a few birds and sold them in the village the next day, he would have at least five pounds to use and would be on his way before Ryan came calling and found Kathleen.

There were no lights on in Ryan's house, making him sure Ryan was fast asleep. Silently, he opened the chicken coop and crept up to the sleeping birds. Fortunately, they made little noise, and he lifted the birds one by one off their perches and wrung the necks of ten of them. He tied their feet together and strung them over a pole he had brought and returned home. As soon as the town came to life, he took the birds to the market and sold them as quickly as he could. Gathering up his belongings, he shut the door and headed to Belfast.

Five days later he was arrested and brought to trial. As it was obvious Kathleen had died from natural causes, Ryan couldn't have charges of murder brought against him.

"Michael McBride, you are charged with theft of chickens from Constable Ryan McMillan. How do you plead?" asked the magistrate solemnly.

"Not guilty, your Worship," McBride smiled. After all, the theft of ten chickens was not going to be all that serious. A spell of six months in jail would keep McMillan away from him.

McMillan took the stand and testified how McBride had been seen selling chickens in the market the day after his chickens disappeared. As McBride had no chickens then it was obvious they were the ones stolen.

"I agree, Constable McMillan. How many chickens went missing?"

"Over two hundred your worship," said McMillan, grinning at McBride.

"He's a flamin' liar," shouted McBride. "It was only ten."

"I think he has convicted himself from his own mouth, your Worship," said McMillan.

"It would seem so," replied the magistrate. "Michael McBride, I find you guilty of the theft of two hundred chickens and sentence you to ten years imprisonment and transportation to his Majesty's prison on Norfolk Island in the New World. Next case."

He slammed his gavel down hard, the noise echoing in McBride's ears as he was led off.

CHAPTER SIX

The ensuing months were worse than Rebecca had expected. McBride made sure she worked hard and struck her when he was displeased. Her body began to swell as the baby grew, and she prayed that any beating would not damage the unborn child. For the first few weeks he made her submit nearly every night, but when she showed not an ounce of passion he bored at the sexual ritual.

"You're a cold bitch," he snarled one night when she moved not an inch as-he lay on top of her.

"I'm sorry you are not satisfied," she replied, but of course she wasn't. At times she tried to think about Robert as he took her, but even that didn't help. When she reached her eighth month he gave up in disgust and visited the women at the local brothel rather than put up with her now huge belly. She was happy he left her alone, but still had to struggle to prepare his meals and clean his house. He had little money and any spare cash was spent on rum and women.

Parramatta was growing rapidly, and Rebecca found one or two friends among the other settler's wives who sometimes came to visit. None of them liked McBride, and they soon stopped coming except Molly McGregor, who visited when Rebecca was alone while McBride worked in his fields.

Molly was a woman of forty with five children, the wife of a Scot who emigrated to leave the poverty and weather of Scotland behind. He owned a farm of some two hundred acres next to McBride's property of fifty acres and constantly bickered with McBride over many small matters.

Molly had seen Rebecca's face after one of the beatings and resolved to try to make life tolerable for her. She brought her clothes and made things for the forthcoming baby, making Rebecca grateful for her friendship.

When she called McBride a thug for the way he treated Rebecca, McBride called her an interfering old hag and told her to get off his property. It was then she began coming around when McBride was out working.

"What else could you expect from an Irishman?" she said to Rebecca. "Why on earth did you marry such a beast?"

"I had no choice," said Rebecca. "I was a convict, Molly, and pregnant. The choice was marry a settler or remain in prison and watch my baby die."

"For what crime were you convicted, child?"

"I could lie to you and say petty theft, but worked the trade in an exclusive Gentleman's Club in London. The authorities decided to make an example of some of us, and I was sent to Botany Bay."

"Then it's not your husband's child?"

Rebecca shrugged her shoulders and bit her lip. She hesitated for a few seconds before replying. Maybe Molly would not want to talk to her once she knew of her past. What did it matter now? "No. I was given no choice but to provide a service for an important man. This is the result."

Molly sat stunned then squeezed Rebecca's hand. "No wonder you had to marry McBride. I don't know if I could have done it. It must be awful having to submit to such a monster."

"What choice do I have? If I refuse he will beat me again. I can't leave as there is nowhere to go. I just lay there while he does it, hoping he will get sick of it."

Molly frowned. The injustice made her angry.

"It is wrong what the authorities are doing to women, Rebecca. They will learn women are a most important part in the development of this country, and they should be shown respect."

"I'm afraid that day is a long way off, Molly," she said and then clutched her belly. "Oh, Molly, I think the baby is coming."

"Is this the first pain?" Molly asked.

"No, it's been happening all day, but none were like this. Maybe every hour or so."

The pain subsided, and Molly eased her onto her bed. "Don't worry, love, I've had five of my own. I know what to do. Just lay back and relax."

Ten minutes later another spasm of pain hit her, and again Molly gripped her hand. "I'll prepare some water to clean you down after the birth," she said, leaving her side briefly.

Molly squeezed her hand at each spasm of pain, and she was grateful she didn't have to endure it alone. The pains began to come closer and closer, each time racking her body until at last Rebecca felt the baby force its way out. The baby made no sound, and she thought it was dead, but Molly soon allayed her fears and placed a small contented bundle into her arms.

"It's a girl, Rebecca, a sweet, tiny angel, and she's fine. What will you call the little mite?"

Rebecca smiled as she looked at her daughter, pink and healthy looking as she lay in her arms. "I'm going to call her Mary. Welcome to the world, Mary McBride. May you have more luck than I've had in my life."

"I'm sure you'll see to that, love," said Molly, smiling proudly. Rebecca lay back, tears forming in her eyes as she looked at her daughter. "May God smile on you, darling," she said as she placed the infant to her breast.

When McBride returned home, he gave the baby a cursory glance and sat down to a meal of cold meat that, unbeknownst to him, Molly had prepared.

"I expect ya to be back on your feet by tomorrow, and I don't want your duties ignored because of the brat."

Rebecca lay back wishing she were rid of him. Molly came around each day, sometimes bringing her young son Campbell who was only twelve months old. Her help was invaluable as she cleaned the house and assisted Rebecca in whatever way she could.

"It will be good to see the young ones grow up together, won't it?" she said as she bathed the infant.

"Yes, she will cherish the company, for I will not bear a child to this fiend I'm married to. I'll see to that."

"You must come and visit us whenever you can get away. Mary will welcome some other children to play with."

Rebecca nodded, determined she would make the best life possible for the child after what she had to put up with to enable her to be born. Within a week she was back to health and continued to keep McBride's home as best she could. At the same time, McBride insisted his conjugal rights must be maintained, and he forced Rebecca to submit once more to a nightly ritual. When she showed no interest whatsoever, he again reverted to the women available for a small fee and bothered her only once a week.

* * * * *

For five years Rebecca took Mary to the McGregor farm whenever she could, and Mary became a close friend with young Campbell and the other McGregor children. Rebecca thought often of clearing out from McBride, but knew it was too early yet. She would have to wait until Mary was old enough to earn money to help keep them. She had heard that land opened up in the south, but money was needed and she had none.

When Mary reached twelve, it was obvious she had inherited her mother's beauty, mixed with her father's handsome features, and Rebecca was disturbed when McBride began staring at Mary. Once, when Mary bathed in a tub, the water only reaching her thighs, McBride burst in and ogled her naked body. She threw her hands across her small breasts, a look of fear crossing her face. He grinned when he saw the first signs of breast formation as Mary hastened to cover herself.

"She's goin' to be a real beauty, that girl. Almost ripe for the pickin'." He grinned lustily and fear clutched Rebecca's throat.

"You keep your filthy hands off her. If you touch her I'll kill you." she screamed, terrified as to what he would do.

He brought his hand back and struck her with a backhand blow, bringing blood to her nose. As she lay on the floor he stood over her. "If you was more amiable, then I wouldn't have to think about her, would I?"

"Get out," she yelled, and McBride left, grinning. Then she knew she had to give McBride a better time, no matter how much she hated it if it was going to protect Mary. Even McBride was surprised at his wife's newfound talents and contented enough to leave Mary alone.

By the time Mary was sixteen, romance entered her life and she was in love. Campbell McGregor had grown into a strapping seventeen-year-old and was as attracted to Mary as she was to him.

"Meet me by the river at night, Mary, after your father has gone to bed." Campbell only had to suggest it, and Mary willingly agreed.

"Poppa goes to bed at nine. I'll be there at ten," she said, excited at the thought of being alone with Campbell. Each night for a month they met, sitting, holding hands, talking and planning their lives until at last Campbell kissed her. Mary didn't have many pleasures in her life, but having Campbell take her in his arms was one of them. The attraction they felt for each other was overwhelming.

Her heart soared when they kissed, and they eagerly explored each other's bodies as they removed their clothes in the privacy of the banks of the river. It needed no prompting from either, and they made love for the first time. Mary's heart soared, and when she was with Campbell she forgot the poverty she lived in.

"I love you, Mary," he whispered in her ear. "We'll marry one day when we get a little older."

She shuddered with the thrill of his warm body on hers. It was a pleasure she didn't know was possible, and she confided in her mother about her relationship with Campbell.

Rebecca was busily peeling potatoes when Mary spoke to her. "Campbell wants to marry me, Mother," she said, and Rebecca smiled when she saw the shine in her eyes. She put down her knife and turned to her daughter.

"And do you want to marry him?" she asked, pleased Mary had found such a nice boy.

"Oh yes, I love him dearly. He wants to go south and claim land where we can set up a home and raise children."

Rebecca was amused. "But he is so young, and so are you."

Mary's face showed her enthusiasm for the dream. She broke out into a big smile as the thought rushed through her mind. "He says we will wait until he turns twenty, then we'll wed."

Rebecca took her hand and stared into her eyes. "Mary," she said carefully. "Campbell is a very nice boy, and he may make an excellent husband, but it is likely he will change as he gets older."

Mary's eyes opened wider. "Change? Whatever do you mean, Mother?" She was quite puzzled in her innocence.

Rebecca shook her head. Years of experience came into play. "You must learn now that men think women were put onto this world to serve them. They will use you at their whim as you can see by the actions of your stepfather."

Mary's mouth popped open. "Campbell is not cruel like Poppa."

"No he's not, at least not yet."

Rebecca's words made her uncomfortable. "But he loves me, and I love him."

"And that is wonderful, but what I'm saying is that sometime in the future, some man will want to use your body as if he owns it. It's a fact of life, and I learned in London years ago that you must take advantage of the fact if the possibility exists." She looked sullen. "Campbell won't do that."

"Maybe not, but if Campbell died or you were left alone for some reason, then a man will want to take advantage of you."

"But Campbell won't leave me."

"Pray to God that he won't, but if he ever does, then you must use men as they use you."

"How?"

"When I was no older than you, I became a courtesan in an exclusive club for gentlemen. I didn't particularly want to, but it was that or die on the streets in poverty."

"You mean you slept with men for money. Mother, how could you?"

"I was taken from the streets of London when I was a child. It was the only way to survive in those days. I worked in an exclusive bordello."

Mary looked stunned. This news did not sit well. "Was it hard to work like that?"

"I was taught many tricks and skills, skills that made love making for a man very pleasurable. I was not expected to enjoy it, for some of them were old men, but it paid well and kept me alive."

"Is that why you were a convict?"

"Yes. Your real father was a gentleman who was very important, and I was ordered to entertain him for over a week. I became pregnant and thought you would die in prison if I didn't get out. The only way was to marry a settler who wanted a wife and someone to use for their pleasure."

Mary sighed. "So you married Poppa."

"I had to. It saved your life."

"Is that why he's cruel to you, because you had earned money from sex?"

Rebecca shook her head. "No, it's because he's a cruel man by nature who has no respect for me, for you, or any woman."

"Does he still use you?" Her voice was soft and caring.

Rebecca tightened her lips. "Only because I let him. He has eyes on you, child, and you must always be on your guard."

Mary gave out a deep breath. "Then it is better that I marry Campbell as soon as possible. When we do you must come with us."

Rebecca hesitated. "Have you been making love with Campbell?"

Mary looked down, her cheeks reddening. "Yes, most times when we meet."

"Then you must learn to prevent having a baby until you are wed. I will show you what to do, and I will show you how to please your husband, for he most likely will be the best chance of a happy life in this vast country."

Mary smiled at her. "I would be happy to have his baby, and I hope it has red hair just like him."

Rebecca gave her a hug. "But not yet. After you're wed."

Mary continued to see Campbell as often as possible and together they made plans of owning a tract of land in the south, possibly along the borders of the river they called the Murray.

"It will be a wonderful life for us, Mary. We'll have our own farm, we can make love whenever we feel like it. We'll raise our children and be rich."

"Oh, Campbell, I can't wait. I love you so much."

He took her in his arms and kissed her passionately. "Let's go to the river where we can make love," he said, smiling at her.

He led her away from prying eyes to the riverbank.

One evening in the barn when McBride had retired for the night, Campbell and Mary lay on the straw.

"When do you think we might marry Campbell?" she asked as his hand went to her dress.

"Soon. I'll be eighteen in a few months. I'll be a man and we can marry and leave. You must not mention this to McBride." As he spoke he lowered her dress until she stepped out of it.

"Not a word," she said, touching his face gently.

He removed the rest of her clothes; then she helped him remove his. The lamp was turned down very low and the place offered a more romantic setting. Mary lowered her hand to his groin and began to stroke him gently. Her mother was right.

"I love it when you do that. Where did you learn it?"

"Mother gave me some instructions. She said all married women should know how to please their husbands."

He closed his eyes as her hand stroked softer but faster. "Oh God," he said, drawing in a breath. "When we build our home we will walk around naked for hours doing just this."

"And there will be no one to see us," she said, enjoying the rapture on his face.

Later, they lay beside one another in the pleasure of the afterglow of their lovemaking. It was a wonderful feeling being in love. The gentle moment was shattered as the barn door crashed open. McBride entered holding his musket, loaded and cocked.

"Get off her, you animal!" he said as if he were a concerned father.

"Mr. McBride!" said Campbell. He quickly dressed as he spoke, embarrassed by his nakedness. Mary grabbed her clothes and covered herself.

"Poppa, I thought you were asleep."

"That's bloody obvious. You must be a slut like your mother."

Campbell frowned at his words. "Mary is not like that. She's a good girl."

"So good she lets you stick your cock into her."

Campbell bit his lip. He had to make this clear to McBride. "We only did it because we love each other."

"We did it because we love each other." McBride mimicked. "The only thing you love is a bit of pussy. I know young men. Any piece you can get, you'll take."

"No, it's not like that, Poppa," said Mary, still holding her clothes in front of her. "We want to marry."

"Wed? He's only a boy and can hardly take care of himself." He turned towards Campbell once again. "She may be a slut, but keep away from her."

"Mary is not a slut. You have no right to talk about her like that."

McBride brought the butt of the musket around and crashed it into the side of Campbell's head. A deep gash appeared, and he fell, stunned.

"If ya come around here again, I'll shoot you for trespassin'. Now get home to that interferin' mother of yours."

Campbell struggled to his feet and moved toward McBride only to see the muzzle of the gun facing his chest.

"Come on, try it," McBride grinned. "I'd love to blow a hole in you."

"Go, Campbell, please go," cried Mary, sobbing loudly. Campbell hesitated as he looked at her. "Please go, it will be all right."

Reluctantly he left, vowing to see her at a later opportunity.

McBride gave an evil grin as he looked at Mary, still on the straw holding her dress.

"Can you turn your back please, Poppa? I want to dress."

He ignored her plea. "So ya like havin' a boy between ya legs, do ya?" he sneered

"We love each other, Poppa, we want to marry."

He turned and spat on the ground. ''You'll not be marrying any McGregor, and you should learn that a man is better than a boy anytime."

He placed the musket down and fell over her. He snatched her dress from her hand, quickly turned her over and bound her hands behind her back with a piece of twine, then held his hand over her mouth as she struggled to free herself. Mary's fought in desperation, as she knew what he was about to do.

When he released his hand she cried out. "Please, Poppa, don't do this."

"Now you'll learn what a man is like," he said as he unbuttoned his trousers and let them slip down Unlike the pleasure she felt from Campbell, she was terrified. She felt he would kill her if she protested. She learned that every word her mother had said was true.

When McBride had finished, he pulled up his trousers. "Now,"' he said as he grinned. "That was better than McGregor could give you." He turned and walked out leaving Mary sobbing on the straw.

Chapter Seven

When Rebecca rose next morning at six, she began her morning routine of preparing breakfast. She made porridge for McBride and prepared his favorite mushrooms and bacon. She knew once his belly was full he was more amiable. As he was missing when she woke she suspected he was out milking their solitary cow.

When he made an appearance, he sat down at the table and began eating.

"You were up early," she said frowning.

"Couldn't sleep. Your efforts in bed were far from satisfying."

She smiled to herself. *Too bad*, she thought. "I'll just call Mary," she said, and McBride glared at her as she left the kitchen.

She found Mary's bed vacant. This puzzled her as Mary always got up early to help her get breakfast. She frowned and worried when she saw the bed hadn't been slept in.

"Mary is not here," she said, rushing into the kitchen.

"Aint she?" said McBride, not interested at all.

Rebecca rushed outside and saw the barn door swinging open in the breeze. Slowly she walked towards it, then a fear came over her, and she began to run. She found Mary sitting on the straw, her back against a timber support, and her eyes still filled with tears. Her hair hung around her shoulders, and straw still clung to her clothes.

Rebecca's heart began to beat faster as she saw the vacant look on Mary's face. "What on earth is the matter, Mary?" she asked, frightened by Mary's appearance.

"He raped me last night, it was awful."

"Campbell?" said Rebecca, horrified.

"No, not Campbell. It was Poppa-Poppa."

Rebecca's mouth went dry; she gasped, "Tell me what happened." She held Mary in her arms as the sobbing began once again.

"I can't, it was too horrible."

Rebecca held her tight as her body racked with the sobs. "You must tell me, child. You must."

Mary looked up into Rebecca's eyes with a pained look on her face. Her body trembled, and Rebecca held her even tighter.

"He found Campbell and me in the barn last night making love. He struck Campbell with his musket and sent him away. Campbell wanted to fight him, but I said to go. Poppa would have shot him."

"Then what happened?" asked Rebecca, fury building inside her.

"Poppa tied my hands behind my back. He said I needed a man, not a boy and then he did it to me. He laughed when he had finished and said I would never marry a McGregor, especially now."

"The bastard," yelled Rebecca and took Mary into her arms. She led her back into the house just as McBride returned to the kitchen with an armful of wood.

"You mongrel," she screamed. "How could you do that to your own daughter?"

"She ain't my daughter, she's yours. I wanted to see if she was any better than her mother, and she is." He smiled. Rebecca wanted to wipe the smirk from his face.

She picked up a piece of wood from the stove and swung it at his head. He caught it easily and then smashed his fist into her face, sending her to the floor, blood running down her lip from her broken nose. He raised the wood as though he would smash her head in but paused and threw the stick away. To kill her would bring big trouble. As she lay on the floor, he brought his boot back and kicked her in the ribs.

Rebecca felt her ribs give way, and she lay there unable to move. He brought his foot back again and repeated the action. She screamed as his boot struck her. Mary rushed forward and threw herself across Rebecca's body to prevent more punishment.

"You've killed her, Poppa, Poppa, you've killed her."

For a moment he worried, but then noticed she was still breathing.

"Serves her right. No woman is going to attack me without punishment. Put her back to bed. You'll have extra work to do now until she recovers, and you better do it, or you'll get some of the same."

Terrified, Mary helped Rebecca to her feet, and together they staggered to Rebecca's bed. Rebecca gave a cry of pain as she collapsed onto the mattress. Rebecca grabbed Mary's hand. "You have to get away from him, Mary, you have to leave. He'll do it to you again."

"I can't leave you, Mother. He'll kill you."

"Never mind me, leave now. Get out before it's too late."

"I can't."

She brought in a bowl of water and bathed Rebecca's face."

"You must go. I'm thirty-eight years old now. My life is nearly over."

"I won't leave you. I won't."

Rebecca sighed and fell back onto her bed with despair for her own situation and fear for Mary. By noon, McBride returned to the house and hitched up the buggy.

"We're goin' into town. You can get some stores while I go to the inn."

"What about mother?"

"The rest will do her good. Now get into the buggy."

They rode into Parramatta without a word. McBride pulled up outside the inn, just behind a covered wagon that held a man and a little girl of no more than three. The big man had a heavy black scraggy beard, dusty clothes and wore a large hat to protect him from the afternoon sun. He sat there staring at Mary as she left the buggy and walked to the store, happy to get away from McBride. The stare took in the swagger of Mary's walk as she carried the basket. From behind she looked to be just what he was after. There was no doubt she was attractive. Any man would have paid dearly to get his hands on her. He made a decision and jumped down from the wagon.

"Stay here," he said to the child, then followed McBride into the pub.

McBride left the buggy and entered the inn, bought himself a rum and sat down alone at one of the tables. A jug of ale was suddenly slammed onto the table. Startled, McBride looked up at the man. He was around thirty years of age with a scar running down one cheek on the sparse amount of skin visible behind the bushy bear. It wasn't a big scar, but a scar just the same, and it gave him a frightening appearance. It made McBride nervous looking at him. He must have been at least six inches taller than he was. His beard all but hid his face, only deep dark eyes caught his attention. *Six foot one at least* thought McBride *and muscles that could break you in half.*

"Mind if I join you?" said the man, sitting down without waiting for a reply.

McBride inspected the man and then looked at the grog again. "Only if you're willing to share your jug."

"My name's Brian Corcoran, I'm moving south to claim some land." He offered his hand, which McBride shook reluctantly and wondered if his fingers would ever work again.

"Michael McBride," McBride answered, suspicious of the man's motives.

Corcoran took a sip from his tankard before speaking.

"That pretty young girl your wife?" Corcoran asked as he poured two drinks.

McBride frowned. "No, me stepdaughter. Why are you interested in her?"

"Just curious," he said.

"You sound as if you're from Ireland." McBride noted the accent, not quite as broad as his own, but it definitely had an Irish twang to it.

"A long time ago. The bloody English shipped me out here years ago. Got my freedom and have moved around."

"Me, too," said McBride. "I got ten years for helpin' myself to a bit of property. You'd think a man wouldn't miss a few chickens, would you?"

"A few?"

"About ten, but they said two hundred or so. I sold them in the market and went to Belfast where they caught up with me."

"The English have no sense of humor, have they?" Corcoran threw his head back and laughed loudly.

"Ya married?" asked McBride as the jug soon emptied, only to be filled again by Corcoran.

"Was. Picked out a woman from the prison and married her. Had her for about ten years before she upped and died last month. They don't let 'em do that any more."

"Yeah, I did the same. The bitch was already pregnant, and I got stuck with her bloody kid. That's her you just saw." The second jug disappeared, and again Corcoran replaced it at his expense although he seemed to drink little himself.

"What's her name?"

"Mary, Mary McBride. Sweet sixteen and she's just been plucked." The grog was affecting McBride, and he grinned with satisfaction at the thought of the night before.

Corcoran raised an eyebrow and asked in a friendly manner. "Was she any good?"

"Wasn't very co-operative," McBride laughed. "But she'll get better. Her mother is incapacitated at the moment so I'm going to make a pig of myself until she recovers."

"She's just the sort of wife I'm looking for, young and pretty."

"Well you won't get your hands on her." McBride frowned at the suggestion. No way was he going to miss out on more of Mary.

Corcoran shrugged his massive shoulders. "That's a pity. I would have paid a lot of money for her. I've got a three-year-old daughter from the other one, and she needs lookin' after. And at times, I need looking after, if you get my drift."

Instantly, he had McBride's attention. The mention of money did that. "Money you say. What sort of money?"

"Well if you're not interested I'll look around. I need someone in a hurry. I'm leaving today."

He began to rise, but McBride grabbed his arm. "I didn't say I'm not interested. What sort of money are we talking about?"

"I'd go to fifty pounds for someone like her. If she was older then I'd drop my price."

"Fifty pounds?" McBride spluttered. He had never had such a sum in his entire life. Christ, he didn't think his farm was worth that if he sold it.

"Yeah, do you know anyone with a young girl who might be interested in the offer?"

"You're leavin' today you say."

"Yeah, as soon as I find a woman."

"She wouldn't be too happy at the suggestion."

"For fifty pounds you might be able to convince her. I could marry her and be on my way before she knew what hit her."

"I think I know a way to convince her." McBride smiled, the alcohol now taking effect. The thought of fifty pounds was very inviting. They went outside and found Mary struggling with a basket filled with supplies. She looked with disgust at the two men waiting for her. Two rogues if ever she saw any. The big one was even more repugnant than McBride.

"Mary. I want you to meet Brian Corcoran, your husband to be."

"G'day, Lass," said Corcoran, tipping his hat.

Her mouth dropped open. "Husband? Are you mad, or just drunk?"

"Neither mad nor drunk, well perhaps just a little tipsy, but I'm now fifty pounds richer."

"I don't know what you're talking about, Poppa, but I am not going to marry this person."

"Yes you are. The deal has been done, and I've got the money in my pocket."

"Take me home," she said, ignoring both men, but McBride grabbed her by the shoulder and dug his fingers into her flesh. She winced.

"You'll do what I say or be responsible for the consequences."

"What consequences?" said Mary, puzzled. What could be worse than what McBride had already done to her?

"For the general health of your mother. What happened to her today will happen quite a lot if you refuse. Maybe she might even die."

Mary's eyes widened, and her face paled as she looked at this evil person she called her stepfather.

"You wouldn't; you can't."

"She's my wife, and I can treat her any way I like. If you don't want anything to happen to her then you'd better do as I say. Brian here is movin' out today."

Mary staggered back against the buggy as if McBride had struck her. "Don't do this, Poppa, please don't do this."

"Well I'll miss the fun we can have together," he said, smirking. "But fifty quid is fifty quid."

The color drained from Mary's face. Rebecca had said he would do it again and that she had to escape, but certainly not this way. Corcoran looked no better than McBride, maybe even worse. She noted he stood not speaking, just scowling at what was taking place.

"I can't," she said, tears running down her cheeks.

"Pity. I'm in a foul mood now. I think I'll go and take it out on your mother. She may even be in the mood for a bit of funny business."

She knew he was serious as he smirked at her.

She bit her lip. There seemed to be no choice. "All right, all right," she conceded. "But only if you promise to leave her alone."

"If you mean by leaving her alone is not hitting her, then I agree. As for the rest, well, she is my wife."

"I have to be allowed to see her before I go."

"That seems reasonable," he said, looking at Corcoran who nodded.

"Sure, but we're runnin' out of time. Let's find a preacher. I have to be on my way before dark."

"I know just the man," said McBride, patting his fifty pounds inside his pocket. "But you'll have to pay him."

McBride took them to the nearest church where Corcoran paid the preacher a small fee. Before Mary knew what was happening, the minister was saying man and wife as she stood there with bowed head. Then the huge, hairy man grabbed her hand and led her outside.

"Now let's go and see your mother and tell her the good news." McBride laughed at his own joke.

They arrived back and Mary rushed to Rebecca's bed. Rebecca's face went white when Mary told her what had happened, and she fell back, devastated.

"I had to, Mother. He said he would kill you if I didn't."

"Not before I kill him," she said softly. "I'll come and find you, Mary, I don't know when or where, but I'll find you. If you can escape from that brute then do so, but wait until you're near a town. If you get lost in the bush, you'll die for certain."

"All I know is that we're heading south, towards the Murray. It's a big country mother, but I'll be looking for you, too. Will you tell Campbell what happened?"

"As soon as I can get out of this bed. Remember what I said, Mary, this man is going to use you so you use him, too. I love you, and one day I'll find you again." Both women had tears running down their cheeks.

"Good-bye, mother. I love you." She let her fingers slowly slip from Rebecca's hand as she moved to the door. Rebecca looked at the huge brute of a man who stood in the doorway.

"If you hurt her, I'll kill you, I swear." she said, staring at him.

He stared back for a few seconds then tipped his hat. "Nice to have met you too, Mrs. McBride."

After they left the small bedroom, Rebecca buried her sobs in the pillow. She had lost the only person she loved and her loss combined with the pain from her made it all seemed hopeless. She whispered into her pillow, Mary, as God is my witness, I'll free myself from this brute and find you. If I die trying, know that I love you with all my heart. She drifted off into a haze between sleep and sorrow.

Outside, the couple approached the loaded wagon.

"I'm sure you'll have a very good time, Brian, I can recommend her," said McBride as Mary climbed onto the bench seat.

"I'll see to that," he said and then addressed Mary. "This is Bridget. You're her mother now." With that he swung his whip and lashed the horses into movement. Mary looked at the frightened child and slipped her arm around her shoulders. If she was terrified of this man, what was the child feeling?

When they had gone, McBride stepped into the bedroom with the wad of notes in his fingers. He sat down and counted them again.

"I'll never forgive you for this," said Rebecca through her pain.

"You think that worries me?" McBride laughed. "It looks like it's just you and me again. Maybe I'll spend some of this on you."

"Keep your filthy money and never touch me again."

"Let's get one thing clear. You're my wife, and you'll do whatever I say. I'll touch you whenever I feel like it, and I've got plenty of rope if you fight me. You're not much good until your ribs heal, so I'll look for my comfort in town for a while. Any arguments and you'll get more of the same." He grabbed her dress and moved his face only inches from her. "Do you get what I'm sayin, girl?"

She said nothing but gasped with pain so he repeated the question more forcibly. "DO YOU UNDERSTAND?"

"Yes," she whispered in a weak voice, but she was already making plans.

Chapter Eight

Three days went by until Rebecca was recovered enough to be able to walk. Bent over and still in pain, she slowly made her way to the McGregor farm. Molly saw her as she dragged herself up the steps and helped her into the kitchen.

"My God, what happened?" she asked, plainly upset to see Rebecca in this condition.

"Can you call Campbell? He needs to hear this, too."

When Campbell appeared and sat on a chair a look of fear spread over his face. "What's happened? Is Mary all right?"

Rebecca tightened her lips before replying. "Something terrible has happened. My husband raped Mary after you left the other night."

"No!" Molly and Campbell cried out together.

"I must go to her," said Campbell, leaping from his chair.

Rebecca bit her lip. This was going to hurt Campbell as much as it did her. "You can't. When I protested to McBride, he beat me up and broke some of my ribs. Then he took her into Parramatta where he met this brute of a man."

"What man?' said Campbell almost screaming at her.

"Go on," said Molly putting her hand to her mouth.

"The man had just lost his wife and offered McBride fifty pounds if he made Mary marry him."

"He can't do that, not to his own daughter. The man is a fiend." Molly took Rebecca's hand and squeezed it.

Campbell tightened his fists, and a look of anguish spread over his face. "Marry?"

"Yes. McBride forced her into it to stop him beating me again."

"I'll kill this brute," said Campbell, snatching up a musket from the bracket on the wall.

"And hang. I don't think so. The man took her in his wagon towards the Murray River to claim land. I swore I would come after her once I'm better."

"Will you be able to find her?" asked Molly. "The country is so big. They could be anywhere."

"I know. It might take years, but I swear if it takes my last breath, I'll find her. She's all I have in the world. Without her I'll die."

Campbell slumped in his chair once again covering his face with his hands. The love of his life was gone and now married to some stranger she didn't even know. God only knows what this man would do to her. His life had been ruined by McBride and this brute.

* * * * *

The wagon moved south for four hours until at last Corcoran pulled it to a halt beside a gentle stream. Mary felt uneasy as Corcoran kept glancing at her when he thought she didn't notice. He looked at the sky and noticed the light was fading. "We'll stay here for the night. Get the canvas out of the wagon." It was said with no aggression, merely as a fact that it had to be done. The surrounding land looked inhospitable, and she felt sure she would get lost if she ventured away.

Mary did as she was told and dragged the canvas to the ground.

"Watch me, Mary, you will have to do this in the future."

She watched as he assembled the canvas over some branches and quickly erected the shelter. He pulled an old straw-filled mattress from the wagon and placed on the ground.

"We sleep in here. Bridget sleeps in the wagon. Get a fire going." Again it was a simple instruction, no intent and no malice.

The thought of what was going to happen horrified Mary. He looked so big and powerful. His eyes were almost the only part of his face visible. The beard hid everything. She gathered some dry wood and soon had a roaring fire going. Corcoran handed her a billy, which she filled from the stream and soon had it and another pot boiling.

"Throw some potatoes in," said Corcoran, indicating with his thumb toward a canvas bag. He produced a bundle wrapped in calico, which contained salted beef. He cut several slices. They were all silent as they ate. Mary watched him warily. It was her first chance to really study him. In Parramatta she had only looked at him with contempt, but now wondered what such a brute was doing with a three-year-old girl. She remembered Rebecca telling her how her father had abandoned her and wondered why this creature hadn't done the same to his daughter. She was pleased, however, that he had no body smell about him. *He must bathe often* she thought comforted by that fact.

For a while they just eyed each other, neither speaking. She had been scared when McBride had taken her, but this seemed even worse. Her hand shook, and she grasped her metal cup with both hands to steady it as she sipped her tea.

"How old are you, girl?" he suddenly said.

"Sixteen," she said, in a voice she tried to hold steady, without much success.

He looked at her smooth skin, fair hair and eyes that showed fear. He frowned at her.

"I know you're frightened, but I won't physically hurt you. You'll soon learn what's required. You are now my wife, and there are duties to perform. We've got a long way to go and life will be hard, but you'll adapt."

Mary glanced over at Bridget who seemed happy to eat and drink. Obviously she was used to camping out in the open. "Where are we going?" she asked.

"South to the Murray. I heard there's good land to claim. Are you frightened of the blacks?"

"I've never met any."

"Shifty bastards. They attack when they think they're safe, but don't be afraid. A ball between the eyes will discourage them."

"Why will they attack us?"

"Some says they're cannibals. Maybe they might want to eat us."

She knew he only said this to frighten her in case she slipped away during the night.

"I have never heard of them doing that. I find it hard to believe."

He gave a grunt and continued eating. With the meal finished, Corcoran stood up and stretched his arms.

"Wash the dishes and get Bridget to sleep. We have a big day tomorrow, and I want to leave early."

Mary finished her tasks and took Bridget to the wagon. She looked at the child and felt sorry for her having lost her mother at such an early age. She was not particularly pretty, but did have a childlike innocence about her. Mary combed her hair and was surprised when Bridget suddenly reached out and hugged her.

"Are you my new mummy?" she asked, still holding her tightly.

"I guess I am," said Mary, her heart going out to the tiny tot. "My name is Mary."

"Goodnight, Mary. Will you be here in the morning?"

"Yes, Bridget. I'll be here."

Bridget smiled and rolled over in the wagon, contented with her answer. She hugged a rag doll as she snuggled down. Mary stayed as long as she could, not wanting to return to Corcoran, but at last she had no choice.

"Let's get to bed," he said gruffly. "You know what's expected?"

She nodded, again her eyes filling with tears.

"You don't have to enjoy it. Just do your duty, and I won't make undue demands. Just now and again will do."

She expected rough treatment, but was surprised that he was reasonably gentle. He sensitively eased her down to the mattress and removed his trousers. She turned her head and shut her eyes as she felt him remove her under garments.

"I'll try not to hurt you," he said, and then entered her. She lay back thinking of what her mother had to put up with and now knew she was in the same position. Three men had sex with her in the space of twenty-four hours. One she adored and the other two forced upon her. It was over quickly, and he rolled off her.

"Did it hurt?" he asked, concerned, which surprised Mary.

"No," she said curtly.

"I won't worry you very often. Only when it's necessary. Men must have it to exist."

How often would that be, wondered Mary as she turned her back to him. *Three times a day probably*. She lay there unable to sleep. Corcoran's heavy breathing interrupted her thoughts. She had the feeling she was trapped forever with no escape.

Eventually she fell into a deep sleep. The next morning Mary woke to find he was not beside her. The tangy smell of the smoke teased her nostrils, and she realized how hungry she felt. He had risen early as promised and had the fire already going. The air was crisp, and the sun appeared to promise them a warm day.

"I've made some tea and some porridge. Get Bridget up, and we'll be on our way as soon as we've eaten."

With Bridget dressed, Mary hungrily ate the porridge as Corcoran sat and watched her. She was aware of his gaze, but elected to ignore him until she finished. The meal concluded quickly, and Corcoran had the tent wrapped up and in the wagon in no time. Little conversation occurred except for Bridget who seemed to adopt Mary quickly.

Obviously the child had missed the company of a female, and she clung to Mary's side as if frightened Mary would vanish.

Mary was curious about this brute and decided to ask questions. "What happened to your wife?" she asked. She expected a curt, mind you own business, or even a smack across the face.

He grunted as he flicked the reins of the horses. "A horse bolted in Goulburn and knocked her down. She hit her head on a rock and died the next day."

"Where did you meet her?" Mary was determined to find out as much as she could, for if he beat his wife then she would certainly be in for the same treatment.

He looked across at her before answering.. "Ten years ago I decided to go to Parramatta to the women's prison and select a wife from the prisoners paraded."

"That's what happened to my mother."

"It was a better choice than rotting in prison."

"Only for some, Mary added thinking of McBride.

"I never made the trip. I met her in a Tavern to ask directions. It developed from there. She had no future so she asked me to marry her. I obliged."

"Was she a whore?" asked Mary now very interested.

"No, but she was an ex-convict. Sent there as a punishment for hitting her employer with a poker when he wanted more than domestic duties."

"I see. You offered a better life than she expected."

"I guess so.

He looked across at her before answering. "Ten years ago I went to Parramatta prison and selected her from the prisoners. She had ten years to serve, and the authorities gave her the choice of marrying a settlers or remaining in prison. I picked her out, and she accepted."

"That's what happened to my mother."

"It was a better choice than rotting in prison."

"Only for some," Mary added, thinking of McBride.

"Anyway, she was just like you. She'd never met me before and was very quiet at first."

"What was her crime? Was she a whore?"

"No, she was a domestic, only fifteen, and the lord of the manner raped her. She struck him with a poker and cracked his head open. He had her charged, and she got ten years. The English always look after the gentry. Nothing was done about the rape."

"How old was she when you married her?"

"How old was she when you picked her out?"

"Eighteen. She'd been abused by the guards and didn't want to die an old maid or resorting to another way to make a living. She got out early for a fee."

Mary understood immediately.

"Eighteen. She'd been abused by the guards and wanted to get out at any price. I was the price."

"Was she happy?"

"Not particularly at first but she took the risk. She didn't know what I was like but she soon found out. I treated her well and we were soon friendly."

He grunted. "Not at first, just like you, but I treated her well, and we were soon friendly."

Mary raised an eyebrow. "Even when you forced yourself upon her like you forced yourself on me."

He scowled at her, and she wondered what he would do.

"Mary, you should understand that men need women. Some are cruel and show them little respect. They're fools. I treated my wife fairly, and she performed her wifely duties, just as I expect you to. I did my best to make life comfortable for her, and she rewarded me with Bridget. I did not regard her as a horse or a mule, but as my wife. She put up with me for two years until she began to realize I was not an evil person. She did not love me, but the day she died was the worst day of my life."

Mary raised her eyebrows at his words. To think someone could care about this person after being married out of desperation seemed ludicrous.

picked out at a prison seemed ludicrous.

"Are you saying you loved her?"

He gritted his teeth before speaking, a sad look in his eyes. "Yes, but she left me with a three year old daughter who needs a mother. I cannot claim land and develop it with a small child at home. I need someone to look after her, and I don't wish to live alone. It was obvious McBride was a fool and would have used you again. I'm sorry I had to take you away from your mother, but I only care about Bridget. I will make your life tolerable, and I won't beat you. That's all I can promise, but I expect you to do your wifely duties as my wife did."

She looked down at her hands in her lap and sad sadly "You took me away from the man I love."

"You're only young, and you'll get over that. Don't try to run off. You'll die in the wilderness."

She remained silent for a few seconds and folded her arms across her chest. "My mother will come after me one day."

"Then she is welcome to live with us if she can ever rid herself of McBride, and if she can find us."

This announcement shocked Mary. She almost fell out of the wagon. "Had I known that I would have asked her to come."

"I don't think McBride would have agreed, and I would have no wish to get into a fight with him. If she comes one day then she'll be welcome." He flicked the reins once again.

Mary sat silently and thought about his words. She had no feelings for this man and regarded him as being no better than McBride. But at least he cared about his daughter and held her welfare above any others.

The second night out the same ritual occurred. The tent was erected and the meals cooked. Bridget was put to bed, and Mary expected she would have to submit once more. She removed her undergarments and lay on the mattress waiting, for the inevitable, but Corcoran pulled up the blanket and blew out the lamp.

"Good-night, Mary," he said. "Sleep well."

Mary thought he was joking and waited for him to take her, but soon all she heard was his heavy breathing as he slept. It was an hour later before she fell into a deep sleep.

Brian gritted his teeth and focused on keeping his breathing even. He certainly wanted her, much more than she thought, but it would be a long journey, and he didn't want to spoil it too much for her. He considered how lucky he was to get a beautiful young girl like Mary for a wife. They traveled for another six days before he claimed her again and as the first time, it was brief.

She lay on the mattress, expecting him to leave her alone as he had for the last five nights, but he touched her on the shoulder.

"Mary, I'm sorry, but I need relief."

She looked sharply at him, eased down her underwear and lay down on the blanket. No sense in fighting it. It had to happen again. He eased himself over her and was incredibly gentle. She looked sideways and soon he finished and then rolled off her.

"Thank you, Mary," he whispered as he turned his back and went to sleep.

Tears gathered in her eyes. Was this what life offered from here on? She thought about Campbell and how she loved him. Being forced to make love to this man was not painful physically, but it wasn't much better than being raped by McBride. At least he apologized which was more than she expected.

One thing she did notice was the way he looked at her when he thought she was unaware. She knew that look ~~of lust~~ in a man's eyes but was confused as to why he didn't take her more often. Any other man would have used her every night or whenever he felt like it.

Once she surprised herself when he hadn't touched her for four weeks. When he came to her she felt an unexpected pleasure. He may not have been Campbell, but she didn't want it to end too quickly. Afterwards, she felt ashamed of herself for actually enjoying his touch. Who would have thought this hairy beast could give her a little satisfaction?

One morning after breakfast she spoke to him. She drew in a deep breath not knowing what his reaction would be. "I have to tell you I am pregnant."

She expected him to be enraged, but all he said was, "I hope you keep well. Is it mine?"

Mary shook her head. "I don't know whose it is. Campbell, McBride and you all had me in one day. I don't know."

"I understand. It matters not; a child is a blessing to be grateful for. It shall be my son or daughter. Is there anything I can do?"

Mary looked at his scraggy repugnant appearance and hesitated before speaking. "There is one thing."

"And what would that be, Mary?"

"Please shave off that horrible beard, and let me cut your hair. I want to see what you look like."

Corcoran burst out laughing. "I suppose I do look like some hairy monster. Get me my razor from the wagon, lass. It's a task that you can do."

She found the razor and some scissors wrapped in cloth, and she heated some water. He lathered his face and sat down after handing her the razor. They both knew she could easily cut his throat, but he didn't even flinch as she made the first cut. She looked into his eyes and saw a steely look as she lifted his chin to expose his throat. The white soft flesh looked inviting, and had it been McBride, she wouldn't have hesitated. However, she made slow smooth strokes and soon his face was devoid of any hair. Except for one small cut, it was a clean shave.

"Sorry," she said. "I haven't done this before."

"Then you've done well," he smiled as she dabbed the small trickle of blood from his chin.

She gasped at what she saw. His jaw was firm and while she couldn't call him handsome, his features did have some appeal. The beard had hidden a strong face, a face of character, and she wondered why he ever grew it in the first place. He broke out into a smile she thought attractive, and he wiped his face with a towel as she stood back.

"Is it as bad as you thought it would be?" he said, running his hand over his now smooth face.

She shook her head and smiled. "No, I'm surprised. You look very different, even with the scar."

"Then if you feel more comfortable, I shall shave regularly. You may cut my hair now."

Mary proceeded and soon had hair falling to the ground as she snipped away. When she was finished, she felt well satisfied with her effort.

"You don't look like an old man at all."

"I'm thirty years old, Mary, old by your standards, but young enough to take care of your welfare—and our child when it arrives. There is another thing I would like you to do for me," he said, liking the expression on her face.

"Yes?"

"Since we have been on the trail, you have not referred to me by my name. I would like you to call me Brian."

For the first time since he took her, she felt less tense and at ease. "Then Brian it will be."

They passed through many settlements where Corcoran replaced their rations, and Mary had a chance to mix with people again. In one such place she waited in the wagon as Brian bartered for goods.

Bridget tapped her on the arm and had a pleading look in her eyes.

"Yes, Bridget. What is it?"

"I'm hungry, Mary. Can I have something to eat?"

"How about a couple of slices of salted beef?"

Bridget nodded, and Mary produced a knife from a basket in the wagon and sliced off a couple of slices of meat.

When she looked down, she saw a scrawny looking dog sitting, watching her with appealing eyes. It sat staring at Mary. It was a tawny colored cattle dog that had been having a bad time by the look of it. Its ribs stood out and it had a scar on its face, probably from a dog fight or where someone had kicked it. Its eyes never left the meat.

She hesitated for a second and then threw it a slice. The dog leapt upon the meat and swallowed it in one gulp. It wagged its' tail, waiting for more. Cautiously, Mary gave it another slice. Bridget jumped down and patted the dog, which in turn licked her face.

"Can we keep him, Mary?" she asked appealingly.

"I don't think so, Bridget. Your daddy wouldn't like it."

"Her daddy wouldn't like what?" asked Brian as he approached with an armful of goods.

"This stray dog. Bridget's fallen in love with it."

"How do you know it's a stray?"

Mary raised one eyebrow, and Brian grinned. "Okay, I can see it's a stray, but a dog would be a burden."

"It would make Bridget happy," she said. "Four months on the trail is a long time for a little girl."

"I suppose it might come in useful when we get to where we're going. All right, Bridget, get it in the wagon."

"I'm going to call it Wolf," she said happily. "Come on, Wolf."

The dog jumped into the wagon, and another member was added to the family.

CHAPTER NINE

Molly came over a week later to check on Rebecca.

"How is Campbell taking it?" asked Rebecca. Her lips were still swollen from the beating.

"He's heartbroken. He wanted so much to marry her. McBride is an animal to do such a thing." Molly lifted the kettle from the stove and poured a cup of tea first for Rebecca, then for herself.

Rebecca nodded. "And she wanted to marry Campbell. Now she is gone forever, married to a man she doesn't even know."

"But why did she do it? It's stupid." Molly stirred two lumps of sugar into her tea and took a cautious sip.

"You saw what McBride did to me. It's not hard to understand. She knew he would do it again and again unless she did."

Molly gave a sigh. "So she sacrificed herself for you?"

"Yes, I would have done the same for her."

Molly paused for a few seconds. "Did you see this man?"

Rebecca nodded. "Yes. He's a brute of a man with a scar on one cheek. He looked no better than McBride. Just looking at him frightened me. God knows what he has done to her. His name is Brian Corcoran. I'm afraid for her, Molly."

Molly shook her head. "What are you going to do?"

Rebecca gave her a cold stare. "I'm going after her when I can get on my feet again."

"But what about McBride?"

Rebecca snarled. "I'll kill him if I get the opportunity."

Molly shook her head. "Then you'll hang, and that will do Mary no good at all."

"Then I'll leave in the night." Rebecca spoke with certainty, crossing her arms and holding them tightly against her cracked ribs.

Molly looked thoughtful. "You must give him no reason for suspicion, or he might lock you up."

"I can't go until I'm well again, but you're right. I must think about this. I'll have no money. The choice I have is to revert to my old profession, but I'm too old to make good money now."

"Is there no other way, Rebecca? It's a ghastly way to make money."

"I don't know. It will be the very last alternative. I'll try to keep my hatred to myself and then make the break."

It was five weeks before Rebecca fully recovered. McBride's brutality continued.

"Now that you're back on ya feet, I feel like doin' it. Let's have a go in the bedroom." She followed him in, thinking of her revenge while he roughly took her again. Revenge was what she wanted, and revenge was what she would get. It was six months before her chance came. During that time, she pretended to be his subservient slave and complied with all his wishes. If he wanted his meal, she quickly prepared it. If he wanted sex, she made it as pleasurable for him as she could.

"I'm goin' to town to try out the new whores," he would say.

"Yes, Michael," she would reply.

"I want my evening meal exactly at six, not five past, not five to."

"Yes, Michael." She would stand with her head bowed.

When she was sure he was confident of his hold over her, she went out into the paddock looking for mushrooms. She knew they were his favorite food, and she hunted high and low until she found what she was looking for. She soon had a basket full but then she looked further. The toadstools stood well clear of the mushrooms, and she scrapped the skin of one with her fingernails until it came up yellow. Smiling, she gathered them too, placing them under the mushrooms she had already picked.

When McBride came home early, she was afraid he would see what she was doing.

"What's for supper?"

"I gathered your favorite mushrooms, Michael. They'll be ready on time."

"Good, we've got an hour to spare before the meal. Into the bedroom, and this time I want your best effort."

She followed him in and removed her clothes. Might as well she thought, it will be his last.

Later, satisfied with her performance, he watched her dress. "If the mushrooms are as good as that, then the day will have been perfect."

"They will be, Michael, they will be."

When she served them they smelled delicious.

"You're not havin' any?"

"I don't like them much, and there was only enough for you. I'll try to find some more tomorrow."

"Good, pour me a cup of tea."

She watched him drink his tea, eat his supper and waited. By ten o'clock he was writhing about his bed in agony clutching his stomach.

"Get the bloody doctor, woman, I'm dyin'," he groaned.

"I would have to go to town to do that. I'll go and get the McGregors to go for me."

The sweat was pouring from him as he rolled in intense pain. "Then go, hurry, before I die."

Rebecca picked up her shawl and casually strolled toward the McGregor farm. When she knocked, a surprised Molly greeted her.

"Rebecca, whatever is wrong?"

"Perhaps if you made me a cup of tea I could explain it to you," she said coyly, and Molly understood immediately. They sat and drank the tea for over an hour chatting casually before Rebecca told Molly of the problem.

Rebecca smiled at her and spoke softly. "It appears Michael has eaten something that he shouldn't have and is feeling unwell."

"Oh, that's too bad. And what has he eaten to make him so sick?"

"I think it was the mushrooms. I usually collect them, but this time he brought them home. You do know how fond of them he is?"

Molly almost burst out laughing. "Of course, but you must be very careful you don't pick toadstools. I hear they can be very dangerous."

Rebecca feigned sadness. "Yes, some of them look just like mushrooms and are most poisonous. He sent me over to ask you to go to town and fetch the doctor."

Molly could hardly keep a straight face. "Perhaps we should go back and see just how sick he is. Don't want to bring the doctor out for nothing."

"If you think that's best," agreed Rebecca. "Perhaps after another cup of tea."

Molly called to her husband, noting the time. "Angus, I'm going back with Rebecca to see how her husband is. She said he was sick. Don't wait up, it's already eleven."

"Couldn't happen to a nicer mongrel," he said, not looking up from his book.

Together they returned to Rebecca's house to find McBride unconscious and breathing spasmodically.

Molly smiled. "What a shame, Rebecca. I don't think he's going to survive the night."

Rebecca shrugged her shoulders. "Perhaps we better wait another hour before we call the doctor."

Molly nodded. "Come back to my place, and we'll have another cup of tea."

"Okay, but if I drink anymore I'll burst."

They waited another hour, then woke Campbell and sent him into town to fetch the doctor. By the time he returned with the doctor, it was sunrise. The physician listened to McBride's chest. He looked at Rebecca sympathetically.

"I'm sorry, Mrs. McBride. I'm afraid your husband has passed away."

Rebecca shed tears and wiped her eyes. "I knew it must have been the mushrooms. I told him I would collect them, but he said he knew best."

"Yes, well, you can't be too careful when you pick them. I've seen the same thing happen to others. I shall have to report it as an accidental death," he said sadly.

Rebecca put her hands to her face as the doctor wrote out the death certificate. They buried him the next day and Rebecca sold the farm within a month.

"Where are you going, Rebecca?" asked Molly as her friend climbed up on her wagon.

"To find Mary. She said they were moving somewhere south to the Murray. I'll look there first."

"It's dangerous country. There's blacks, bushrangers and all sorts of undesirables ready to take advantage of a single woman."

"What a wonderful word."

"What?" said Molly.

"Single. Nothing could be more dangerous than McBride, and I'm well rid of him. Besides, I have his musket and pistol. I'll write when I can." With that she urged the horses forward and turned south.

* * * * *

The sound of the shot rang out and Mary held her fingers to her ears as the musket discharged. The kangaroo fell immediately, and Brian rushed forward to the carcass.

"It looks like kangaroo steaks tonight, Mary," he said proudly.

Mary looked at the man she had wed. She thought it would have been a horrible nightmare being married to such a disgusting looking person, but now that he kept clean he wasn't as bad as she might have thought. Since her stomach had swelled, Brian had done most of the work, and had even left her alone sexually. It was a part of his nature she had not expected, and she wished her mother had been lucky enough to have been claimed by such a man.

She was aware he felt strongly about her, but he couldn't compare to Campbell. She held hope that one day Campbell would come for her, and they could set up a love nest somewhere in this vast land. The only problem was the oncoming baby. How would Campbell react when he saw it?

As he skinned the carcass, Mary grabbed his arm, a hint of warning in her action. "Brian, look over there."

He looked to see a party of five blacks standing, watching, and holding spears. He quickly reloaded his musket and fired over their heads. They just seemed to disappear into the scrub.

"Will they attack us?" she asked, afraid.

"If they wanted to we would be dead now. The shot was just to let them know to keep away."

The further the journey went, the more Mary felt at ease in his presence. No longer did she fear he would treat her badly. Not once had he made a gesture of hitting her, even though she had made a few mistakes. Once, she dropped the flour into a stream and waited for punishment, but a shrug was all she received.

"Accidents happen, girl. Don't be concerned."

While she held no love for him, she at least liked him and felt pleased about the consideration he offered her. It had been a month since she'd had to submit to him, although she knew he was having trouble controlling himself by the way he longingly looked at her. She expected him to approach her every night, but he began to sleep in the wagon, while Bridget moved into the tent with Mary.

One night Mary left the tent and joined Brian in the wagon.

"Is something wrong, girl?" he said with concern in his voice.

"No. You have treated me well. I see the way you look at me, and I know you want me. I decided to relieve you in this way."

She slipped her hand to his crotch and almost immediately he responded.

"Mary, please, don't torture me."

"Is this torture, Brian?" she asked and began to stroke him gently. She gained a little pleasure to hear him draw in a deep breath then he lay back. He tried to lift himself up but she pushed him back and continued. It was stimulating her, too, and she had to admit, she had missed his taking her in the last few weeks.

"I think you needed this. I'm your wife, after all, and I have a duty to carry out." He suddenly reached out and pulled her near him.

"Thank you, Mary. I didn't expect that."

"I confess I've missed when you take me. I have a short time to go, but if you wish, I'll let you if you are very careful."

"Then if you agree, I'll take you up on your offer one more time before the baby is born."

"I agree," she said before returning to the tent.

Three nights later he approached her. When he did take her she felt strangely relieved. It was becoming more pleasant each time, and she felt pleasure in the act.

Bridget became very attached to Wolf and he responded by following her everywhere. Mary began to like the dog herself, especially when she fed him. He would wag his tail and lick her hand. There was no hint of savagery in him. The journey was becoming easier as they progressed. Because of her swelling belly, she couldn't give Bridget the attention she deserved, and she felt grateful they had taken in Wolf.

One night Brian handed her a cup of tea and smiled at her.

"Mary, I want to get to a place and build a cabin before the baby comes. I don't want you to give birth out in the open."

"We only have two more months now, Brian. We must find a place soon."

"We'll stop at the next water."

As they came across the river, Mary looked a little apprehensive. The swiftly flowing water looked dangerous to cross. Debris washed downstream, and the water was muddy and discolored.

"The water is running quickly," she said nervously.

"It's been in flood. See where the water mark has been."

She looked at the mark on the tree trunks and could see the water had dropped at least four feet. The grass on the banks lay flat where the water had cascaded over it when in full flood.

"What river is this?" she asked.

"I think it's called the Murrumbidgee. The land looks good, and I think we'll stay here. Maybe I'll claim land if it's pleasing to you."

"But there is no pasture."

"There will be if I clear it. Let's cross."

He eased the horses into the water, fighting against the current as they struggled to make the other side. Brian stood up, wielding his whip and urging the horses on. The water reached the top of the wheels, and Mary clung to the side of the seat as they made slow progress. She watched it swirling around the wagon at a furious pace as it surged downstream but felt confident it wouldn't turn the wagon over. It swept against the sides, creating eddies as it fought to find a way around the impediment of the wagon. The very sight of the swiftly running water made her nervous. Suddenly she heard a loud splash and looked around to see Bridget flaying in the water.

"Bridget," she screamed and leapt into the water with no thought of her own safety. Wolf also leapt in. Brian looked back, his face turning white at the sight of both Bridget and Mary being swept downstream.

"No," he screamed at the top of his voice. Immediately he jumped into the torrent trying to reach his family. Brian tried to reach both of them. Suddenly the water was over Mary's head as she screamed for Bridget, who was nowhere in sight. She flayed desperately, the water, a muddy brown as it swept over her head depriving her of oxygen.

"Mary, Bridget," she heard Brian call as he desperately felt for both of them. The weight of her waterlogged dress began to drag her down, her belly hindering any movement she might manage. Over and over she turned as she swallowed water and gulped for air, knowing she was in desperate trouble. Then just when she was ready to give up, she felt Brian's hand grab her dress and lift her to the surface. When she came up she could see they were a hundred yards downstream from the wagon, which was still in the middle of the river with little protection from the waters.

Brian swam toward the bank with his arm under her chin until she felt solid ground under her feet once again. At last he managed to drag her to the bank and she collapsed, exhausted, trying to regain her breath.

"Mary! Mary!" he shrieked, afraid she was dead. He let out a muffled sob and pulled her to him, hugging her tightly. She opened her eyes.

"Bridget! Where's Bridget!" she cried, but she could see the expression of anguish on his face.

"She's gone Mary, she's gone!" he cried, and she pulled him close as he buried his face into her shoulder.

"No, oh no!" she wept, looking at the water in a vain hope she would see the child.

It took them half an hour to regain their breath. Brian lifted her gently in his arms.

"I've lost her, Mary, I've lost my little girl." His eyes filled with tears, and he tried to wipe them with the back of his hand.

"Maybe she could have been washed ashore. You must go and look."

"What hope would she have?" he choked as he spoke. "I'll get you back to the wagon and set up camp. Then I'll go and look for her body."

Through tangled brush and mud sucking at his boots, Brian moved two miles downstream. His heart was heavy with despair. He had come all this way to give his daughter a good life and had lost her in the blink of an eye. He dropped to his knees and held both hands to his face, unable to face her death.

The sound of Wolf howling caught his attention. He hurried forward only to gasp when he saw her body lying in the mud by the edge of the river.

"God, no," he sobbed.

The child's hair and face was covered with mud, her clothes soaking wet. Wolf stood over her licking her face as if trying to revive her. Suddenly he heard her groan.

My God, she's alive, he thought, rushing forward again.

He picked her small body up in his arms and hugged her tightly, sobbing into her shoulder, almost squeezing the life from her.

"Wolf pulled me out, Daddy. He grabbed my dress."

Gratefully he patted the dog and carried Bridget back to the campsite.

Mary cried when she saw Brian carrying Bridget. She rushed forward, taking her from Brian's arm and hugging her.

"Bridget, Bridget. Are you all right?" she said, still holding her tightly.

"Wolf saved me, Mary," she said happily, "I thought I would be dead."

"It was well that we found him, wasn't it?" Mary said, smiling broadly and looking at Brian while still hugging the child. "Let's get those wet clothes off you and get you clean."

That night after supper, when Bridget had gone to bed, Mary looked across for Brian. He was nowhere to be seen. She walked in the direction she thought he had gone. She found him sitting on the bank of the river, tears running down his face, his hands over his head and knees brought up.

She watched him sobbing for a few minutes, this big man showing such emotion, and quickly went back to the camp, leaving him in his solitude. She knew the pain he suffered at the near loss of his daughter. This was a sensitive man, she thought. She wouldn't have believed it. He arrived back at camp an hour later to find Mary had put Bridget to sleep in the wagon.

"You put her in the wagon?" he said surprised, the tear stains still on his face.

Mary moved to him and put her arm around his shoulder. "You need comforting, husband, if you can manage it, and there is no need to hurry."

She took his hand and led him into the tent.

Afterwards, he held her in his arms and turned his face into her shoulder. She could feel the tears running onto her as he sobbed.

"I thought I'd lost her, Mary, I really thought she was dead."

"But she's not, Brian." She patted his shoulder as he lifted his head and stared into her eyes. It was a look of love.

"And I almost lost you as well. I couldn't live if I lost you both." He held her tenderly then.

She lay awake in the dark for over an hour. He couldn't love her. When Campbell came she would have to leave. She knew that would break his heart.

Chapter Ten

The heavy cloudbank obliterated any light the moon could have given, plunging the night into complete darkness. It gave her an eerie feeling as Rebecca huddled around the fire peering into the shadows with her musket alongside her. She had been afraid before, but not of being alone in the bush. There had been noises, and she had a terror of snakes, one of which she had seen before nightfall. The wind softly whistled through the trees, giving a ghostly atmosphere. She knew the search would be long, maybe years, but she was determined to re-unite with Mary once again. Mary was now her only reason for living.

The money she had received for the farm was over sixty pounds, a sum she knew would keep her going for many months, but eventually she would have to find some way of making money. It was a problem she would face when the time came. Molly's warning of blacks and bushrangers still lingered in her mind. She turned at every sound in the bush. It was scary being out here alone. A single woman alone in the bush would be an easy target. She gave the musket a pat of re-assurance.

As the sound of horse's hooves became clearer, she immediately gripped the musket in readiness. When the rider came into view, she raised it, hoping she could manage such a heavy weapon. He pulled up quickly when he saw the firearm.

"Stay right where you are," said Rebecca coolly.

"Mrs. McBride! Don't shoot, it's me, Campbell."

With relief, Rebecca lowered the gun. "Campbell! What are you doing here?"

"I'm coming with you to find Mary."

"But your mother, she'll be upset."

"I talked with her, and she agreed. I'm eighteen now, and I'm going south to claim land and to find Mary."

"But she's married."

Campbell scowled. "Forced into marriage is no marriage. I'll kill him when I find them and then marry her."

Rebecca had never seen him like this.

"Campbell, it may take years to find her. The country is so big."

"If it takes years then I don't care. I'll claim land, get it established and then find her. I looked for you because it's safer for two to travel."

"Are you sure you want to do this, Campbell? You're so young."

"I'm a man now, Mrs. McBride, and I'll protect you as we look together. I love Mary, and she loves me. I need a woman like Mary to establish my position in life."

Rebecca considered his offer. "Very well. You're welcome to join me, but I insist that you do one thing."

"What's that, Mrs. McBride?"

"Call me Rebecca. We're going to be together for quite a while, and I don't want to sound like some distant aunt."

He grinned "I agree heartily, Rebecca."

"Good, then come and have some supper."

As they ate she noted Campbell was obsessed with killing Corcoran. "When I think that she is at the mercy of such a man I want to scream."

"He's a brute of a man, Campbell. He won't be easy to kill."

"There will be ways. I'll ambush him on the trail and save her; then we'll start our life together as we planned."

"You have to be careful they don't hang you. The man may be a brute, but as far as I can see he's committed no crime."

"No crime? He's stolen the woman I'm going to marry. He's probably convict stock. He's going to suffer."

Rebecca looked at the boy, disturbed by his venom.

* * * * *

The land they on which they squatted was heavily timbered, and Brian cut many trees in his haste to erect something to give Mary shelter. The crude hut gave them reasonable protection and kept out the rain that fell infrequently. He selected a site above the flood line on the trees, but it took him almost two months to complete and Mary's time was almost at hand.

"Are we going to live here forever?" she asked as he completed the structure.

"No, the soil is good, but I want to go to the colony of Port Phillip. I'm going to build you a grand home one-day, and it will be many miles from here on the banks of the mighty Murray River. It will have wooden floors, a fine roof, and a room where you can bathe. I'll see to it that you have elegant clothes and all the things you need."

Mary smiled. While she liked Brian and his dreams, she still thought about Campbell and longed to have him hold her in his arms once again. She wondered if that would ever happen. How would Campbell take to the fact she was now about to be a mother giving birth to a child that might not even be his. Would he just forget her and take up with another woman? The chances of seeing him again seemed remote, and she wondered if he would seek her out at some point.

She had seen a side of Brian she had not thought possible. He was kind and considerate, but feared he might kill Campbell if he dared to take her away from him.

But what of Bridget? Leaving her would not be easy. She had come to be very fond of the child, and she knew Bridget was fond of her. It would be heartbreaking to lose another mother in her short life. Mary suspected it would break her own heart, as well. Still, the thought of a life with Campbell excited her and there was also her mother.

Would she be able to escape the clutches of McBride? Would McBride eventually kill her? They were questions she had no answer for, but she would think about them after the birth.

The thing that disturbed her more was that Brian often touched her hand and let it linger. There was no "Let's go into the tent," just a soft loving touch. It wasn't the touch that disturbed her, it was how it shot a thrill up her spine. It shouldn't affect her like this, but it did. It gave her a warm feeling to know he actually cared about her.

"Brian, you make such grand plans, but you must realize that you took me away from the man I love. I don't think I can ever forgive you for that.

"It's been nearly nine months since that happened, and I'm sorry, Mary, but I had to have a mother for Bridget. When the child is fifteen, I promise I will let you go if you still wish to leave by then. That's still some eleven years away yet and things can change. The man you love will have moved on by then and may not even remember you. If you want to seek out your mother, then I'll assist you with that, too, but for now you're stuck with me for better or worse."

"You've been honest with me, Brian, but I must tell you that if Campbell comes looking for me ~~then~~ I'll go with him."

"Perhaps we'll cross that bridge when we come to it," he said, "but first things first."

Two days later she got the first pains.

"Brian, the baby is coming," she screamed, as a pain she couldn't describe hit her.

"Into the hut, lass," he said, taking her hand. He eased her down onto the grass and hessian mattress he had made. Twenty minutes later the pain hit again, and he gripped her hand as she squeezed, her knuckles turning white. For three hours the pains came and went, each time getting closer and closer. Bridget watched wide-eyed as Mary's face contorted in agony. After another hour, the pains were five minutes apart, and Brian knew her time was close. Suddenly, Bridget screamed as she pointed to the bush.

"Black men, Daddy, black men."

Brian rushed to the opening to see a group of six aborigines all armed with spears not more than twenty yards away. He picked up his musket and fired over their heads in an effort to scare them away, but they became infuriated and rushed at him. He fumbled, quickly trying to re-load as one brought back his arm and hurled his spear. It whistled through the air, catching Brian high in the shoulder. He dropped the musket and staggered back, falling to the floor.

Mary screamed, this time with fright, when she saw the blood beginning to ooze down his arm, the spear still penetrating his shoulder. As the blacks rushed in, one with a club raised to smash Brian's head she thought, *I'm going to die, my baby is going to die, we're all going to die,* and waited for the killing blows. As the man raised the club, his blow was halted by one of the blacks, a man with grey hair. He spoke in some language she could not understand.

The grey-haired man looked at Mary with her huge belly, and at Bridget cowering against the corner of the hut. The only aggression came from Wolf who snarled at the intruders. Brian was groaning, trying to pull the spear out, and the man with the club, anger showing on his black face, picked up Brian's musket and smashed it against the doorframe. The grey-haired man stood over Mary and placed his hand on her belly just as another pain hit her. He stood up and again spoke to one of the men, then bent over and ripped every stitch of clothing from her body. She thought he was going to rape her, even in her condition and prayed to God it would be over quickly.

Instead, the blacks sat on the floor as if waiting for something to happen. Ten minutes later a completely naked middle-aged black lubra, probably a senior woman of the tribe, entered the hut and then another woman entered. They spoke their language while the men removed Brian and Bridget, leaving Mary alone with the women. Brian sat outside the hut holding his shoulder. After removing the spear, one of the men placed some sort of plant herb on the wound on Brian's shoulder.

Another hour passed and then another, and then he heard the cry of a newborn infant as the two lubras ran out with smiles on their faces.

The grey-haired man pointed to Brian and again spoke to his men, indicating he was to enter the hut. There he found the naked Mary with a small, unclad child in her arms, suckling her breast.

She looked up with joy as he entered. "It's a boy, Brian, a little boy."

He moved to her and touched the child on the head, kissing it gently. Then he lent over and kissed Mary, an action that stunned her, and she could see tears in his eyes.

"He's beautiful, lass, and he looks just like you."

She tried to see a likeness to Campbell, McBride or Brian, but could see none. She hoped there would be just a shade of red hair, but the child was completely bald and gave no indication of his future coloring.

"We have a son, Brian. Will you claim him?"

"Yes, lass. I'll do my best to make his life as full as I can. What do you want to call him?"

Mary smiled. "My true father's name was Robert. I'll call him that."

"Robert Corcoran, it is then.

"It a fine name, don't you think?" replied Brian.

Mary fell back, contented he would see to it that the child would not suffer in any way because of the doubt of his paternity. When she looked out of the hut the blacks were gone.

"Why did they help us? I thought they would kill us."

"It was my fault. I panicked when I saw them as I thought of your safety. I fired over their heads to scare them off, but they thought I was trying to kill them. With good reason, I suppose. When the old man saw you, he knew I was only trying to protect you and Bridget. I guess they're not savages after all."

"If only some of our own people were as gentle."

Brian nodded and took some clothes out of the wagon for Mary and the baby. He boiled some water and washed Mary's body down before dressing her. Bridget sat looking in awe at her new brother. The family had increased by one.

Chapter Eleven

For another week, Rebecca and Campbell pressed on in an endeavor to find some trace of Mary. Rebecca realized Campbell was no longer a boy, even though he still held a youthful appearance. He spoke of his plans of accumulating great wealth and becoming an important man in the society of the new land.

He sat holding a mug of tea with a superior look on his face as he stared at her with a crooked grin. "The opportunities are in the Colony of Port Phillip, and I hear the city of Melbourne is growing each day on the shores of Port Phillip Bay. The people will want wool, meat, and resource materials for their buildings. I intend to take the opportunity."

Rebecca looked confused. "But how can you do that and look for Mary, as well?"

He gave a grunt. "They go hand in hand. Mary is important to me. She will be my wife and bear me children. A man of importance will need a beautiful wife to complement his position. Mary will be perfect."

This was new to Rebecca. "I thought you wanted Mary because you loved her."

He took another sip from his mug before answering. "I do love her. I love her dearly, and I want to release her from the bondage she finds herself in. As soon as I dispose of her husband and claim her, she'll be eternally grateful and will be my queen."

"And where do I come in all these plans?" Rebecca asked warily, the first pangs of doubt entering her mind.

"A woman must be close to her mother, it's only right. When I'm rich, I will set you up in a cottage close by, and you can visit whenever you like."

Rebecca sighed. If Campbell thought she was going to be some little old lady allowed to see her daughter only by the grace of her husband, then Campbell had another think coming. He was still young and would learn that nothing works out the way you want it. She intended to be more than a visiting mother; it was her only child he was talking about.

Just after darkness had set in, it happened. Rebecca had a fire going to prepare the evening meal while Campbell was adding to the pile of firewood. Suddenly, two men rode up with pistols drawn, both wearing dusty coats and broad hats. They were bearded and rough looking, like the man who had claimed Mary.

"Get your hands up before we kill you," one shouted and rushed to the pair. Campbell tried to reach his pistol, still in its holster by the wagon, but the second man brought his gun down on his head, opening a wound on his forehead. Rebecca feared for their lives as the blood began to cover Campbell's face.

"Shoot him," snarled the first man, but Rebecca screamed and threw herself over Campbell's prostrate body. Still conscious, his eyes opened wide as he thought his last moment had come.

"Please don't shoot," cried Rebecca. "He's my only son. My husband has just died, and he's the only one I have left in this world."

The bushranger nodded and the other quickly tied Campbell's hands behind his back and then lashed him to a wagon wheel.

"We want your money, woman, where is it?"

"I don't have any," said Rebecca trying to cry louder.

"Shoot the kid," he said. "We haven't time to play around."

The other aimed his pistol at Campbell and fired, the shot missing his head by inches hitting the side of the wagon.

"No, please," implored Rebecca as the man began to take aim again.

"Are ya goin' to tell us?"

She nodded, knowing they would kill Campbell if she didn't.

"It's in the wagon, hidden in a tin."

He nodded and barked at her. "Get it and no tricks."

She reached into the wagon, and saw her pistol lying alongside her trunk. For a moment an idea came to her, but one of the thieves quickly dashed it.

"Don't even think about it, lady," the man said and opened the trunk he had pulled from the wagon. There he found the tin containing the last of Rebecca's money.

"This is more like it," the other shouted. "Are we goin' to have her?"

The man rubbed his chin as he looked at her. "No, she's too old. Must be close to forty. We'll look for something younger down the trail."

The words stunned Rebecca as she realized they were quite young men. They actually felt as though she was past it. She was relieved. They mounted and rode off, leaving her standing there. She ran to Campbell and wiped the blood from his face and untied his bonds.

"I'll go after them, the bastards. I'll kill them," he said as he sprang to his feet.

"You'll do no such thing. You'd never find them in the dark and more than likely they'd kill you. It's obvious they do this for a living and would have no hesitation in killing you if the opportunity arose again."

"But our money, did they get it all?"

"You mean my money. Yes, they got it all. We're now stone broke."

"Then what are we going to do?"

"Stop in the next town and start earning some. What else can we do?" He sat down, resigned to the night's events.

* * * * *

Mary looked at Brian coyly. "Do you know what day this is, Brian?"

"Sure. Wednesday." He grinned and watched her reaction.

A frown spread over her face as she glanced at him. "Yes, but the date?"

"You mean is it Robert's first birthday?"

She compressed her lips together and knew he was fooling her. "You knew; you didn't forget."

He laughed at her concern. "No, I didn't forget, and I've caught a fine cod to celebrate. I'm afraid I don't have a present for him."

"It doesn't matter. The important thing is you remembered. It doesn't seem like a year since he was born."

Again, his eyes went to her face with that look of adoration but she tried to ignore it. "The year's gone quickly, and you've recovered well, but now it's time to move south again."

"To the Murray?" She raised her eyebrows at this announcement.

"Yes, to the place I'm going to claim. I'll still have enough money to buy a large holding, but we must get there before it's all sold."

"Then we have to pack our belongings."

"Yes, this place has been a good shelter for us, and I didn't want Robert on the road until he was old enough to cope, but now it's time."

Again he surprised her by his actions. Most men would have gone no matter how it affected their family, but he had stayed and considered their welfare.

The crude cabin had given them shelter over the winter months. At times, Brian had left her alone with the children while he made a journey into the nearest settlement some four days ride away and returned with important supplies. She was overwhelmed when he had brought back a new dress for her and more importantly, new shoes. The dress was a little large, but she made some minor alterations, and it fitted well. He also brought back some clothes for Bridget and a rag doll that she treasured.

Now packed and about to leave, Mary frowned. "How will you find your way to the Murray?"

"Have you ever heard of a man named Charles Sturt?"

"No, who is he?"

"An Englishman who made an historic trip down this very river. He sailed along it in a small boat until he came to the Murray. We'll follow the river to its end, and there we'll look for our land."

"Brian," she said slowly.

"Yes."

"Can I ask you some questions about yourself?"

He looked at her and grinned. "I wondered how long it would take. A lot longer than I thought. Go ahead." He climbed into the wagon alongside her after tying his horse behind.

"Where did you come from, and how did you get to Australia?"

He gave the horses a flick with the reins then looked at Mary. "I guess you have a right to know. I was a lad of fifteen in Killarney in Ireland. We lived on a small plot of ground we rented from our English landlord. It was a bad year, and my father took ill and died. When my mother was unable to pay the back rent, the landlord sent her to a debtor's prison. The day he evicted us, I struck him with a shovel and knocked him to the ground. I was arrested and given ten years deportation to Van Dieman's land. I survived and released the day I turned twenty with a conditional pardon. That meant I was free, but couldn't return to Ireland. I left that awful place and came to the mainland."

Her eyes opened wider at this revelation. "But you would not have had any money."

He shrugged his shoulders as he looked at her. "No. I was given work in clearing land and grew rather strong as you can see. I learned that was the only way to make a life. Claim land and build a family."

Her words came out a little slower and perhaps a little nervously. "Is that why you took your first wife?"

"I heard there were women to be had at the prison. As I had little hope of finding a wife in the free women, especially as I was an ex convict then this was the only sensible thing to do."

She sighed at his words. "So you went to Parramatta."

"Yes. I found Rose there, and she was in much the same position as your mother. She was being abused by the guards and had to give herself for decent food." He gave the horse another gentle flick. "When I picked her out I could see she was repulsed by the thought of living with a total stranger. She expected nothing and relieved when I treated her humanely."

Mary tightened her lips before speaking. "You used her just as you use me?"

He shot her a sharp glance hoping she'd understand. "I'm a man, Mary, and I have feelings just as all men do. It seemed a just reward for taking care of her. I made no great demands of her, only relief when I could bear it no longer."

"How did she take it?"

"Much the same as you. She put up with me as she had no choice, but I made life as comfortable as I could. She bore me a child in the second year, but he died of fever."

This certainly surprised her. "You had another child?"

"Yes. I was heartbroken when I lost him, and Rose could see I really cared. It wasn't long before I fell madly in love with her, and we built a good life together."

"Did she love you?"

"She never said so, but I knew she liked me, and that was enough."

"Then Bridget was born."

"It was a wonderful day, and I love her dearly. When Rose died, I knew I had to find a mother for Bridget, or I would lose her too. That's why I picked you."

"You never gave a thought as to how I would feel."

"I did, but Bridget's need was more important, and I could see McBride was a villain who would abuse you. I'm sorry you had to leave your mother, as I was when I had to leave mine, but as I said, if she finds you, she's welcome."

She paused again. "You gave McBride fifty pounds. How did you get such a sum?"

"You see this scar?" he said, pointing to his cheek.

She nodded.

"A month before I came to Parramatta I was alone with Bridget, and had ten pounds, my entire savings. It was all I had in the world, and I was desperate. I needed someone to look after Bridget, and I needed money."

"You stole?"

He laughed. "No, lass, I earned it the hardest way."

"How?" Her eyebrows shot up then a small frown creased her brow.

"Bridget and I were in Goulburn one afternoon, and I could see a crowd gathered at the fairground. As she had no fun in life and missed her mother, I took her to see some clowns."

"Yes. Go on," said Mary. She leaned forward, anxious to hear what he was going to say.

He stared ahead as he spoke. "Men were gathered around a ring, and I watched a bare knuckle fight in progress. People were making bets as to who could stand up to the champion, Ironbark Cassidy. He was knocking people out with ease. When they ran out of opponents his manager became angry and called the spectators cowards. He saw me and challenged me."

This was getting interesting. Mary listened intently. "You fought the man?"

He still stared ahead, remembering. "At first I refused, but then he asked me if my mother let me out to come to the fair. The rest of the crowd laughed, and I got angry. He said I would get five pounds if I could last three rounds, so I accepted."

"Five pounds is not a huge sum." It was a long way short of the 50 pounds he had paid for her.

He shook his head in agreement. "No. But I thought I had nothing to lose as I was down to my last ten pounds. I asked how much I would get if I knocked Cassidy out, only to be greeted with howls of laughter."

"What happened then?"

"The bookmakers accepting bets shouted they would give me odds of 100 to 1 such was their confidence, and 50 to 1 if I lasted ten rounds. As I had nothing to lose, I accepted, and the bets were made. I wagered my entire savings."

Mary frowned, having no understanding of prize fighting. "How long did a round last?"

"As long as it took one man to knock the other to the ground. If one couldn't rise by the count of ten, then the match was over."

"Go on," said Mary, She placed her finger tips together and stared at him, wanting him to continue.

Brian gave her a little grin. "The fight commenced, and Cassidy knocked me down with his first blow. Everyone laughed, but I got to my feet and after a few minutes rest, the second round started. This round lasted seven minutes as I tried to avoid his blows. Again I was knocked down, and again the fight was re-commenced."

"Did you get any blows on him?" By his size she thought he might have had some success.

"Very few at first, but then I hit him on the nose, drawing blood. This seemed to infuriate him, and he rushed at me. He swung wildly, and I landed one to his chin, knocking him down."

"Did he get up?"

"Yes, but the bookmakers went quiet as no one had ever done this to Cassidy before."

"What happened then?" Mary's gaze never left his face. She had heard about such contests, but of course had never seen one.

"The fight went on until the ninth round, but Cassidy was getting the better of me. For every blow I landed, he landed five. When I lasted the tenth round, the crowd was going wild, for I had just made five hundred pounds. Of the ten rounds, Cassidy had knocked me down eight times while I had knocked him down twice. His knuckles were bleeding, as was my face for he had hit me so many times I lost count."

Mary put her hand to her mouth in horror. "Was Bridget watching?"

"Yes. There was nowhere for her to go. By the time we reached the fifteenth round, my eyes were blackened, and my face covered with blood, but Cassidy was beginning to tire. He had not fought for this length of time before. I knocked him down in the sixteenth round, and he sat gasping for breath. The bookmakers were screaming for him to get up."

"And did he?"' Mary leaned forward and placed her hand on his arm in her eagerness to hear the rest of the story.

Brian nodded. "Yes, but then I had a stroke of luck. The man who acted as my second whispered in my ear that Cassidy drank a lot and for me to stop trying to hit him in the face, but to hit him in the belly."

She frowned again. "What's a second?"

"A man who wipes the blood from your face and gives you advice between rounds. It seemed Cassidy's manager had been cheating the man, paying him less than promised. For the first time Cassidy started to back away from me just to get his breath. Then I hit him in the stomach, and my fist almost disappeared. His eyes went funny, and he dropped his arms. I swung again with all my might and hit him flush on the jaw. I heard a sickening crunch, and I knew his jaw was broken. He fell down and never got up."

Mary's mouth popped open "You mean you had won one thousand pounds?"

"Yes, that's how I had the fifty pounds to pay McBride for you. He split my cheek open, and this scar is the result. It took a month for my face to heal."

"How much do you have left?"

He laughed at her question. "Why, are you planning on stealing it?"

Mary's cheeks reddened. She had no such thought.

"No, —I mean—I just—"

He laughed loudly again. "I know what you mean, Mary. I have eight hundred and thirty pounds left. It will be enough to buy land when we get there. Any more questions?"

"Not at the moment," she said, watching the sparkle in his eyes. The thought of Campbell meeting such a man frightened her.

Chapter Twelve

Ireland 1830

Brian looked out of the window of his home at the rain swept countryside of Ireland as he shivered in front of the fire. The house he lived in with his parents was made of stone with a thatched roof and a dirt floor. As a lad of almost fifteen, he was big for his age, but painfully thin, a common occurrence with the starved population of Ireland in 1830. The only living child of Elizabeth Corcoran and her husband Patrick, Brian had worked hard on his father's small plot of ground to help forge out a pitiful living.

The farm was rented from their English landlord, as most of the other properties were, and life had been hard for the entire family. His brother and sister had succumbed to the ravages of years of starvation and had died. His brother had been only five and his sister just a year older. Now his father had fallen to pneumonia and lay in his bed dying. His mother had asked him to run to the village and fetch both the doctor and the priest. Brian had covered the one and a half miles in cold blinding rain and had to plead with both men to follow him home. Reluctantly they agreed, saying they would come as soon as they could. The doctor had to have his supper, and the priest had some confessions he had to hear. Brian ran back again in the hash conditions and, together, he and his mother waited an hour before the two men appeared.

Brian had removed his wet clothes at his mother's insistence and sat in fresh, but worn clothes with a blanket around himself listening to the men talk as they hovered over his father. The smell of burning peat ran through the house as it had only one room. Each bed was isolated by a curtain from the next to give some privacy.

The sound of his father wheezing with each breath he took brought fear to Brian. His mother sat with tears streaming down her face, knowing her husband did not have long in this world.

"Perhaps if you made something hot to drink, Mrs. Corcoran," said the doctor as he sat with his patient. Anything to keep her occupied as her husband lay dying. When the doctor left, Father O'Brien began to give the last rites. They all knew the end was near. For another ten minutes the unfortunate man gasped for breath until at last he gave a strangled cry and stopped breathing. Elizabeth clasped her son in her arms and sobbed hysterically. Brian was stunned. He was now technically the head of the family.

They buried Patrick Corcoran the following day in a solemn service as the rain fell in a slight mist, adding even more misery to the mourners. At the end of the week, the first notice of back rent arrived. The landlord demanded two pounds five shillings. When Elizabeth pleaded for more time to raise the money, she received no sympathy from the landlord. Another week passed then another as the debt began to grow. Brian sold the pig for ten shillings, but that was swallowed up with a demand for the rest.

They managed to make small payments of two and three shillings by selling everything of value they could find, but eventually the bailiffs arrived and arrested Elizabeth for the debt incurred. The debtor's prison was a forlorn, miserable place from which few returned. As an example to others that rent must be paid, the bailiffs burned the cottage to the ground as an angry crowd stood around shouting.

"Arrest the woman," shouted the bailiff, and two men took her to a small wagon that had bars surrounding it.

"No, let her go!" howled Brian and rushed toward the English Lord who sat on his horse smiling broadly.

People tried to hold him back, but he broke free and picked up a shovel covered with manure. "You bastard," he cried and swung the shovel at the man, knocking him from his horse. He continued a flurry of blows before two bailiffs restrained him.

The man staggered to his feet, blood streaming down his face. He touched his chin and looked at the blood, then turned to the bailiffs.

"Arrest him. I want him charged with attempted murder."

His trial was a formality and over quickly. His age had no bearing on his sentence. He was found guilty and sentenced to ten years to be served at his Majesties penal colony in Van Dieman's Land in the new country.

He languished in prison for three months in frightful conditions and celebrated his fifteenth birthday in isolation. Later, five convict ships left the shores of England, taking over eight hundred prisoners who were held in conditions not fit for animals. Three weeks out, Brian caught the attention of one of the convicts, who thought a fifteen-year-old boy would suit him. He grabbed Brian one night and forced him to the deck. He hadn't expected that Brian was capable of hurting him and found his face smashed as Brian swung a wooden pin left lying on the deck. He laid the man out. Both Brian and the man stood before the Captain to receive their punishment.

"Twenty lashes each," came the order, and both were dragged out to the rigging.

"Here, put this between your teeth," a sailor said and shoved a piece of wood into his mouth. The sailor then brought back his arm and sent the lash biting into his flesh with an agonizing blow.

Brian screamed as it felt like a hot piece of steel was placed on the broad of his back. The flogging continued with each blow bringing an indescribable pain and leaving his back red. By the fifteenth blow, the flesh parted and ribbons of blood streamed down his back.

Mercifully it ended, and although barely conscious, he felt strong arms carry him below decks. Eventually they reached Port Arthur in Van Dieman's Land. The prisoners were roughly manacled and ordered down the gangplank. The long line seemed endless.

"Out into the yard," an order came, and he followed the other prisoners with leg irons shackled to his feet.

"Where are we going?" he whispered to an older man who stood alongside him.

"To work like slaves for the bloody English on roads and buildings," the man said. "Just keep your nose clean and do what you're told, and you won't get into trouble."

It was here he found out just what hard labor meant. Up before sunrise, he spent long hours swinging an axe to make fence posts, breaking rocks with a heavy sledgehammer to make gravel and carrying heavy bags of rock and gravel on his shoulders.

A week later another convict had a scuffle with Brian over who would carry the next load. He took a swipe at Brain.

He never got any further as Brian swung his fist back and struck him in the face. The man roared and knocked Brian to the ground.

The other convicts gathered around to watch the encounter, as did the guards. It broke up a boring day for them. The man was much bigger and heavier than Brian, and Brian swung his fists without making contact. Blood ran down his face, but he refused to give in. One man stood watching with interest. When he was knocked to the ground he picked him up and whispered in his ear, "Keep away until he tires, then kick him in the groin."

Eventually the guards broke it up before the man killed Brian.

Both stood as the Governor paced back and forth poking each man with his cane.

"It appears neither of you show much respect for the rules. Twenty lashes each."

Both were dragged away, and the punishment inflicted. When Brian recovered, the same man took him aside. He was puzzled by the man's friendly approach. No one had ever been friendly to him since he arrived.

"Listen, lad, if you want to survive then you had better learn to fight," he said as they sat together.

"How do I do that?" Brian replied, cautiously.

"I used to be a fighter back in England before they brought me out here. I can teach you if you like."

Brian looked at him sharply. He knew he had to fight to survive. "I can't pay you," said Brian.

The man gave him a grin. "No one can here. I don't want anything. I had a lad like you back home before they transported me. I taught him."

What was there to lose? "What's your name, mister?" he asked curiously.

"Colin Treadwell. Do ya want help?"

"Yeah, these blokes had better learn I'm no sissy. Every night for a month Treadwell taught him the fundamentals of boxing.

As Treadwell had conquered more than one of the convicts in previous fights they all became wary of Brian, even though he was still undeveloped.

Since they shared the same cell, Treadwell gave him valuable instruction each night.

"Use your left like this, lad," he said, poking his left fist at Brian. "Then when he drops his hands, counter with your right."

Every night the instruction went on.

"Now we learn how to evade wild swings," said Treadwell, and showed Brian how to bob, step back and move forward. "Remember, if you show a passive stance it will give them confidence. Don't take a backward step. Always keep moving in, just watch the wild swings."

The next time he was attacked, Brian did much better and sat the man on his backside. Brian got in several hard blows, drawing blood before he was knocked down. Colin stepped in to save him further punishment, and again Brian received the mandatory lashes.

By the time he was eighteen, he had a reputation that he wasn't a man to be trifled with. During his years at the prison he had taken over two hundred lashes. The scars were always visible on his back, and this fact warned others to leave him alone.

After five years, he was allowed to work as a farm laborer on some of the land generously handed out by the Colony Governor as reward to his cronies for favors given. Brian learned about sheep, land control and pasture growth, facts he filed away in his mind to be used in some way on his release.

On his twentieth birthday he was released with a conditional pardon and he was free to leave the prison. He was determined to escape this evil place that had been his home for the last five years, the place where he had seen floggings, executions, brutality and uncivilized behavior he hadn't thought possible. He worked as a free man and labored on land until he had enough passage to take him to Sydney town.

In another six months work he had earned enough to buy a wagon and seek land offered to ex-convicts in an endeavor to open up the country. He had the urges of any young man and visited the whore houses at times, but he desperately wanted a woman to give him a family.

When drinking in an inn one day, a man mentioned that women from the prison in Parramatta, were available to marry and if interested then he had better turn up on the following Saturday.

On a bright sunny day, walking along the street his attention was gathered by one of the ex convicts he had just worked with on one of the farms. The work had run out and now it was time to find a new job.

"Brian, are you looking for a bit of entertainment with some of the women in the town?"

Brian studied him. He was about Brian's age and had been agreeable when they toiled together.

"No, I want to save my money. How else can I buy land and build a future?"

"Christ, that could be years away. You have to have some fun while you're waiting."

"I want to find a wife to start a family. Then I can think about getting some land."

"A wife? Hell that would be a burden like a weight around your neck."

"Haven't you thought about finding a girl to live your life with?"

"Not while I'm having fun with the women who give their favours so cheaply."

Brian shook his head. This man had no thought of his future.

The man frowned. "Look if you're serious I know where you can pick up a wife-and it won't cost you anything."

That caught Brian's attention. "Where?"

"The women's prison near Parramatta. Twice a year they parade the women for men who are seeking a wife. If they agree then they are released from that hellhole, married and are on their way."

"Really. What are they like?"

"Don't know for sure. Some will be pretty scrubby, some whores, some thieves some violent."

"And some may have been put in there because of some minor infringement with the gentry. That's how I finished up there."

"I guess so. It's pot luck."

"How do I get to Parramatta from here?"

"Not sure. Ask in the tavern. They would know."

Brian nodded and went to the tavern across the street. He entered to see five or six drinkers sitting at tables smoking and talking with glasses of ale in front of them. His attention was caught when he saw a man of perhaps forty, dirty beard, dirty clothes and holding the arm of a young girl behind the bar as she struggled to break free. The girl looked to be around eighteen years old and had a furious look on her face.

"Come on Rose. It will be the easiest five bob you've ever made. We go out into the stable for five minutes. I'm happy and you are five bob richer."

"I said let go of my arm." She struggled to break free but the man had a firm grip on her.

Brian could see what was going on and frowned as none of the other drinkers intervened. He strode to the pair and glared at the man.

"What do you think you're doing with my fiancée?"

The man gasped as he looked at the size of Brian and cringed at the frown on Brian's face.

"Fiancée? Shit I didn't know."

"Are you all right Rose?" asked Brian remembering her name.

"I am now. Thank you." The man let go and stared at them both.

"How long have you been engaged?" he asked Rose not believing Brian's words.

"Two weeks. We're getting married on Saturday."

Brian looked surprise at her words. "And if you ever try to annoy her again then you'll leave here with several teeth missing. Understand?"

The man nodded and left in a hurry, much to Rose's delight.

"Thanks. I guess I can get you an ale on the house."

"You own this place?" he asked surprised.

"God no. I work here two days a week. It's the only thing between starvation and me. My name is Rose Wallis."

"Brian Corcoran," he replied offering his hand.

"Fiancée?" she said smirking.

"Wedding?" he replied.

"If you can lie then so can I."

He laughed. She certainly had a sense of humour.

"I wonder if you can give me directions to---"

"Parramatta," she said before he finished.

"How did you know that?" he said again surprised.

"You're Irish, that means you're an ex convict. Not many free Irish in this country. You're going to get yourself a wife from the prison."

"What else do you know about me?" He smiled at her knowledge.

"Not a lot but there have been three others in here today asking the same question. You must all be desperate."

"Desperate? I would rather think that we're looking to the future to build a family."

"Do you know what sort of women you're likely to get from the prison?"

"I think so. Some will be whores, some criminals, some innocents who were sent there because they offended the English. You seem to know a lot about them."

"That's because I was one of them. I was sent there for seven years when I was fifteen."

"But you can't be more than eighteen now." Brian frowned at her words.

"I got lucky. Many more women were being sent and the place was over crowded. The Governor let me and a few others have four years off our sentences. There was a fee to pay of course."

"And you are telling me this because---?"

"You did me a favour and I feel sorry for ex convicts who struggle to survive like I do."

"I know. It's a struggle but much better than being back in Ireland. Do you know when the prison is presenting the women?"

She smiled. "Yes, the day of our wedding."

"Saturday," he said nodding. "How long does it take to get to Parramatta?"

"Three hours in your wagon. You do have a wagon don't you?"

He nodded. "I need one to get south to buy land."

"Buy land? You must be rich?"

He laughed again. "Not yet but maybe one day. First things first. I need a wife to help me when I get a farm."

"So you need a slave to work for you?" He could see the smirk on her lips as she spoke.

"Not a slave. A partner who I hope can give me a happy life as I will try to give her one."

"With the side benefits," said Rose waiting to hear his reply.

"Don't know how else you can get children."

"I guess not. Of course you realize the wife will not want to sleep with a total stranger. It will just be a way out of prison."

"I'm very aware of that. It will be part of the bargain. I won't worry her as much as she might think."

"And that will be how often?"

"Hell, you are a very nosey person. What's it got to do with you?"

"Just letting you know how the woman will react."

Brian frowned. This was getting out of hand. "That will be between her and me. Is there somewhere I can park the wagon until Friday. That will give me a bit of time to spend a night there and get organized once I get there."

"Down the street. You will see several wagons parked there. You can buy feed for you horses and let them rest up. Can I help you with anything else?"

"No, that's all. Thanks for the information."

He began to turn away but Rose spoke to him. "Just how fussy will you be to find a wife?"

"She doesn't have to be a raving beauty. Just a nice person with a sense of humor and a willingness to work hard with me."

She laughed. "Good luck with that."

He turned and walked out.

For the next two days Brian waited. To fill in time he went to the tavern again but found Rose was not working those days. As he walked down the street he ran into her.

"Still here?" she asked giving him a nice smile.

"I leave at eight tomorrow. It will give me a day to get organized once I get to Parramatta.

"Then this is the last time we will see each other."

"I guess so. It's been nice to have met you, Rose."

"And you too Brian. Good luck."

"Thanks." He tipped his hat and watched her walk away. When she stopped and looked back he smiled to himself.

Next morning Brian was up at seven. He paid for a room in the tavern as this would be the last time he could afford such a luxury. He gathered his clothes, dressed and left for the wagon. When he neared his wagon his fists clenched. His horses had already been hitched to the wagon. Someone was trying to steal it. He was shocked to see Rose sitting in the seat at the front.

"You're late. You said eight o'clock."

"What are you doing here?" he asked astounded.

"I hitched up the horses after feeding them. I've been thinking about what you said. It will be a waste of time going to Parramatta to find a wife as you can find one here."

"But I don't know any women here." He stared at her, still surprised.

"God, maybe I'm making a mistake. I thought you might be intelligent."

"What are you saying?" he asked staring at her.

"I've decided you can marry me. I have no future here and I like what you're saying about having a family and buying land. I also liked your answers to my questions. If I stay here then I'll finish up an old maid or worse, having to earn a living another way."

Dumbfounded he stood staring at her.

"Get up here man and let's find a minister who will do the deed. Then we can try to start to find enough money to buy that land you're talking about."

Still shocked he asked "Are you sure?".

"Decisions had to be made. You will find me honest and hard working. As long as you don't want kids too soon then I can put up with you if you can put up with me. Do we have a deal?"

Brian nodded. "I guess I could do a lot worse."

"Me too. Now let's get moving. I already quit my job so there's nothing to hold me here."

He grinned and mounted the wagon beside her.

"You're a very confident woman"

"I learnt if you make a decision then you have to work through it. You seem to scrub up well so what is there to lose?"

"I see. Where are we going?"

"The church is at the end of the street."

"I guess I can buy a cheap wedding ring." He liked her attitude. She was no mouse.

"I don't care about a ring. Anything will do."

"Do you know what you are getting yourself into?"

"No more than you. Are we going to sit here all day?"

He climbed up beside her. "Let's go."

The wedding was held that day and they looked at each other before Brian started the wagon to leave the town.

They drove until early evening. Brian unloaded the wagon and erected a makeshift canvas tent. He started a fire and boiled some water.

"Do you know how to cook, Rose?" he asked.

"I said I was a domestic in England,"

"Okay, you peel some potatoes while I cut some salted pork."

They ate as the sun began to set, and Brian gathered up the dishes and washed them.

"Time for bed," he said. "We have a long day tomorrow."

He led her to the tent, her face tight with tension. She didn't seem so confident now.

"I guess we can get this over with," she said nervously.

"You can get changed while I tie things down on the wagon. When you're ready, give me a yell."

She did as he told her. She lay on her back as he climbed onto the mattress and pulled up the covers. She waited for him to touch her, but he bid her goodnight, rolled over and went to sleep.

Rose stared at the sky wondering why he hadn't taken her. She expected it and was ready.

It was a week before he took her, surprising her with how gentle he was. As they prepared for bed, Brian touched her arm. Rose looked at him, startled.

"When we agreed to marry I said I would expect you to perform your wifely duties. My needs for a woman are great, Rose, and I wish to look for my release. I don't wish to upset you, but I want you to adhere to your part of the bargain."

She raised one eyebrow. "I wondered why it took so long."

"I promise I won't hurt you."

"I know you will try not to."

"Would you like the lamp out?"

Rose nodded and lay on her back as he reached over and plunged the tent into darkness.

The next few years showed her Brian could be a gentle giant if he wanted to be. The physical day-to-day survival was hard, but she felt grateful for the peace she now felt. She was indeed a happy woman. She began to look forward to their lovemaking for that is what it developed into. A strong bond began to develop between them.

One morning as they drove the wagon Rose claimed his attention by grabbing his arm. "I have some news."

He looked at her in surprise. "What is it, Rose?"

She smiled at him as she spoke. "We've been married for nearly five years now, and you have treated me well, better than I thought."

"I'm pleased you feel this way. You've treated me well too. It's been a good bargain." he said, acknowledging her words.

"I must confess, when we married I never thought I could feel such happiness. I could only see a life of misery, but you've changed all that."

He smiled at her, thankful for her words. "I think we both made a good decision. You've made me happy, too."

"Can I ask you a question?" She waited for his answer.

"Of course you can."

"Do you love me?"

He paused before answering. "Yes, but why do you ask?" This was a most unexpected question.

She leaned across and squeezed his hand. "Because I'm expecting a child in six months."

Brian pulled up the horses and drew her into his arms. "A child? That's wonderful. I couldn't be happier."

When the baby was born, Rose watched fondly as he held his son in his arms. It amused her the way he fussed over her. He looked the proud parent who wanted to show off his son.

A very concerned Rose woke him one morning. "Brian, the baby is sick."

She opened the blanket to show him a red rash all over its body.

"What do you think it is?' he asked. He placed his hand on the baby's head.

"I think its measles. He's burning up. We have to get him to a doctor."

"But we're almost thirty miles from one," he said, anguish showing in his voice.

She touched his arm. "I know, we must hurry."

Brian packed the wagon as soon as he could and turned toward the nearest town. By the time they reached it the baby was dead. Both felt a shock never experienced before. Rose burst into tears as Brian tried to comfort her. She thought he might blame her, but found he was even more attentive than before she became pregnant. As they stood at the grave Rose pulled his arm around her shoulder as they stared at the little coffin lowered to the ground.

"We'll have another, Brian, I'll try to give you another son."

"Any child is welcome, Rose. We have to try and put this behind us."

Twelve months later she gave him the good news she was pregnant again. She was happy to see the joy in his face. When a little girl was born, they felt happy to have a healthy child once again.

Bridget, as they chose to call her, brought them closer together than even Brian thought possible. For the next three years they wandered around with Brian seeking work wherever he could. He still promised to build her a grand house one day, but she knew that would probably never happen. Rose didn't care; she was happy and free.

She became very fond of Brian although she never actually said she loved him, frightened that something would happen if she made such a commitment. While cooking the evening meal one day, he rushed to her.

"One of the men I work with said there is land for the taking in the Colony of Port Phillip, along a river called the Murray. The Government wants to open up the area and are offering settlers the land as incentive to move there."

"It's your dream. We should do it."

He nodded. "Thank you for agreeing. We'll move out tomorrow."

"How else are you going to build me this grand house you spoke of?"

"Then we'll leave tomorrow," he said, overjoyed.

The next day they gathered up their belongings, and Brian drove the wagon down the main street of the town.

"Stop for a moment Brian, I want to get something from the store."

He pulled the wagon to a halt, and Rose leapt from the wagon to hurry across the street.

Brian rested his elbows on his knees as he gazed at his wife, someone he felt deep attachment to. It was the first time he had ever loved anyone, and the last seven years had been the happiest in his life.

"I won't be long," she called, smiling at him. A yell caught his attention. His eyes widened with fear as he saw the horse bolting down the main street, its rider lying on the road. Rose walked across the road and looked up at the last minute. The horse was just a blur as it toppled her. Her body lifted from the ground and sent hurtling into the air. Brian blinked as her head crashed to the ground with a sickening thud. Everything occurred as though in slow motion to him. There was nothing he could do but watch in the split second it happened. The horse continued on, but Brian gave it little consideration as he looked at his wife's prone body.

He leapt from the wagon and gathered her in his arms. Blood trickled from her mouth, and her eyes were shut.

"Get a doctor!" he screamed, and then tenderly lay her down and put his coat under her head. A crowd gathered, and after a few minutes a man pushed his way through.

"I'm Doctor Cresswell. Out of the way, man," he said to Brian.

"Is it bad, Doc?" he asked, fearfully. Blood was beginning to flow faster from her mouth and nostrils.

"Looks like her skull is cracked. Let's get her to my surgery."

Brian picked her up gently and carried her to the doctor's place, only fifty yards away. It was half an hour before she opened her eyes. Her hand gripped Brian's like a vice.

"What happened?" she said softly, her voice barely audible.

"A bolting horse hit you. You've hurt your head," whispered Brian, his eyes moist with tears.

"Brian," she gasped. "You must promise me something, please promise me."

"What is it, Rose?"

"Promise me you will take care of Bridget, no matter what happens, you must take care of her."

"I love her as much as I love you, Rose. I'll always take care of her."

"Brian, I want you to know that I lov..."

He looked into her shining eyes, and then saw the life leave her as they suddenly went dull. The pressure of her hand relaxed, and she lay there staring up at him. He felt the hand of the doctor on his shoulder.

"She's gone, Mister. Corcoran, she's at rest." He closed her eyes as Brian broke into deep sobs, his face buried in her bosom.

They buried her the next day in a simple ceremony, and as the funeral attendants left, Brian stood staring at her grave with Bridget holding his hand.

"Is Mummy coming back?' she asked sadly.

"No Bridget. Mummy's gone to heaven. It's just the two of us now."

For two days Brian sat in the pub and drank himself stupid. "Leave me alone," he said aggressively when the doctor grabbed his arm and led him outside into the sunshine

"I'm sorry, Mister. Corcoran, here's me thinking you were a man of honour. It looks like I made a mistake."

"What do you mean?' he asked, surprised.

"I heard you promise to look after your daughter for always. Your wife would be disgusted at your behaviour if she could see you."

The words stung, and he turned towards the doctor. "I miss her."

"So does your daughter, but that's no excuse. Bridget is your concern now. You must honour your promise."

Brian sucked in a breath. *Bridget?* He hadn't given her a thought in his own grief.

"Where is she?" he asked, trying to clear his head.

"She's with my wife and has been since you started drinking. Don't you care about her?"

"Of course I care. I must go to her."

The doctor paused for a few seconds. "Have you given any thought to having Bridget adopted out? We might be willing to take her." The doctor lit his pipe as he let the suggestion sink in.

"And why would I do that?" asked Brian, still numb with the drink.

The doctor blew smoke into the air. "You are now a single man and having a child must be like having a chain around your neck. You can't work land if you have her to look after. We can relieve you of that problem."

"No, I love her, and I'll get by somehow. I have to see her now."

The doctor's wife frowned when she saw the condition he was in, but Bridget ran to him and threw her arms around his neck. "I want my Mummy," she said pitifully.

"I know, sweetie. I miss her too, but as I told you, she's in heaven now and is safe."

"Our offer still stands," said the doctor, looking at his wife, who stood tight-lipped.

"Thank you but I can't do that. Where would I go to seek land in the south?" he said, still hugging his daughter.

"Try the local magistrate. He should be able to tell you the rules."

Brian found him in the courthouse. A small man with a rather large potbelly sat working on some papers. He looked up when Brian entered.

"And how can I help you, sir?" he asked, looking over the spectacles perched precariously on the end of his nose.

"I've heard that there is land to be had on the Murray River. I wonder if you can advise me as to how I may obtain some."

"I think you may be a little late. The Colony of Port Phillip is soon to be named after our new most gracious Majesty, Queen Victoria. While the land in New South Wales has been leased along the Murray, the land on the other side of the border is available for purchase. Large tracts of land are now gone in New South Wales so I suggest you raise some capital and buy in Victoria, before that's gone, too. The opportunity is there if you're willing to take the risk."

Brian heeded his words and returned to his wagon. He had to get money, and quickly or it would be too late.

"Where are we going, Daddy?" asked Bridget as he urged the wagon forward.

"To try and earn some money, pet, so we can buy land and make a new life."

He headed toward Sydney, picking up work on the way. He never bothered to shave as he fell into his bed each night in exhaustion, and soon had a grubby, hairy, abhorrent appearance about him.

After three days he knew he couldn't look after Bridget properly and farm land. He had to find a new wife, or he would lose both Bridget and his dream. His plan was to return to the prison at Parramatta and seek a new wife, but when he reached Goulburn he found out the prison no longer offered women as wives. Things were getting serious as he was now down to his last ten pounds when Bridget grabbed his arm.

"A fair ground Daddy. There's a circus. Can we go?"

He looked at the pathetic face of his daughter who was in for a sad life unless he did something about it.

"Why not? I can see some clowns," he said, smiling at her cherub face.

He parked the wagon and led Bridget to the fair ground to see the animals and clowns.

It was then that he saw the crowd gathering for the prize fighting.

Chapter Thirteen

Rebecca and Campbell broke camp the next morning and headed for the nearest town, one that held no more than two hundred people. Those on the street gave them a curious glance as their wagon entered on the only avenue.

"Where are we?" asked Campbell as she pulled to a stop.

"Cockatoo Creek," she said pointing to a sign. "We'll have to find some work."

"In this place?" Campbell was not impressed with what he saw.

"Yes, you go to the top of the road while I ask here. Surely there will be some sort of work we can get."

Campbell did as she suggested and left her to begin seeking work at her end of the town.

There didn't appear to be any women in sight, which Rebecca found curious. She entered the first shop that sold hardware— saws, axes, rope, and a variety of tools. The man behind the counter almost dropped his pipe when he saw her.

"Strewth," he exclaimed, his gaze never leaving her. "Can I help you, lady?"

"I'm short of funds at the moment, and I wondered if you had any employment available?"

He gave a grin. "I don't have anything but you shouldn't have any trouble earning money in this town. It's full of timber cutters."

"I notice there are not many women around," she said frowning.

"Many is not the word, try none." He began to make her uncomfortable as he ogled her.

"Thank you for your time. I'll try the next shop."

He laughed. "You'll get the same answer and think about it, you can earn serious money seein' you're a woman."

Rebecca knew exactly what he meant but continued along the street and received the same response. Every man who passed her tipped his hat, and one winked at her. When Campbell met up with her halfway down the street he told her what she already knew. No work available.

"What are we going to do? There's no work, nothing," said Campbell disillusioned.

"I think we're in desperate trouble. We're going to starve unless we do something."

"I suppose I could hunt for food," said Campbell. "But that's not going to get us far."

Rebecca sighed sadly. "I have no choice," she said at last. "I'm not going to starve. I'll never find Mary unless I do it."

"What do you mean?"

"Campbell, do you know what I was transported for?"

"No."

She watched him carefully, not knowing what his reaction would be. "It was for being a whore. Not a street whore, but a courtesan in an exclusive club. As much as I said I would never return to that life, I now have no choice. There are many men here and no women. If we are to get money you will have to protect me."

"How?" he asked, frowning. The news that Mary's mother had been a whore did not sit well.

She gave it more thought. "You will seek the customers and then stand guard outside the wagon. Can you do that?"

He shrugged his shoulders. "I suppose so. How much will you charge?"

"These men will not be rich. I will try for five shillings a turn."

He gasped. "That sounds high."

"If we don't get customers then I can always drop the price. Let's get started, try the pub first."

Rebecca drove the wagon to the outskirts of the small town and dropped the canvas covers. Campbell went into town to try to get customers.

When he entered the solitary inn, he could see twenty men standing around, drinking. He approached one, a man of about thirty in a checked shirt and heavy cord trousers. The man was drinking with two others. Campbell whispered in his ear.

"Are there any women around who sell their favors?" he asked, and the man burst out laughing.

"Mate, if there were, you'd be at the back of the queue. There ain't no women around for miles."

"Then a woman offering such a service would not be void of customers?"

"I'd be her first customer," he said grinning.

"What if she were an older woman of say thirty-seven or there abouts?"

"Mate, if she was sixty then it wouldn't matter, as long as she can lay on her back, then I'd have her."

"Bloody oath," he heard others say as they listened in on the conversation.

He grinned at both men. "I have such a woman with me. She worked in service in England many years ago."

That brought interest. "How much?"

"She charges five shillings a time."

One man almost choked in his beer. "Shit, that's dear."

"I guess you could call it a seller's market," said Campbell grinning.

"It's a bit steep," said the man.

Another slammed his empty glass on the counter, almost shattering it. "Not for me," he said. "Where is she?"

"Follow me and I'll show you." He led the man and others who joined them to the wagon where Rebecca opened the covers.

"These gentlemen wish to buy your services, Rebecca."

She had prepared herself by combing her hair smoothly. No grey showing yet. It fell to her shoulders, giving the impression she was only around twenty years old. She glanced into a mirror and felt satisfied no serious wrinkles had settled into her face. Lifting up her breasts she noted they still had not sagged as some women's had after giving birth to children. She tied a sash under them to hold them in place. Satisfied she stepped out to meet the men coming toward her. The men stood agog when they saw her.

"Welcome, gentlemen. The fee will be five shillings. Form a queue and please pay my companion before entering."

The first customer quickly handed Campbell his five shillings and entered the wagon. Rebecca closed the covers and sat the man down. There wasn't time for the niceties of the Gentleman's Club. She undid the man's trousers. He was already for her before they fell to the floor of the wagon. Rebecca pushed him to the makeshift bed and finished him quickly. He left with a smile on his face and another quickly took his position. Within the hour, Rebecca had fifteen customers, and Campbell had three pounds fifteen shillings his pocket. News spread quickly and the next day another twenty turned up. By the end of the week, Rebecca was sore, but they had over thirty pounds when she ceased to work.

"Why are you stopping?" asked Campbell, as he counted the money.

"Perhaps you would like to bare yourself for such men, while I collect the money?" she said angrily.

"I'm sorry, Rebecca, I wasn't thinking. It must have been horrendous for you to have to do such a thing. Are we ready to go on?"

"No. One of the men said the reason there were so few in the town was that gold had been discovered in Bathurst. We need a substantial income to resume our search, even if Bathurst is in the wrong direction."

"You're going to do it in Bathurst?" he said incredulously.

"No, this was the last time. I'm going to open a bordello, and I'll hire younger girls for the task. There will be many miners with money there, and we'll make quick money before we're closed down."

He frowned at her words. "Who will close us down?"

Rebecca shook her head. "In any large town there are people who try to force their morals on others. I think I can keep going for a couple of months before the puritans begin their cries."

* * * * *

Bathurst was a hive of activity, with miners strolling the streets and people bartering in the stores for goods and food. There had been several shops erected quickly and crude signs painted on boards offered their wares. This time no one took the slightest interest in their arrival.

As soon as Campbell alighted from the wagon, a young woman, brightly dressed, her bust almost protruding from the top of her dress approached Campbell.

"Hello handsome, are you looking for a good time?"

Campbell's mouth dropped open. "Pardon?"

She sidled up to him and rubbed her leg against his. "Are you looking for a woman? I can have some fun with you for a shilling."

Rebecca saw what was going on and walked up. The woman frowned. "Is this your mother?"

She answered for him. "No, but I'm interested in your proposal."

The woman, who looked no more than nineteen, glanced curiously at her. "You mean you'll pay for him?"

Rebecca gave a laugh. "He can pay for his own fun. Are there many girls offering their services here?"

She gave Rebecca a curious look. "If you want to compete, you haven't much chance. There are at least twenty here who are younger than you."

"And all charging a shilling, I presume."

The girl nodded. "Competition is hard, and a girl has to make a living with all these miners around."

Rebecca spoke slowly trying to get the girl's interest. "How would you like to make twice that much a customer?"

The girl stared at her. "What do you have in mind?"

"Round up all the girls you can find and tell them to meet me on the western outskirts of town at six o'clock. Tell them I can double their prices."

"Who the hell are you?"

"Rebecca McBride. I've had a lot of experience in this trade. Are you interested?"

"Nothing to lose I suppose," said the girl.

"What's your name?" asked Rebecca.

"Dora Leving."

"See you at six then, Dora."

When Rebecca arrived there were fifteen girls at the meeting; all young and all eager to make money. Rebecca climbed onto the wagon and waited for them to quiet down before she spoke. "My name is Rebecca McBride. Twenty years ago I worked in an exclusive brothel in London and learnt that men will pay good money for good service. If you work for me, I can guarantee you twice the money you earn now, but you will have to do as I say."

"Tell us more," said Dora, and others nodded.

Rebecca felt she was getting somewhere. "I will hire a house and charge the customers ten shillings, of which I will give you five."

"Are you serious?" one girl asked.

"Very. You must never steal from them or be offensive. If there is any trouble, Campbell here will take care of you. You will work in the confines of the house, and never offer your services away from the house, for to do that would take away custom from the other girls."

A murmur went around the group. "They won't pay ten shillings," one yelled.

"They will if there is no other service available. This way you will be working together instead of fighting each other for customers. Discuss it together for a minute and tell me of your decision."

The women began a healthy debate and thirty minutes later after much shouting and arguing they agreed they would give it a try. Rebecca stood with her hands on her hips and spoke confidently to them. "Remember, girls, it means no more of it in a back alley somewhere, but in a comfortable bed. At five shillings a time, you can be fussy about who you take on. This won't last forever so you will have to work hard and make your money quickly before the puritans cry foul."

"Yeah, okay," said Dora. "We'll give it a try."

Rebecca rented the largest house she could find and opened the door for business three nights later. With the supply cut off in the streets, men began to attend, and the reputation of the house grew immediately. The girls found the men were willing to pay the high fee for the comfort available.

Rebecca took Campbell aside. "I'm going to get grog in, but I want you to stop drunks from entering."

"I can do that," he said, smiling. He felt he could handle any drunk without too much trouble.

On the third night they heard a scream from one of the girls, and Campbell rushed to the room.

"You fucking bitch." One of the customers stood over a girl lying on the floor and holding her face. Blood ran from her nose. His face contorted, and his fist cocked when Campbell rushed into the room.

"What's the problem?" Campbell asked, frowning, as the girl tried to get to her feet.

His face still red, the man snarled at Campbell. "She wouldn't suck my cock. For five bob she should do what I want."

Campbell looked at the girl.

She struggled to her feet, still holding her face and spoke bitterly. "He grabbed my hair and pushed my face down. I told him he was hurting me, but he didn't stop."

The man slapped her across the face again. Campbell took out his pistol and hit the man over the head. Then he sunk his boots into the man's body.

Rebecca came running up and grabbed his arm. "Campbell, that's enough," she shouted. She checked the man to see if he was still breathing and let out a sigh of relief. A dead body was the last thing she needed.

"Get him out of here."

The man gave a groan as Campbell lifted him to his feet, carried him down the stairs, and threw him out the front door.

When she was alone, she worried about Campbell's attack on the man for it appeared he had relished it. It disturbed her for she had never seen this part of Campbell's personality before.

By the end of two months they had over one thousand pounds, but Rebecca could see the writing on the wall, as some of the respectable citizens began to grumble about the tone of the town and the moral fiber beginning to decay. It was an article in the local newspaper that convinced her. The headlines read, "Whores bringing the town into disrepute. Debauchery must end."

She made a quick decision and called Dora over when she was free.

"What's the trouble, Rebecca?" she asked.

"I've decided to move on, and I wondered if you would be interested in buying the business."

"What?" said Campbell, slamming his fist onto the table. "We're making a fortune, and you want to move on."

Rebecca glared at him. "I only went into this to have a stake to find Mary. If you want to buy the business then I'll sell it to you. I thought you wanted to help me find Mary."

He backed off a little. "I do, it's just that we're making good money."

"And maybe the fact you're using the staff for some fun," said Dora.

Campbell's face reddened as he looked at her with a deep scowl on his brow.

Rebecca looked at him with sadness in her eyes. She knew what young men were like, and it seemed Campbell was no different. "I understand, Campbell, you're a young man, and you need a woman. I would hope you would cease such behavior once you're married to Mary."

He drew back haughtily. "It's a wife's duty to take care of her husband, not to question his behavior."

Rebecca began to have some serious doubts about young Campbell. She turned back to Dora.

"Well, would you like to buy the business?"

"How much are you asking?"

"Five hundred pounds, but I must warn you. The good town's people will try to close you down soon. I don't believe you have any more than two months before they sway the city fathers."

Dora smiled. "Half the city fathers are our customers. Very well, I'll take the risk, but I've only got four hundred and eighty pounds."

Rebecca nodded. "I'm sure one of the others girls will go partners with you."

Dora agreed. "Two hundred and fifty pounds lessens the risk, and if you've made over a thousand in a couple of months, then I'll more than get my money back. It's a deal."

Rebecca had her money, and she and a reluctant Campbell were on their way the next day.

"If you had stayed another month then we would have been rich," said Campbell, sulking as he drove.

"Mary is more important to me than making money. I would have thought she was more important to you, too."

Campbell had a bland expression on his face. "She is, but the extra money would have helped."

"Campbell, there's one thing I want you to promise me."

"What's that?"

"That you will not tell Mary how we got our money."

"Don't worry. I don't want anyone to know my wife's mother worked in that trade." He glanced at her as if she was no better than the whores of the brothel.

Rebecca bit her tongue. She wanted to come back at him but let it slide. There were more problems to face than worrying what Campbell thought.

Chapter Fourteen

The journey along the river was difficult. They had to find their way around trees and over small gullies that the rain water ran in to get to the river, and sometimes they had to turn inland to pass the dense bush. The country had turned into rolling hills, slowing their trip considerably. As soon as Brian thought they could, he headed back to the north until he found the Murrumbidge again. For four weeks they traveled, stopping to camp for several days at a time to give the children and Mary time to rest. Each day was different as the country continually changed. Open plains gave way to thick forests, then back to open plains again.

It was Mary who spotted it first. She grabbed Brian's arm and pointed to the skyline. "Brian, is that a fire?"

"Looks like it, and a fairly big one, too. I'll make for the river until it passes or burns itself out."

Even from such a distance they could feel the radiant heat. Smoke spiraled into the air and carried upward burning sparks floating gently down to the ground again. Mary held her nose as the acrid smell tingled her nostrils.

Thankfully the fire headed away from them, but the burnt trees by the river made them grateful they hadn't been there an hour earlier. They proceeded through the blackened trees carefully. The smell of the burning foliage was strong. It was amazing how quickly the beautiful countryside had turned into a charred blackened scene. Brian suddenly pulled the horses to a halt and peered through the smoke, which drifted close to the ground.

"What's wrong?" asked Mary.

"Look there, ahead." He pointed at what looked like the burnt out hulk of a wagon. The wheels still smoldered, leaving blackened timber supporting the iron rims.

"Wait here," he said, picking up his musket. He cautiously approached the remains of the wagon. Two dead horses lay still in their harnesses and there amongst the ashes were two bodies, that of a man and a woman.

"What is it?" called Mary, fear clutching her throat.

"There are two people dead."

"Settlers?"

"It looks like it." He inspected the bodies and then froze. "These people didn't die in the fire; they've been shot." He could see the head wounds where the bullets had hit them. He looked around, but saw no sign of the perpetrators of the crime.

"I'll have to bury them." He looked around and held the broken handle of the musket tightly. He heard a noise and quickly brought the gun to his shoulder, but lowered it when he saw the boy. He stepped from behind some rocks, his eyes wide with fear.

"It's all right, son, we won't hurt you. Mary, come quickly."

The boy shivered with fear, and Mary rushed to him, holding him close.

"Are you all right, boy?" she asked softly.

He nodded, still fearful as he looked at Brian's tall figure.

"What's your name?"

"Sean, Sean Wilson," he said in a trembling voice.

"Are those your parents?"

He nodded without speaking.

"Who shot them, Sean?" asked Brian.

"Some men. Pa was trying to get away from them. They've been following us for days."

"Why"

Sean looked to the ground. "Don't know. Pa wouldn't say."

"How long ago, son?"

"Three hours. They lit the fire and rode off after they shot them."

"How did you get away?"

"Pa pushed me off and told me to hide, just before they caught up. I hid in the rocks."

"How old are you, Sean?" asked Mary.

"Ten."

"And you're sure you don't know why those men were chasing you?"

He looked at the ground and refused to answer. It was obvious he did know but wasn't about to tell them.

"What will we do with him, Brian?" Mary frowned after they buried the bodies.

He pulled his lips tight and stared at her. "We can't just leave him here. He'll die."

"It's awful. Ten years old and all alone." Mary's eyes took on a sad look.

"Do you have any kin we can take you to, Sean?"

"No, there's no-one."

Brian sat thinking for a few seconds and then said to Sean, "Wait here for a few minutes, lad."

When they were out of earshot Brian turned to Mary, "Mary, it's up to you, but I think we had better take him with us. He has no one to take care of him."

"You mean to sort of adopt him?"

"I know it will be harder on you, but I just can't leave him here to die."

"Brian Corcoran, when I first saw you I thought you were the most disgusting creature I had ever seen. Now I find you have a soft and caring heart. I think it's wonderful of you to take him in. He's frightened and has no future. I'd be pleased to help look after him."

Brian nodded. "Then it's settled. You talk to him. He's scared stiff of me." He walked away and replaced the shovel in the wagon, leaving Mary with Sean. She put her arm around Sean's shoulder to comfort him.

"Sean, how would you like to come and live with us? We're going to claim land on the Murray and build a new life. We'll take care of you until you grow up."

"What about him?" he said pointing towards Brian.

"He's not as rough as he looks. He's taken care of me as he will you."

The tears ran down his cheeks at the realization of losing his parents, and he wiped them with the back of his hand.

"Will that be all right?" asked Mary.

"I suppose so," he sniffed, still looking warily at Brian.

"Everything will be fine." She smiled encouragingly at him and led him to the wagon.

"Hop in, Sean," said Brian in his deep voice, and he watched Sean sit beside Mary, as far away from him as the boy could get. He grinned as he urged the horses forward. Sean took a last look at the graves holding a rough cross Brian had made.

It was another week before they saw signs of civilization. "There's a town ahead; see the houses," Brian said.

"Thank God, can we rest here for a while?"

"Yes, I'll have to report what happened to the police, and we have to stock up. It will give us a chance to ask directions to the Murray."

"What is this place?" asked Mary.

"It's called Hay," said Brian, noticing a signpost on the road. "How would you like a hot bath and a soft bed to sleep in?"

"It sounds wonderful."

"Then we'll stop the night at the best inn we can find."

They found suitable quarters for the night, and as Mary soaked in a hot tub, Brian made inquiries as to the next stop in his journey. The innkeeper was more than willing to give advice.

"You say you want to get to the Murray by following the Murrumbidge," he said as he sipped an ale.

"That's the way Charles Sturt went."

"That's true, but the country has opened up since he went through years ago. The land is not very productive in that direction."

"Then where do you think we should head?"

"I'd go towards Echuca. There's still good land to be had if you have the money, and it's becoming a major port for the riverboats. They go all the way down to South Australia."

"But why Echuca?"

"Because it's easy to send your goods off to market by the riverboats or train to Melbourne. It will give you access to both Melbourne and Adelaide."

Brian thought about the idea and then decided. "In what direction is Echuca?"

"Due south from here. You won't come across the Murrumbidgee again, but you'll find some other rivers."

"Thank you. I'll leave next week," said Brian. The man certainly seemed to know what he was talking about.

* * * * *

Rebecca and Campbell found the going easier as they came to pasture country and on the way to Victoria. They passed through the small townships of Cowra and Young, each time stopping for supplies and a well-earned rest. While Rebecca was content to sit quietly and plan her next stop, Campbell began to visit the pubs and gamble.

The first time he came back twenty pounds richer, but then he began to lose heavily. Rebecca was sure he also took advantage of the time to find whores willing to give him pleasure for a shilling or two, but she didn't say anything. By the time they got to Wagga Wagga, he was almost broke. The seven hundred pounds he'd had was now down to fifty.

One day, Rebecca found twenty pounds missing from her bag and frowned. She knew only one person who could have taken it. Without actually accusing him of theft, she started keeping her money on her person.

At the next town Rebecca sat by the wagon as Campbell got ready to go to the pub. He rustled through the wagon as if searching for something. The noise began to get louder. "Where the hell is it?" he muttered. He burst out of the wagon and scowled at Rebecca before leaving for town. When she went inside the wagon she shook her head. Her box had been opened, and her clothes scattered all over the floor of the wagon. Her beads, her combs, her personal items had been tossed everywhere in Campbell's frenzied search for her money.

At last they reached the border town of Albury and found the Murray.

"It doesn't look so mighty to me," Campbell said, as he looked at the stream. "It's only half the width I thought it would be."

"That's because this is the start of it. I heard it gets wider when you move downstream."

Rebecca stopped inside a store and made inquiries concerning the Murray River. The storekeeper took off his hat, scratched his head, and stared at her. "Shit, lady, it meanders all the way to South Australia. There's plenty of towns along the way, but it will take you years to see it all."

"Do you know if there is any land for sale?" she asked, hoping Corcoran might have settled on a place close by.

"Plenty if you have the money. All the towns are growing. They want people to settle and develop the state."

"I think we'll move along the river tomorrow to continue to look for Mary," she said to Campbell that evening.

Campbell had another interest. "Have you read the newspaper? It said there's gold to be had in a place called Ballarat. It's supposed to be the richest strike ever."

"What's that got to do with us?"

"I'm almost broke, and I need cash to claim Mary and build a fortune. You can't continue by yourself. It's too dangerous for a woman alone. We should go to Ballarat to find some gold then we'll find Mary."

Rebecca laughed at his suggestion. "You go; I'm going to find Mary."

"No, you're going with me." His brows furrowed.

"Sorry," she said, ignoring him, but he grabbed her by the throat and pushed her back onto the ground. She struggled, but he was much stronger than she.

He put his hand under her dress and released her when he found her purse holding it up in triumph. "I'll look after this in case someone steals it."

Rebecca reached desperately for it. "It's mine! Give it back!"

He slapped her hard across her face, and she fell to the ground again, shocked. He stood over her and gloated, as she lay supported on her elbows. "I don't think so. From now on I give the orders."

"You'll only waste it on gambling and women," she said, getting to her feet

He gave her an arrogant sneer. "I'll gamble if I want, but to save money you could give me relief."

"What!" she gasped.

"It makes sense. As you said, I'm a man, and I need relief. Why should I waste money on whores when you can deliver for free?"

Her mouth dropped open in shock "You can't mean that. You said you were going to marry Mary. If she knew you had sex with me that would be the end of your ambitions."

"She doesn't have to know. It would save me the time of looking for whores."

"Never!" she said angrily. "I have to find Mary."

"On foot?" he asked, grinning. "I'm taking over the wagon so you have no choice."

"I can't find her on foot and without money."

He laughed loudly. "No you can't. I need someone to do the cooking, washing, and ironing."

She knew she was beaten. She would bide her time and take the wagon at the first opportunity. Claire's words kept coming back. Always agree with the customer.

"I'll go with you provided you leave me alone, and you promise to resume the search once you've made some money."

"Very well. You're probably too old anyway. I like them young." He smirked at her as if she didn't dare defy him.

"How long do you expect us to stay there?"

"Just long enough for me to find some gold."

"If it was that easy then everyone would go there."

"Shut up. From here on I'm in charge," he snarled, and Rebecca went quiet. They headed for Ballarat the next day.

After they had been traveling for a day, Rebecca became exasperated. "Where are you taking us? Do you have any idea where Ballarat is? It's not on the river?"

He produced a map he purchased in Albury and pointed out a possible route. "We'll head for Echuca, cut south to Bendigo and then to Ballarat. Look at the people heading that way."

* * * * *

Mary and Brian continued south until they came to another small township named Deniliquin, built on another river. They stayed a week, camped by the banks of the Edward's River, heartened with the knowledge their journey was close to ending.

"We'll be in Echuca in a week, Mary," he said excitedly. She was caught up in his enthusiasm.

The week went quickly, but not quickly enough as far as Mary was concerned. Finding their way through the dense trees was not easy with a wagon. Finally, they came over a rise, and there it was, the Murray River. Brian pulled the horses to a stop, and they took in the sight, neither speaking for several minutes. The wide and peaceful river had a slow flow winding its way towards Adelaide.

It was a sight Mary thought she would never see. A river over six hundred miles through virgin bush land from the place of her birth. Gum trees down to the water line cast a shade across the water. In places high banks and eroded soil exposed tree roots, giving a skeletal look to the trees.

"It's so peaceful Brian. It's a lovely place."

A piercing scream from a riverboat whistle caught their attention as it went by, its crew giving them a hearty wave. Mary and the children waved back excitedly. The boat held a huge rotating paddle and a funnel on the roof where smoke from the boiler escaped.

"What sort of boat is that?" asked Sean as he continued waving.

"It's a river boat paddle steamer." said Brian. "They carry goods up and down the river picking up produce from the various farms. You'll see many when we find a place to live."

"Which way to Echuca?" he called to the boat as loudly as he could.

"Ten miles upstream," came the reply, and Brian turned the horses toward their destination. They found a river crossing where a punt carried people, wagons and goods across the river to a thriving community. They had to wait in a long queue of wagons for their turn to cross. A huge wharf on the other side seemed to be a hive of activity. Paddle steamers tied up for unloading. People hurried to their various businesses, giving the impression this was a big commercial district. It was an exciting atmosphere.

Brian halted the wagon on an open tract of land.

"Mary, take the children into town and see what they have. I'm sure they will enjoy the freedom and the sights."

"And where are you going?" she asked, puzzled.

"To find a land agent. I want to see what land is available."

Bridget jumped up and down, a huge smile breaking out on her face. She looked in awe at the activity going on.

Mary tied a bonnet to her head as she fidgeted, wanting to leave the wagon.

"I'd better tie Wolf to the wagon first," Mary said. Wolf whined as they walked off, then he settled down to sleep.

It was good to be in a civilized town once again.

The sign on the window read, 'William Grant Government Land Agent.' Brian entered immediately. He noted a man who sat at the desk, writing in some sort of journal when Brian entered. Brian saw the sharp look he gave him and felt embarrassed by his grimy appearance with just a hint of a beard starting to grow back. He rubbed his chin, knowing Mary would be nagging him to shave his face soon. He thought the agent had seen many settlers coming to his office, all seeking land but few with money in their pockets.

"Good afternoon, sir," he said, respectfully. "Can I help you?"

"Yes. My name is Brian Corcoran, and I'm after good land for sale."

Grant threw down his pen and gave the prospective customer his attention. "You've arrived a little late to claim the best. Most of the pasture land is already sold, but I do have some heavily timbered land still available. If you have money I'm sure it will interest you."

Brian paused. "You have no pasture land at all?"

The agent stuck his thumbs in his waistcoat before speaking. "Yes, I do have some, but it's very expensive."

Brian frowned. "How much do you have and what's the price?"

"I could offer you two thousand acres of pasture land for ten shillings an acre and timbered land for three shillings an acre."

Brian's heart sank. He only had seven hundred pounds left. "Is there no other available?"

"I'm afraid not, unless you are prepared to pay a higher price."

"It would take me years to clear the timbered land for pasture growth. How much of that do you have left?"

The agent looked up at him. "I'm afraid no one wants to purchase that sort of land. As you say, it will take years to clear unless you can pay for a large gang to do the job for you. It could be a good investment though. I can sell you three thousand acres next to the two thousand acres of pasture land. You could work this and cut down the timber at your leisure,"

"Where is this land?"

"Fifteen miles west of here on the river. You may have come that way."

"Can you take me there to see it?"

"Of course, Mister. Corcoran. I can take you now if you like."

"Tomorrow will do. I have a wife and children with me. I'd like to set them up somewhere while I investigate the land."

"Then tomorrow at say eight a.m. Is that satisfactory?"

"I'll see you here tomorrow." Brian tipped his hat and left.

Brian found Mary and the children still investigating the shops. Mary had bought each child an ice, and Bridget had most of it over her face. Mary looked a little embarrassed because she had spent some of his money, but he had given her three shillings in case she needed something. He grinned as he told her of the offer.

"You don't have that sort of money do you?" she asked.

"No. I have enough to buy the timbered land and two hundred and fifty pounds for the pastured land. If he will give me a chance to pay off the rest in twelve months then I can manage it, providing the land is suitable."

"When will you see it?"

"Tomorrow. I'll leave you here with the children while I drive out with the agent." Mary shrugged. "All right, we'll find a place to camp for the night. I can't spend money for an inn. We'll want every penny we can get."

CHAPTER FIFTEEN

Brian left Mary and the children by the river while he went with Grant to see the land. A sudden thought entered his head, and he grinned as he dug into his pocket and gave her two pounds. "What's this for?" she asked, surprised.

"You've had a hard long journey to get here, Mary. Buy yourself and the kids something while I'm away with the agent."

"Can we afford this amount to spend on a whim?"

"You all deserve some fun. I'll be away for most of the day."

Mary pocketed the money gratefully. It had been nearly two years since he had claimed her. Brian had given her money before when they had reached some of the towns on the way, especially if she asked for small amounts to spend on supplies. But this was the first time she'd had such a large sum to spend. She relished the chance to buy the odd luxury.

Before he left for his appointment with the land agent Mary pointed at a tree stump by the riverbank "Sit down," she said.

"What for?"

"If you're trying to make an impression on the land agent for credit then you had better scrub up. I'm going to cut your hair, and then you're going to shave and change your clothes."

He scowled at her and then grinned. "You're a hard woman, Mary McBride, I don't know how I got stuck with you." He did as he was told.

"I do," she said with a smile. "I'm not cheap you know. I think you would have had to spend at least fifty pounds."

"I think I got a bargain," he said as she began cutting.

Mary carefully cut his hair, lost in thought. *He called me Mary McBride, even though he knows Campbell is coming for me one day and that I'll leave. It will be hard for me to go for I have a family to take care of. Bridget, Robert and now Sean. Can I take them with me when I go?* She did know one thing; life hadn't been anywhere near as bad as she had thought it would be when she first married this man.

She put down the comb and dusted the hair clippings off his collar. Now he looked respectable for his appointment with the land agent. Brian met Grant and left for the inspection of the land. Mary decided to see the shops in Echuca and spend some of the money he had given her. It was the first time she had been alone in a town since he had taken her and the thought of shopping and taking in the sights excited her. She wandered from shop to shop, with the baby on one arm and Sean and Bridget tagging along behind her.

* * * * *

Brian gazed at the pastureland that went all the way down to the banks of the Murray. It was on the Victorian side of the border, and it was just what he wanted. The rich soil, the high grass gave promise to a bright future for all of them. The red gum forest of the timbered land alongside the pasture would require years of hard work to clear, but if he bought both, then he would have five thousand acres of prime land in a few years time.

"Well, Mr. Corcoran. What do you think?" asked Grant after the inspection.

"It's just what I want, Mister. Grant, but I have a problem."

"You don't have the money," sighed Grant.

"Not exactly, but I do have a proposition. I'll buy the timbered land outright, and give you two hundred pounds for the pasture land, the balance to be paid in twelve months."

Grant frowned at the suggestion. The man was either a fool or very confident in his own ability to succeed. "That will leave you a deficit of eight hundred pounds. How will you pay it in such a short time?"

"I don't know yet, but I'll get it." Brian said with certainty.

Grant paused for a few seconds, turning the suggestion over in his mind. Money was tight at the moment, and he didn't want to lose the possibility of a sale. "If you put the timbered land up as collateral then you have a deal. The interest will be three percent."

Brian thought hard. He would also need more cash to stock the land and to build a home. At least he had timber on the property to use as building material, but a lot of sheep would be needed to pay off the land debt.

"Very well, Mr. Grant, it's a deal." How he was going to handle the arrangement he had no idea, but he wasn't going to let the opportunity slip by. Thank God for the thousand pounds he earned in the fight.

They shook hands and then headed back towards Echuca with Brian wondering how he could meet his commitment. It left him fifty pounds in his pocket; every bit of which he needed to buy food for his family.

* * * * *

Rebecca and Campbell came to the outskirts of Echuca. They had passed many people heading for the gold fields, and Rebecca hoped there might be some news of Mary, but no one had seen or heard of a man named Corcoran with a young girl in the towns of Corowa or Yarrawonga. She pressed on in a vain hope she would be lucky. In each place, the ritual was the same. Rebecca would ask at each shop about a brute of a man with a young girl and a small child, but none proved fruitful.

"We'll stay a few hours and get some supplies, then head off again," said Campbell.

"Can I have some of my money to buy a few things?" She scowled at having to ask for her own money and felt humiliated. He pulled out a pound note from his pocket and gave it to her.

"Here, don't spend it all. I'll meet you here in an hour. Don't be late, or I'll take the wagon and leave without you."

"Where are you going?"

He gave her a grin. "You won't give me comfort so I'll find someone who will."

For a moment she considered staying in town and letting him go on without her, but then rejected the idea. She began to ask questions at the shops for news of Mary.

* * * * *

Mary entered the millinery shop to look at the latest in clothes. A particularly nice blue-colored bonnet attracted her, and she sighed, wishing she had the money to buy it. Bridget and Sean stood alongside her, bored. Shopping was not on either's list for excitement. Bridget grabbed her hand and looked up at her. "Will we be here long, Mary?"

Mary looked down and smiled. "Not long, sweetheart. Just let me see a few things. Maybe we might be able to buy you a bonnet one day. Something that will match your pretty eyes."

* * * * *

Rebecca waited patiently for the storekeeper to finish serving another customer so she could question him. At last he gave her some attention. When she received a negative reply to her questions about Mary, she moved on to the millinery store.

Mary was still daydreaming, when Sean grabbed her other hand, excitement written all over his face.

"Mary, Mary, come quick," he said, his eyes alight with pleasure.

"Good heavens, Sean, what's the matter?"

"There's a circus at the fair ground, please, can we go?"

Mary looked at Bridget's face, which also lit up with excitement.

"Can you wait until I've looked at the shops?"

"Please, Mary, can we go now? There's clowns and animals and all sorts of things."

Mary smiled at their pleasure "All right, let's go," she said, not wanting to disappoint them. The clothes were out of her price range anyway. She took Bridget's hand and left the store seconds before Rebecca entered.

* * * * *

Rebecca saw her tall figure in the distance, but not her face. Her walk seemed familiar. For a moment she thought it was Mary, but then she saw the baby in her arms, and the two children hand in hand heading towards the fair ground. She knew this could not be Mary, as the woman obviously had three children. Disappointed, she entered the millinery store to make further enquiries. When she found no trace of Mary, she waited at the wagon for Campbell's return.

"Did you waste the money?" he said in an unfriendly tone when he arrived.

"No, but I did see a woman who looked a bit like Mary."

He spat on the ground then pointed to the wagon. "But it wasn't. Get aboard, we're leaving."

Rebecca continued talking about the woman she had seen. "She had three children with her so it couldn't have been her."

"Unless they were triplets then it certainly wasn't." He flicked the reins, and the wagon began to move toward Bendigo.

* * * * *

When Brian returned to Echuca, he finalized the deal with Grant and handed over the money. He was now a landholder, and he knew a lot of work would be needed in the near future to fulfill his dream. As he looked for Mary and the children he heard the noise of the fair ground, busters shouting, children laughing and knew he would find them there. Sure enough, the children were watching some clowns painted up in their colorful make up and juggling wooden pins, throwing them high into the air. A band played and kept the crowd in a happy mood. Families held children, balloons in hand, and eating floss.

He came up alongside Mary. She smiled when she saw him. "You're back? How did it go?"

"Good and bad," he said raising an eyebrow. He knew what her next question would be.

"Don't like the sound of that. Better tell me."

When he finished telling her of the deal he had struck she looked worried. "How will you pay the rest?" she asked, frowning.

"I will try to get work on the wharf."

"What sort of work?" she asked in a dubious tone.

"The usual, unloading the river steamers. I'll also build a crude hut to live in until we have sufficient funds for the proper house I promised you."

"I think that is going to cost more money than we have."

"I have to house my beautiful wife and family. I'll get there. You just wait and see."

"I think you will," she said softly. The beautiful wife comment made her uncomfortable. When she left it would break his heart.

They walked around the fair ground watching the fun until they heard shouting taking place where a large crowd gathered.

"What's going on over there?" asked Mary.

Brian's face lit up immediately, and a small smile began to break out. He knew full well what it was. "Just an exhibition for men," he said. "Why don't you take the children into the tent to see the circus?"

"Don't you want to see it, too?"

"No, I have some business to attend to. I need to see Grant about some more details," he said keeping his expression blank.

"Oh?" Mary raised her brow in concern.

"Nothing important. Enjoy yourself and watch the show."

After Mary and the children left, Brian returned to the crowd. Men stripped to their waists as the boxing troupe knocked out the locals one by one. Several men stood around with bags over their shoulders taking bets and giving odds to the local men, who all wanted to try their skill on the boxers of the troupe.

One by one the unskilled men were knocked out, some of them lasting only a few seconds, much to the delight of the bookmakers who were making money with ease.

With the last fighter disposed of, the man who was in charge stood up and called to the crowd to be quiet.

"Gentlemen, we have here today the bare knuckle heavy weight champion of Victoria, the all powerful, all conquering, Bone Crusher Molloy. I will give the sum of twenty pounds to any person who can stay on his feet for three rounds with Bone Crusher."

Brian looked at the man and understood his nickname. Over six foot three and weighing at least sixteen stone, with huge biceps, he stood with a bare chest, his arms folded. He stared at the crowd, daring anyone to challenge him. His head had been shaved, and his arms were oiled and shining. The crowd drew silent.

No one stepped forward, and the manager pressed. "Come, come, gentlemen. Is there no one amongst you with the courage to face Bone Crusher? I will offer a prize of fifty pounds if one can go five rounds with the champion."

Brian sidled up to the bookmakers and asked casually, "What odds will you give me to take him on?"

Eager to make some easy money, the man looked at Brian and grinned. "I'll give you odds of twenty to one if you can stay with him for ten rounds."

Brian dug into his pocket and produced his last fifty pounds. "I'll take the bet."

A cheer went up from the crowd as they heard the announcement from the caller.

"Gentlemen, we have a challenger. This gentleman will fight Bone Crusher for a wager of fifty pounds at odds of twenty to one if he can last ten rounds. Give the man a cheer."

The crowd responded as Brian climbed into the ring and removed his shirt. Just then Mary and the children returned. The circus had already started, and she would have to wait for it to conclude before she could take the children to the next one. Her eyes widened as she saw Bone Crusher and Brian in the ring. A sudden pain of emotion swept through her. This brute would kill Brian. No one could stand up to him. The back of her hand went to her mouth. She didn't love Brian but certainly didn't want to see him beaten to a pulp. Then she wondered why she cared so much. She bit her lip but resolved to stay and watch the slaughter. He would need help once the battle was over. She hoped it would end quickly for Brian's sake.

When Brian removed his shirt, she was stunned as she saw the scars on his back. She had never actually seen him naked from the waist up. When he washed in the various rivers he did so by himself. He always gave her privacy, and she had returned the favor.

The flesh had scarred badly, leaving red ribbons criss-crossed across the broad part of his back. This man had suffered great pain before.

He turned and was shocked when he saw her watching. He called. "Go away, Mary, you mustn't see this."

"I'm staying," she said, still holding the baby in her arms with Bridget and Sean alongside her.

The referee called them together. "A round will be completed when one is knocked down. If he can't get to his feet by the count of ten then he has lost. No kicking, spitting, or gouging. Now go to your corners."

Bone Crusher stood staring into Brian's eyes, a smirk on his face. His voice was slow and menacing. "I am going to hurt you, my friend. When the pain gets too much, stay down."

"Really?" said Brian, "I heard you were a cream puff."

Bone Crusher scowled.

The announcer spoke in Brian's ear. "What's your name, mate?"

"Brian Corcoran."

"You're Irish, aren't you? What part?"

"Killarney," replied Brian

"Ladies and Gentlemen. In the red corner is the champion Bone Crusher Molloy, a man who has never been defeated in eighty-one fights. In the white corner, we have the Killarney Mauler, Brian Corcoran, who is having his first fight. They will commence at the sound of the bell"

Laughter and applause rang out as the fighters returned to their corners. Brian's second whispered in his ear. "Try to keep away from him as much as you can, mate. If he hits you, go down, as that will be the end of the round. He's got a murderous right so watch him carefully."

"What's his belly like?" asked Brian.

"He has them drop bags of flour on him to toughen him up."

Shit, Brian mumbled under his breath, *there goes that theory.*

The fight began with Brian warily circling Molloy, trying to keep away from his fists, but the man was skillful and left his guard down to entice Brian to come closer. When he did, he hit Brian a crushing blow to his face that split his eye open. Mary shuddered at the blow and turned her head away. Molloy moved in closer and hit Brian with three rapid lefts to the face then followed up with a right, knocking Brian to the ground. The first round was over in the space of two minutes.

The second wiped the blood off Brian's face and doused him with a wet sponge.

"I told you to keep away from him. He'll kill you if you stand and fight."

Brian nodded, knowing the man was right. The fight continued after the second round. Brian's face was reduced to a bloody mess as left after left caught him on the nose, the eyes and the cheeks. When he caught Molloy with a wild swing, the crowd cheered, and Molloy became infuriated. He caught Brian with another right and sent him crashing to the ground again.

The rounds continued, and Brian took a terrible beating, but refused to give in. By round five he had caught Molloy no more than eight times while he continued to take a murderous beating. Mary prayed he would not get up after each round, as this would bring an end to the fight and save him from more punishment.

The crowd began to get behind Brian, all admiring his courage, and all wincing as each blow from Molloy struck home. In the seventh round, Molloy got careless and dropped his hands a little. After all, his opponent didn't seem to have much left.

Brian saw his chance and swung with all his might. His fist caught Molloy flush on the jaw, sending him to the ground, and the crowd cheered loudly, pleased that at last Molloy was getting some of his own punishment back.

The referee counted over Molloy, and Brian prayed he would not get up, but at the count of eight, Molloy shook his head and rose to his feet. His second led him to his corner and worked feverishly on him, as this was the first time he had ever been knocked down.

Round nine opened with both fighters warily watching each other, but then Molloy regained the initiative by hitting Brian with a flurry of punches to his eyes. Blood was now pouring from the cuts on Brian's face. He could barely see, and Mary almost screamed in frustration. Tears threatened to drop. She prayed for it to end soon, otherwise she might be a widow. Sean stood with his mouth open in awe while Bridget had tears in her eyes seeing what was happening to her father. When Molloy sent him to the ground again a hush fell over the crowd as they all hoped and prayed Brian could hold out for one more round to win his bet. At the count of eight, he staggered to his feet, but it was obvious he was beaten. His second worked on him vigorously as he tried to regain his senses.

"I think you had better throw in the towel, mate. You've had enough," said the man.

"What round is this?" asked Brian desperately, hardly able to see through his swollen eyes.

"It's the ninth. The tenth is coming up. You have to stay on your feet for another round. If he knocks you out you've lost. Chuck it in now."

"No," Brian gasped. "I'm finished if I don't make it."

"It's your funeral," said the man sadly.

The bell for the commencement of the tenth round went, and Brian staggered out, barely able to hold his hands up. Molloy hit him again in the face, and Brian clung to the man in a desperate effort to keep from going down. The referee separated them, and Molloy hit him again. Again Brian clung desperately. Molloy got careless and left his arms down, thinking Brian was finished. Brian swung and caught Molloy on the eyebrow, drawing blood as the flesh parted. The champion stepped back, trying to wipe it from his eyes, but Brian was unable to take the initiative.

The round progressed. Brian's eyes were beginning to go glassy, and he could keep his hands up no longer. Molloy hit him with a left and then a right, but he too had lost most of his strength and stood back as Brian slid to the ground. The referee began to count, and Brian could dimly hear his voice as the count progressed. Four, five, six, he could hear, but it seemed so far away. He looked in front of him and could make out Mary through the bloody haze, her face covered in tears.

When the count reached eight, he grabbed the rope and pulled himself off the ground. When the referee said nine, he found himself on his feet as the bell went for the end of the tenth round.

"Christ, you made it mate," said his second. "I thought Bone Crusher had killed you."

Brian collapsed on his stool, unable to raise his arms again. When the bell went for the commencement of the eleventh round, he staggered to the center of the ring like a hopeless drunk as Molloy stood there with his arm brought back. Brian now had no defense at all and waited for the final blow. Instead of smashing him to the ground, Molloy gently pushed him with both hands, and Brian staggered back and fell, unable to get up. He was counted out and the crowd cheered wildly. Never before had they seen such a contest. Brian woke to hear the announcer call, "The winner and still champion by a knockout in the eleventh round, Bone Crusher Molloy. But I'm pleased to say that Corcoran has won his bet, as well as the sum of fifty pounds."

A loud round of applause rang out as hands carried Brian to the fighters' tent. When he opened his eyes he could just make out the distorted features of Mary washing his face with a wet sponge, the tears still running down her face.

"Christ, you look awful," he said, trying to smile. "You've got red eyes."

"Yours are black," she said. "That is, what I can see of them."

His face was unrecognizable, his nose broken, his eyebrows cut, and his eyes almost closed.

"I got the money, Mary, over one thousand pounds plus the prize money. I did it for you."

"And you nearly got yourself killed. Don't ever do that again, Brian Corcoran."

"You sound as though you care."

"I just don't like seeing people hurt," she said, embarrassed. "Not even you. Can you get on your feet? I'll take you home."

"Not until I've collected my money." He stood up, every muscle in his body aching. He was about to leave the tent supported by Mary when Bone Crusher walked in.

"You've got guts, Corcoran. We could give you work in our troupe if you need it."

"Thanks, but I think you've cured me of any such ambitions," Brian said.

"If he even thinks about it then I'll give him a beating, too," Mary added.

"Then good luck, Corcoran. You've got a good man there, lady," he said as they brushed past. Mary's cheeks reddened at his words.

They collected the money, and she put her arm around him leading him back to the wagon. Sean carried the baby, his eyes staring at Brian, not believing what he had seen.

Mary left Brian and paid the money to Grant, depositing the rest in the bank in Brian's name. She wondered if Campbell would have taken such punishment for her.

CHAPTER SIXTEEN

Rebecca had never seen so many people confined in such a small area. The sound of picks being driven into the ground, the curses and yells, the hustle and bustle of people moving in a hurry, the smells of fires burning and food cooking was mind boggling.

The rattling of cradles as miners sieved the soil looking for the precious metal. Wagons and tents were lined up alongside each other as people sank shafts into the ground, desperate for success. As they passed through the area, Rebecca watched traders trying to sell goods to the diggers.

Meat hung from hooks exposed to the elements as women lined up with baskets, all waiting their turn to purchase the precious food.

There were signs indicating a hot bath for the price of sixpence and huge pots of boiling water on fires behind the tents. The smoke from the fires drifted into the air and tingled the nostrils. Another sign advertised haircuts for three pence, and a man sat on a chair in the open as another trimmed his hair with scissors.

Campbell looked at her when they passed another tent that simply said, "Women available." A man stood outside advertising the wares, guaranteeing a good time for all concerned. A well-built woman holding a blank expression stood alongside him. It reminded her of when she was in Cockatoo Creek and flat broke. She shuddered when she thought of it.

At last, Campbell stopped, and Rebecca could see a pub in the distance with a store near it and several more buildings.

"Where are we?" she asked.

"A place called Eureka. This is where big strikes have been made."

"If it was easy then all these people would be rich."

Campbell ignored her and selected a site for the wagon. "Make a fire and cook some supper. I'll go and find out the lie-lay? of the land."

He headed straight for the pub and returned two hours later. Rebecca had made supper from vegetables and salted beef.

When he returned, Campbell sat down to eat. "You have to stake a claim and register it at Ballarat. It costs thirty shillings a month. I'll pick out a site tomorrow and start digging. You'd better make yourself comfortable. We'll be here for quite a while."

Rebecca knew the search for Mary would have to be put on hold. It was two weeks before Campbell began to get discouraged. He'd sunk a shaft down to twelve feet and hadn't even seen a color of gold.

"I might have to try somewhere else," he told Rebecca. For twelve weeks he tried different sites and uncovered the grand sum of ten shillings worth of gold. He went to the pub at night to drown his sorrows and would stagger home in the early hours of the morning.

The more he drank, the less work done. Rebecca became bored with no money and nothing to do, so she sought employment in the pub as a barmaid and waitress, serving food to the diggers.

Campbell made a few friends with some of the other drunks. One night he told of his disappointment at not finding gold to Blaster Harry, a digger known for his skill in using blasting equipment to clear the tons of quartz hiding the precious metal.

"That's cause ya don't know what ya doin'" Harry laughed. "How much money have ya got?"

"Why do you want to know that?"

"I figured as I'm getting a bit low on cash, and my back is starting to pack in, I could take you in as a partner if you're so minded."

"How much do you need?" asked Campbell.

"If you can give me two hundred quid, you've got a half share in my mine."

"Have you found any gold?"

"Nothin' substantial, but it's showing promise. I've seen these signs before."

Campbell saw it as a way to make progress. The man was right, he knew nothing of mining gold.

"You've just got yourself a partner, Harry."

He told Rebecca of his investment that evening after the pub closed.

"You just wasted the last of my money on a drunken miner." Her voice came out as a shriek, and her face told how she felt.

Campbell scowled at her. "It's a good investment."

"And what are we supposed to live on now?" she said, slamming her empty plate onto the crude table, so hard the salt shaker fell to the ground.

He sneered. "I admit we are low on funds, but I've noticed the needs of the diggers are not catered. You could go into business again as you did in Cockatoo Creek."

Rebecca's face reddened. She bit her lip trying to contain herself. She clenched one of the chipped plates and made a motion as if to throw it at him. Campbell didn't want anyone to know his intended bride's mother was a whore, but was quite content to use her to make money for him.

"That part of my life is over. You'd better find some other way of making money."

"Don't you want us to find Mary?" he said, a hurtful tone to his voice.

"I sometimes wonder if Mary is better off married to that brute than to be tied up with you, Campbell. You're not the boy I knew in Parramatta."

"Who are you, a whore, to be criticizing me?" he snapped. "I've half a mind to throw you out to fend for yourself."

"Give me what's left of my money, and I'll leave now."

"There's only twenty pounds left, and I need that. Your job at the pub keeps us going so you'll stay until I'm ready to leave." He turned and left her.

For another three months, Campbell worked with Harry in the mine. As rock blasted away, they found encouraging traces of gold, bringing a smile to Harry's face.

"That's forty pounds worth this week." He grinned broadly as he inspected the rock.

"That's not that much," frowned Campbell.

"But it's very promising," said Harry, always the optimist.

He taught Campbell how to use the blasting powder, a skill that made Campbell very nervous, and Harry often poked fun at him in the pub, but by the end of nine months, they had four hundred pounds between them.

Rebecca still worked at the pub, often caught up in the tales of some of the diggers. She was popular, she always had a sympathetic ear for their woes and a ready smile to light their faces.

"Did you see the fight yesterday?" asked one digger, downing his ale one evening. "It went on for half an hour until they both dropped."

"You call that a fight? I saw a brutal affair in Echuca about a year ago where one of the men was battered to a pulp. The stupid bastard wouldn't stay down. He had guts, though. He won over a thousand quid in bets if he could last ten rounds."

"Was that the one with Bone Crusher?"

"Yeah, Bone Crusher Molloy. He really belted this other guy, but couldn't put him away."

"Some blokes have no brains." The man ordered another drink.

"Yeah, they called him Mauler Corcoran or something like that. Big bugger he was, but no match for Molloy."

Rebecca almost dropped the glass she was filling. "Did you say Corcoran?" she asked.

"Yeah, an Irishman with a scar on his cheek. He'll have a few more by now," he laughed

"Did he have anyone with him?" Her fingers began to shake, but she dropped them down below the bar out of sight.

"I saw a young girl. Must have been his daughter for she was only about nineteen. She wiped the blood off his face after."

"A young girl. Was she pretty?"

"Yeah, a real angel. I couldn't work out how an ugly lookin' bloke like him could have such a pretty daughter."

"She couldn't have been his wife, could she?" Rebecca's eyes opened wide with excitement.

"I suppose she could have. She had a baby with her."

"A baby?"

"Well a kid about two or three. I thought it must have been Corcoran's, but who knows."

Rebecca's heart soared. It had to be Mary. She decided she would leave at the first opportunity, but was reluctant to pass the information on to Campbell.

"I'm leaving tomorrow, Campbell," she told him the next day.

"Leaving? You can't, you have no money."

She bit her lip and then told him, "I heard in the pub about a fight in Echuca nearly a year ago with a man named Corcoran. He had a young girl with him and a baby. It has to be him, and the girl has to be Mary."

"Mary? Are you sure?"

"Yes. I want you to give me some of my money back. I have to go to her."

"No. The mine is just starting to pay. We'll go in six months if it doesn't come good."

Rebecca tightened her fists and scowled at him. "But it's Mary. You said you loved her."

He shrugged indifferently. "I need money to claim her, and the baby worries me. She'll have to give it up when she marries me. I'm not looking after Corcoran's brat."

"But we'll lose her." Rebecca was aghast at his attitude. Mary might be married to a brute, but Campbell didn't seem to offer a better solution than Corcoran.

"It was Corcoran's intention to settle on the Murray. We'll find them when the time's right. Now that's the end of it."

She could see he wasn't going to change his mind. Men had been giving her orders for years, and Campbell was no different.

* * * * *

It took two months before Brian looked anything like normal. They moved to their land, and he erected another temporary home from the red gum timbers of the property. It was not much better than the humpy he had built on the Murrumbidgee, a far cry from the grand house he promised her.

The problem was lack of funds as he had little left with which to stock the place. With the small amount of cash he had left, he bought two hundred sheep to graze the pastured land while he began the task of clearing the timber.

The slow progress and hardness of the red gums told him he would be there for another fifty years before it was all cleared.

"It's a hopeless task, Mary. Maybe it was a mistake to buy the timbered property. The red gum is as hard as iron, and without the proper equipment, I'll be clearing it forever."

"I'll help you, Brian," said Sean innocently. Since the fight, he had gained enormous respect for Brian and no longer feared him. He followed Brian wherever he went, and together they roamed the property enjoying each other's company. Brian looked at him as his own biological son, and that made Sean proud.

"Thanks, mate, I could do with all the help I can get." He smiled at Sean, not wishing to hurt the boy's feelings. Mary looked at them both fondly as she, too, liked the boy immensely and pleased he had overcome the trauma of the loss of his parents.

Both Sean and Bridget had taken to Wolf like bees to honey, and the pair of them romped around in the freedom of the land without fear. The house may have been crude, but it was a good place for their well-being. There were few blacks, and the ones who lived in the area were friendly.

They all enjoyed the evenings seated together for their evening meal. Later, Mary would sit in the light of the lamps and knit, while Brian would play checkers with Sean or read stories to Bridget. He even took care of Robert whenever he soiled himself, relieving Mary of that burden so she could do other chores. This simple routine seemed to give them comfort in their lives in the wilderness.

One night after Robert and Bridget were in bed, Brian spoke gently to Mary. "It's going to be hard, Mary. I wanted to make a good life for you and the children, but I'm worried."

"How much money do we need?" she asked, concerned etched on her face.

He gave a sigh as he settled into his chair. "At least another thousand to clear the land and stock the place properly. Another thousand after that to build the house I promised you."

She looked sharply at him. It was more than she had realized. "That's a huge amount, Brian. There must be some way."

"I can get it for you," said Sean, eagerly.

"When you get big you'll be a great help, Sean." Brian patted Sean's head sadly, but his heart gladdened by Sean's enthusiasm.

Sean persisted. "No, I know where there's a lot of money."

"And where would that be, Sean?" asked Mary.

He paused for a few seconds. "It's hidden, and only I know where."

"What do you mean?" asked Brian, puzzled.

"Those men who killed my parents. They were after the money."

"Money. What Money?" both Brian and Mary asked together.

Sean looked ashamed and told them. "My father stole the money from them. That's why they were chasing us."

"Who's they?" Brian had always suspected Sean had not told them exactly what happened when they found him.

"We were traveling in our wagon when one day Pa went to look for some rabbits to shoot and came across this camp. There were three men there, and they were arguing about some money they stole from a bank somewhere. Pa listened from behind some bushes and saw them with the money in a saddlebag. One of the men sat guarding it while the other two argued. He heard them say they would divide it up the next morning and split up."

"What happened then?" said Mary, beginning to understand Sean's reluctance to tell them when they first found him.

"Pa told my mother and crept back in the night to the camp. The man guarding it had fallen asleep, and Pa crept over and took the bag with the money in it."

"And they saw him?" Mary shivered.

"No, he came back, and we loaded up the wagon and left in the night. They must have seen our wagon tracks later and came after us."

"What happened then?" Brian felt every nerve ending tense up, waiting in dread for the answer he knew was coming.

"They followed us for three days. Pa knew they were close. He gave me the bag and told me to hide. I watched from the rocks."

"And they shot your parents." Brian nodded. It all fell into place.

"Yes, they were angry when they couldn't find the money and didn't believe Pa when he said he knew nothing about it. The leader shot them both and started the fire. They didn't know about me."

Brian sucked in a breath. "And what did you do with the money?"

"I put it in a hole behind some rocks where it wouldn't be found."

Brian looked at Mary with a raised eyebrow. "Do you think you could find it again, Sean?"

"I think so. It's where you found me."

"That would take us weeks to get back there and weeks more to return," said Brian.

"I can't go back with the children, Brian," said Mary anxiously.

"I know. I'll take Sean back, and we'll find the money. Can you manage by yourself?"

She sat, nodding. "I guess I'll have to, won't I?"

Brian turned to Sean with enthusiasm. "Will you go with me, Sean?"

"Yes. You need it, and you've looked after me well."

He patted Sean on the head. "You're our son now. We'll build this place together."

The next day they took two horses and food and left before sunrise.

Chapter Seventeen

Brian and Sean had been gone for over two weeks; however Mary had no time to be idle. She chopped wood for her fire and tried to make the house more comfortable while looking after Bridget and Robert. There were the sheep to tend, the garden to till and many other things to keep her busy. On those quiet restful moments, she would sit by the banks of the Murray and take in its beauty. She couldn't have picked a better place.

If Campbell ever did come for her, then this is where she wanted to settle with him. He had lived on a farm all his life, and she was sure he would come to love this place, too.

Daydreaming by the gentle river, she was startled by the sound of a riverboat coming around the bend. She was used to seeing them. The boats made their way back and forth from Echuca and Adelaide, carrying cargo of wool and goods to the markets of the city.

The loud ear-piercing scream of the whistle certainly gained her attention, and surprising her when the boat began to move toward the shore, giving another toot. She could see people waving to her from its deck. When it tied up, a well-dressed, elegant looking man wearing a top hat accompanied by several others came ashore.

"Excuse me, madam, is this the property of Brian Corcoran?"

"Yes, sir," she answered. "I'm Mrs. Corcoran, however my husband is away at the moment."

The man frowned, obviously irritated. "When do you expect him home, madam?"

"I'm afraid he may be away for several months, sir. Can I be of any help?"

"Perhaps if we went to your home we can discuss the purpose of my visit."

Mary nodded, now curious. "Your name, sir?" she asked.

"I apologize, Madam. My name is Sir Henry Fox. I'm the Governor of South Australia. I've just made a tedious journey from Adelaide."

Mary's mouth dropped open. Never did she think she would be entertaining such an important man.

He introduced the other men and then followed Mary back to the hut. "I'm afraid my home is not of the quality you are used to, Sir Henry," she told him, nervously twisting her hands in her apron. "It's only a temporary abode. My husband wishes to build me a grand house one day."

"And that day may be sooner than you think, Mrs. Corcoran."

Mary had no idea what he was talking about.

"This gentleman is Captain Cadell, one of the first riverboat men to navigate the Murray. You may be seeing quite a lot of him in the future. This country is opening up quite rapidly and as Governor of South Australia, it is my job to see that trade and commerce is directed towards my colony."

"How will that affect my husband, Sir Henry?"

"As you probably know, the mouth of the Murray is some distance from Adelaide. Goods transported by the river boats are then taken to Adelaide by horse and cart, a very uneconomical way of doing things."

Sir Henry produced a pipe and lit it as he spoke. Mary listened to every word.

"If this means transportation could be improved, then the stations producing wool on the Lachlan, the Murrumbidgee and the lower Darling rivers would divert their produce to Adelaide. Do you know what this would mean?"

Mary shook her head, trying to understand.

"Why, it would open up the whole interior and direct the trade to Adelaide and overseas markets. South Australia will prosper."

"But I still don't see how..."

"It would affect you," he said, smiling at her wonderment.

"Yes?" Mary still couldn't see the relevance of his presence. "I'll make some tea."

The Governor waited until she poured tea to her visitors before continuing.

"I've approved a railway to be built from Murray Bridge to Adelaide. To build this railroad, Red Gum sleepers would be needed. Mr. Corcoran's land is covered with Red Gums, and I have a proposition for him."

"And that is?"

"I will buy the trees on his property to make these sleepers. The offer will be a good one, but if he is not interested then I will look elsewhere."

Mary was certainly interested. "But we have no equipment to cut these trees," she said slowly.

He looked at his companions then returned his gaze to Mary. "I will supply the labor and clear his land, provided we can start immediately."

Mary sat back, amazed by the offer. "And how much would you pay for the trees, Sir Henry?"

"You have over three thousand acres here. I will buy the timber for the sum of four thousand pounds. Do you think Mr. Corcoran would be interested in such a proposition, Mrs. Corcoran?"

She almost coughed in her tea. Was she hearing right? It was too good an offer to refuse. "I'm sure he would, Sir Henry, so much so, I can speak for him. You may begin whenever you wish."

He clapped his hands together, and a broad smile broke out on his face. "Then I will pay the sum of four hundred pounds now to seal the bargain if that is satisfactory."

"It will be most satisfactory, sir," she said, her eyes opening wide.

With the deal now sealed, a week later the place was teeming with men. A sawmill was constructed, and the task of felling the trees began. Mary watched, fascinated, at the way the logs were cut and made into the sleepers. Boats made constant trips to their destination. The Governor even had a small jetty built for easy access to the land. Used to seeing the land covered with trees, Mary was amazed how quickly they disappeared leaving the ground bare. She wondered if Brian would recognize the place when he returned.

She made several trips into Echuca to bank the money and buy one or two luxuries she felt entitled to. If Brian complained then she would face that when he returned.

She discovered the news of their good fortune spread in Echuca. On several trips, she found herself the centre of attention, something that had never happened before.

Subsequent checks were paid as the timber was taken, and she couldn't believe how their bank balance had grown. With half the timber gone, she had placed two thousand pounds in the bank, a sum unheard of in her short life. It would be interesting to see Brian's reaction if or when he returned.

* * * * *

The journey back to the Murrumbidgee was long and tedious, with Sean unused to riding a horse for that distance. Brian stopped as often as he could to give the boy time to rest, but at last they reached the river at Hay.

"How much further do you think it will be, Brian?" asked Sean, weary of the trip.

"Quite a while yet, lad. It's still some hundreds of miles to where we found you, and the problem is it will have changed since then."

"Why will it have changed?" said Sean, puzzled.

"The place was burnt by the fire. In the twelve months since we have been there, the trees will have sprung new growth. It will be difficult to find it again."

"Will the old wagon still be there?"

"That's what I'm counting on. It's unlikely that it would have been shifted unless another flood went through. We'll just have to wait and see."

As they made their way along the river, they suddenly heard a shout and two horsemen rode out in front of them, both brandishing revolvers.

"Stay where you are," one shouted, pointing a gun at Brian's head. The man was dressed in dirty clothes and wore a large bush hat covering most of his forehead. That and the bushy beard made it hard to distinguish any features. The other similarly dressed man was shorter by at least six inches, although this did nothing to lessen his aggressive nature.

"We want your money. Hand it over and keep away from that gun," he said, watching the revolver Brian had in a belt on his saddle.

"I'm afraid we haven't much," said Brian, afraid for Sean's safety.

"Empty your pockets and let's see."

Brian did as ordered and produced the grand sum of two pounds ten shillings.

"Is that all ya got?"

"My son and I are looking for work in any town we can find. It's all we've got in the world," said Brian, trying to seek sympathy.

"Bloody waste of time," snarled the second man in disgust as the first searched their saddlebags.

"Don't shoot," said Brian, anxiously. "The boy is only eleven years old."

"Piss off," snarled the man. "The nearest town is eight days away, and there's no work to be found."

"None at all?" said Brian.

"No. Now get."

"Could you leave us ten shillings so we don't starve? I'll go on a bit further, and if the land is poor, I'll go south again."

"Here's five bob," said the bushranger and threw him some coins. "Don't say we haven't got a heart." He grinned, and they rode off.

"Who were they, Brian?" asked Sean, relieved.

"Just two men down on their luck, Sean. I've been in the same position once or twice."

"Would they have killed us?"

"Only if I had tried to stop them. There's nothing to be gained by chasing them. Let's continue." They re-mounted and rode off again.

For another month they searched the area along the river, but it looked unfamiliar, and Brian felt frustrated. One night they camped as usual along the bank of the river, and Sean walked off to look for firewood. It was then he noticed the remains of the burnt out wagon and ran excitedly back to camp.

"I found it, Brian, I found it!" he cried loudly and led Brian back to the wagon. The place was different, with scarcely a sign of the fire left. Wattle trees had exploded in brilliant golden blossoms, the trees had regenerated, and only some blackened trunks gave an indication a fire had gone through. The wagon was only a shell, and the rims of the badly rusted wheels were visible. The skeletons of two horses lay where they fell. Sean rushed to the two graves Brian had dug and looked sadly at the mounds now almost sunken to ground level. Brian put his arm around the lad's shoulder to comfort him.

"We'll look around first thing in the morning," he said. "We need a good night's rest first."

At first light Brian made a damper and boiled the billy. He frowned when he looked at the meager rations they had left. Without that money they would have to live off the land and return home empty-handed. When they finished eating, they doused the fire and began to search.

"The rocks were that way," said Sean as he scrambled up a slight rise. "I could see what was going on when I was hiding."

They searched the area, but found nothing.

"Are you sure this was the spot?" Brian asked.

"Yes, I put the sack in a hole in the rocks and covered it." He began turning over as many rocks as he could find. Brian was right, it did look different. They searched for an hour, and just as Brian was about to give up, Sean gave a yell.

"Here, I found the hole."

Brian looked where Sean had moved the rock and could see a hole, similar to a rabbit warren. He peered down the opening.

"Can't see a thing, Sean," he said, trying to reach down as far as his arm would go. "We haven't even got a shovel."

"I can get in there if you hold my legs," Sean said, and began to push his body into the opening.

"Just a minute, mate. If you're going in there, then I'd better tie a rope around you. I don't want you to get stuck."

He tied the rope around Sean's waist and fed it in as Sean entered the opening. After the first four feet, the opening dived almost straight down, and Sean found himself falling. Brian grabbed the rope tightly and took the pressure of Sean's body.

"Are you all right, son?" he yelled as the boy disappeared from sight.

"It's almost a straight drop, Brian. It's some sort of a cave. It's very black." His voice was hardly audible.

"I'll lower you right down until you reach the bottom," Brian replied and carefully let the rope out. At last he felt it go slack as Sean hit the bottom.

"Sean, can you hear me?" he yelled, but received no reply. After ten minutes he thought it was time for Sean to come up, money or no money and began to pull on the rope.

When there was no weight on it, he panicked and pulled faster and harder until the rest of the rope came out of the hole. He held up the end and saw it had been untied.

"Sean! Sean!" he yelled and put his ear to the opening. At first he heard nothing, but then a muffled cry came as he strained his ears. Desperately he looked around for some means of sending the rope back down and picked up a rock. He tied the rope around it and began lowering it back down. He waited for another ten minutes and then pulled on the rope again. This time he felt a slight tug. It took almost all his strength to lift him, but at last Sean's head appeared, and Brian grabbed him, lifting him from the hole. He hugged the boy tightly.

"Are you all right?" Brian asked, now composed.

"I'm fine. It was dark, and I couldn't see anything. I felt around, but the rope wouldn't let me move so I untied it. Then it was gone when I felt my way back." The tears streamed down his young face as he bravely tried to stem the flow.

"Never mind, Sean, at least we got you back safe and sound."

"But I found it, Brian. I found the sack." He held it aloft as he pulled it from the belt in his trousers. Quickly they opened it, and Brian couldn't believe what he saw. There, neatly bound, were two large bundles of bank notes, and when they counted it there was five thousand pounds. Now he had the money to clear the land.

Sean watched him lay the money inside the billy and cover it with the last remains of their tea. "Why don't you put it in your saddle bags?" he asked innocently.

"Because we were held up once and that's the first place they look. I'll keep ten pounds in my pocket so if it happens again then that will put them off."

The next day they made for home.

CHAPTER EIGHTEEN

Campbell was sick and tired of the constant digging in the mine. Every night he looked at his hands and soaked them in brine. His dreams of being a country grazier began to fade. The work was tedious. Blaster Harry would drill deep holes into the sides of the quartz and set his powder charges. The blast would bring down more quartz, and Campbell would have to shift it to the crusher and search for any sign of gold. Once they found a nugget valued at three hundred pounds, but when it was shared between the two of them, it didn't come to much.

Rebecca's money had shown a return of only two hundred pounds, none of which Rebecca had seen. The only money she had was the money she earned in the pub, and she was determined Campbell wasn't going to get his hands on that.

Several times Rebecca was sent into Ballarat for supplies, which gave her the opportunity to open an account in one of the banks and deposit her hard-earned cash. As soon as she thought she had enough then she leave, back to Echuca to follow the lead she had about Corcoran being beaten in a fight.

* * * * *

Campbell had just carried another bucket of quartz to the crusher when he heard Blaster Harry hoot with excitement.

"You beauty!" he yelled. "Campbell, come and see."

Campbell rushed down the ladder to see what excited Harry, a feeling of elation suddenly grabbing his stomach. "What is it?" he asked.

"Look, there on the ceiling," said Harry, pointing. "A seam! It must be worth a bloody fortune."

Campbell looked up and saw the glint of the precious metal reflecting the light of the lamp. It seemed his prayers had been answered. "How much do you think it's worth?" he asked.

"At least ten thousand pounds. We're bloody rich!"

Campbell's mind began to turn over. Half of ten thousand wouldn't set him up, but it was a good start. If he only didn't have to share with Harry, then things would be perfect.

"What's the next step?" he asked.

"I'll drill two holes here and set a small charge. That should bring down enough rock to let us get at the gold. I'll start drilling, and you get a small amount of powder, about half a billy full will do, and for Christ sake don't tell anyone about the find."

Campbell nodded and climbed the ladder to the powder keg, leaving Harry to begin further drilling. As he emptied some of the powder out of the keg, an idea hit him. He carried the billy full of powder to Harry then cut a fuse to burn for ten minutes. He then placed it into the full keg and carried the keg to the mine opening. After tying a rope around it and lighting the fuse, Campbell lowered it gently into the mine.

"I'll be back soon, Harry," he yelled. "I'm going to get a bottle to celebrate."

"Righto, Campbell," Harry yelled back. "The holes will take at least another hour to drill."

Campbell walked away, grinning. Ten minutes would just about give him enough time to reach the pub. Rebecca was behind the bar when he walked in.

"Knocked off for the day already?" she said. "It's only eleven o'clock."

"Harry's blasting a drill hole so there's not much I can do at the moment. Give me a bottle of ale and half a pint to drink now."

"Celebrating are we?" Rebecca asked, puzzled at Campbell's sudden good mood.

"You never know when fortune smiles upon you in this place." He grinned as he raised the glass to his lips. The explosion of the powder rumbled across the ground. All the drinkers in the pub felt it, even though it was one hundred yards away. Glasses rattled on the shelf, and Rebecca looked out of the window.

"What the hell was that?"

"It sounded like Harry used a little too much powder," Campbell said, sipping his ale.

Dust was seen rising into the air from the shaft opening. Rebecca turned to him and said, "You've struck gold and killed Harry, haven't you?"

"I don't know what you're talking about. I'm just having a quiet drink here with you."

People were beginning to run in the direction of the shaft, but Campbell seemed in no hurry to see the results of his work. A man rushed into the pub and called to Campbell.

"There's been a big explosion in your shaft! You'd better come quick!"

"I knew Harry was getting careless," he said casually, and walked back to the shaft.

Dust infiltrated the air, and the crowd had to wait another half an hour before anyone could climb down. Campbell accompanied two others into the darkness to see the result of the explosion and was surprised at the devastation that had occurred.

They found what was left of Harry splattered against the walls of the tunnel. One of them gazed in awe at the ceiling.

"Look at that!" he said, amazed. "It's a bloody seam. Harry died a rich man."

"Lucky for me I wasn't with him," said Campbell, barely able to contain his glee. "It looks like I'm the one who's rich now as we were equal partners."

The men removed their hats in a silent prayer for Harry and then returned to the surface to give the others the news. Rebecca stared at Campbell. Now he was set for life.

After the funeral, Campbell began working the mine with added zest. The fallen rock was cleared, and the seam exposed. He surmised many weeks of hard work lay ahead to extract the gold, but he knew it was going to pay rich dividends. A month after the explosion saw him with over four thousand pounds in the bank.

His only concern remained with possible thieves entering the mine when he wasn't present, so he hired guards to mount a twenty four-hour vigil to protect his interests.

At nights he would dress up in the finest clothes he could buy in

Ballarat and looked every bit the wealthy grazier. He took great delight in showing Rebecca the wad of notes he carried, but laughed when she asked for the return of her money.

"As soon as the seam runs out, we'll go and look for her together. I can see that will be at least another six months."

Rebecca knew he did not intend to give her back the money he had taken.

One night, Campbell remained in the pub, drinking heavily, and totally drunk when the pub closed. Rebecca supported him and led him back to the wagon and hut he had constructed near the mine as added comfort.

She laid him on his bed, removed his boots and about to throw a blanket over him when she noticed the wallet poking out of his coat pocket. He was snoring heavily, and it was obvious he wouldn't wake until morning. She removed the wallet and lightly touched what must have been over four hundred pounds.

Should just about pay the interest on my money she thought as she smiled and took the money placing the empty wallet back in his coat. This was the chance she had been looking for. She hitched up the wagon as silently as she could and drove to Ballarat. As soon as the bank opened, she withdrew her money and headed to Echuca. If Campbell wanted to pursue her then he would have to leave the mine behind, and she knew he wouldn't do that. She was pretty sure_he wouldn't want to go to the troopers. There had been talk about the explosion not being an accident. The fact he was in the pub when it happened took some of the suspicion from him. Campbell would be nervous Rebecca would tell the troopers what he had done, and although she couldn't prove anything, she could stir the whole thing up again.

* * * * *

After several days of travel, Brian frowned and grabbed Sean's reins. "Don't say or do anything. Just stay close to me."

Brian looked up to see the same two men who had robbed them on the trip out.

"Well, well. We meet again, mate," said the tall one, again pointing his revolver at Brian's head.

"You got all our money last time," said Brian, edging in front of Sean.

"Then how have you been surviving for the last couple of months?" he asked.

"I went to that town you told us about and found some work. It's run out, and we're heading home to my wife."

"With some money no doubt," he grinned.

Brian moved his hand as if to feel his wallet in his coat, a gesture that the other man noted.

"He has got some," he grinned. "Give me the wallet."

"Look, I've worked bloody hard for this money. My wife expects me to bring something back."

The man cocked his gun, and Brian reluctantly handed over the wallet.

"Ten pounds! Well this is more like it," he laughed.

"It's all I have. You can't take it all." Brian produced a mood of mock horror, pleading with his eyes.

"You're right," he grinned. "It would not be a Christian thing to do. Here's five bob back again." He threw the coins on the ground, and together the two bandits rode off laughing.

Sean leapt from his horse and gathered up the coins. "What would you have done if they found the money, Brian?" he said, still shaking.

"I'd have killed both of them. They're the most careless bushrangers I've ever seen," he said, pulling his revolver from his saddle. "The tall one was looking in the wallet, and the other one was watching him. I could have pulled out this gun and shot them both."

"Why didn't you?"

"I've seen enough killing to last me a lifetime, Sean. They're both young men, and I didn't want to kill them for ten pounds."

"But five thousand pounds would have been different?'

"That's our future, and no one is going to take that away from us."

Sean was silent for a while, but then spoke to Brian. "Can I ask you something, Brian?"

"Sure, son."

"When you were in that fight with Molloy I saw scars on your back. How did you get them? I asked Mary, but she didn't know either."

"And she wasn't curious?"

"She was, but didn't want to ask you."

He smiled to himself at the fact Mary had discussed him with Sean. The burning question as far as he was concerned was did she care?

"I was a convict brought out from Ireland when I was only fifteen. On the ship one of the other convicts tried to steal my rations. I knocked him unconscious and was given twenty lashes. When I reached Van Dieman's Land, I learned that the only way to survive was to take care of yourself when others tried to take advantage of you. I kept to myself as much as I could, but there was always one or two who thought a young lad was easy meat."

"You were attacked often?" asked Sean.

"At first I was, but when I fought back they learned that to pick on me was going to be painful. One of the convicts taught me how to use my fists, and as I grew stronger I was left alone."

"But your back?"

"The scars you see are the results of the floggings."

"Did it hurt?"

Brian grinned at Sean's innocence. "Like a hot knife being laid on your back. After the first twenty you're usually unconscious. They throw salt into your wounds to stop infection and then leave you for a week or so to see if you survive."

"Didn't you want to kill them?"

"Only the guards, but that's why I sympathize with rogues like our two bushrangers. I know what it's like to be hungry."

"But they might have shot you."

"Then I would have gone down fighting and more than likely taken both of them with me."

Sean rode on with this man he now so much admired, glad that Brian was taking care of him.

Chapter Nineteen

The sight of the Murray, slow moving and peaceful as the water moved on its journey toward South Australia, brought a smile to Brian's face. He eased the horse to a stop and looked again, mystified.

"Are we in the right place?" asked Sean.

Three quarters of the trees were gone, and men were still sawing and carting the red gum to the sawmill. It was almost as if he were a stranger on his own property.

"I think so," he said, looking at the activity. He rode past, not believing what he saw and at last reached the house to find Mary studying some papers.

"Hello, lass," he said. "We're back."

She looked up, delighted to see them both return. "So I see. What do you think of the difference?"

Mary ran to him and embraced him, then did the same with Sean.

"I can see it's saved me a hell of a lot of work, but do you mind telling me what's going on?"

"Just after you left, the Governor of South Australia paid me a visit and wanted to buy your trees for a railroad. You weren't here, so I sold them. I hope you're not angry."

"How could I be angry? You saved me years of work."

"As you can see I bought myself a few things to make the house comfortable. I put the rest in the bank in your name."

"You deserve a few luxuries for being left alone for so long. Just how much did they pay you?"

"Four thousand pounds," she said tentatively, expecting him to explode.

"Did you say four thousand?" His brow frowned, and she became nervous.

"How much did you expect? I'm sorry if I did wrong, but I had to make a decision, or the Governor would have looked elsewhere."

"I expected to get about five hundred pounds for the lot. I'm proud of you, Mary. The four thousand pounds and this will let me build you the grandest house you've ever seen."

He put the sack on the table and watched her eyes as she opened the bag. She gave a little gasp in wonder as the money spilled out onto the table.

"You found it?"

"Yes, and you can buy all the clothes you want for both you and the children and anything else you need."

"Brian, this means you can now stock the cleared land with sheep!"

"Yes," he said, well satisfied. "I'm about to become an important man in the community. I'll also be very proud to have the most beautiful wife a man could want to help me build this place into a thriving property."

Mary felt strangely elated to see him back. She had actually missed him in the four months he had been gone, and she had hardly thought about the day Campbell would come for her. She noticed he had even kept his face clean, which she had not expected. This did not look like the evil brute who had bought her for fifty pounds, two and a half short years ago. She could see the look of desire in his eyes as he watched her face. She knew what he wanted, especially after four months. Mary looked at him, then at Sean, a slight smile spreading across her face.

"Sean, take the children to see the saw mill in action," he said, not taking his eyes off Mary.

Mary's heart raced a little stronger as Sean left the room. She didn't feel revolted at all about what was going to happen. In fact, she felt a stirring within herself as she stared back at Brian. She wouldn't admit it, but she missed the thrill of having him inside her. "Stay at least an hour, Sean, the children will enjoy seeing the mill working," she said softly.

She leaned over and touched Brian's face gently. He moved to her side, placing his hand on the side of her face and lowered his lips to hers. "I've missed you, lass, you'll never know how much."

"I think I do, but you'd better show me." She took his hand as he led her to the bed.

* * * * *

A month later, the house construction began. Mary oversaw the plans, at Brian's insistence as this was going to be her home. She had never considered he would consult her, as most men made any decisions of such importance by themselves. As they inspected the plans stretched out on the table he spoke quickly to her. "The architect has done a good job, but is there anything he has missed that you would like included?"

"A few more cupboards," she suggested, and then pointed to a room near the back. "What's this room for?"

He threw his head back and laughed. "It's a room where you can enjoy the privacy of a hot bath. There will be a basin fitted with running water attached. All the mansions have them."

"And this small room next to it?"

"It will be the lavatory. You won't have to go outside to relieve yourself. There will be a pipe that takes the sewerage away to a tank fitted into the ground."

She smiled at his words, amazed at the idea of indoor plumbing.

"We have another two weeks before construction can start. Study it carefully and tell me if you want anything else added."

When the construction began, Mary walked up the hill every day to where the building was taking shape to see its progress. It had everything in it he had promised. When the veranda was completed, she had to agree it would be the finest house she had ever seen. It had six bedrooms, a large dining room, a bathroom, and a huge kitchen along with other additions.

"Do we really need so many bedrooms, Brian?" she asked one day during the construction.

"We seem to have a habit of collecting strays," he said, grinning. "I just want to be prepared."

"Is that the real reason?"

"I thought one day we might send for your mother if she can get away from that scoundrel she's married to, that is if it pleases you. Why don't you write to her and invite her to come? By the time it reaches her the house will be well finished."

She gave a squeal of delight and threw her arms around him. "I miss her so much," she said. Brian enjoyed her embrace, even though he knew it was because she felt grateful for his gesture. There was always hope she would show some love for him; he certainly loved her.

"I know. She would be proud to see her grandchild, and if you can bring her here then she's welcome."

Mary looked down knowing he was going to be angry. "She might have news of Campbell. If he comes with her then I'll have to leave."

"I'll fight him if he comes," he said sharply, his brow furrowing in anger. "Bridget still needs you and so do Robert and Sean."

"You would keep Robert from me?"

"Would your precious Campbell want him? Robert has black hair just like me. Is there any resemblance to that man?"

She looked down at the floor and didn't answer.

"Tell me, is there? The man has made no effort to find you. He's probably married with a family himself, and it's unlikely he will ever come. Better get used to that."

"It's true you're Robert's father. He has your features, but you wouldn't keep him from me, and Campbell will come, make no mistake about that."

Brian stared at her coldly. "We're talking about something that won't happen. Let's enjoy our life together and be happy." His mood changed instantly, and Mary breathed a sigh of relief.

When the house was completed, they moved in. Mary felt like one of the privileged people of the community as few had a home like she now had. The farm was stocked with the best Merino sheep that Brian could afford while Mary began to grow fruit and vegetables to serve their table. She even planted some grapevines with the idea of making their own wine.

Mary often traveled with Brian and always delighted when he bought her clothes to befit a lady. It was a far cry from the poverty she had lived in on McBride's property, and she knew she was lucky Brian had not turned out to be the brute she thought he was. They both became well known, Brian for his elegance and gentlemanly conduct, and Mary for her beauty and soft heart.

By the end of the first twelve months, Brian was asked to sit for a position on the local council; something he never thought would be offered to an ex-convict. Now he began to feel Echuca was his home.

* * * * *

Rebecca found the journey long and tedious. She was always afraid that Campbell would come after her. He would come one day, for his infatuation for Mary was strong. Now he had money he would need someone of her youth and beauty to cement his place in society. The problem was that Mary knew nothing of his change in character and probably still pined for him. She would remember him as the young, handsome, vibrant boy who had won her heart before she was snatched away by Corcoran.

But would Campbell be any worse than the fate that had befallen Mary, married to a monster of a man who would buy women like goods at the market with no feeling for her or her family?

The track to Echuca was filled with danger for a woman traveling alone. She passed a few wagons heading toward Ballarat, probably with hope of striking it rich.

In reality she was glad to get away from the despair and most of all, Campbell. She camped off the road at night hoping to avoid any unwanted attention from men riding to the gold fields, but kept the pistol she had close by. Her money was well hidden in a secret compartment she had forged into the bottom of the wagon. She kept ten pounds in her purse in case some bushranger held her up, hoping this would satisfy him.

The first three nights passed without trouble. When she reached Bendigo she spent some of her cash on a soft bed in one of the Inns. The next day she headed for Echuca hoping to reach her destination in two more nights.

That night she settled down away from the main track and prepared her supper for the night. Always alert, she kept her pistol close by under the blanket spread out on the ground. The aroma of the soup she made caused her mouth to water as she dished it out into a bowl ready to eat. Already the sun had gone and that period between utter darkness and fading daylight was upon her.

She instantly became alert when she heard the sound of a horse, and she slipped her hand under the blanket just in case. The horseman rode up slowly, hunched over the mane. She relaxed when she saw it was only a young boy, maybe sixteen or seventeen years old.

"What do you want, son?" she said, frowning and looking over his shoulders for any more intruders.

"Sorry if I frightened you, lady. I smelt your supper, and I haven't eaten for nearly two days. I don't suppose you could spare any?"

"You're alone?" she asked, cautiously.

"Yes, I'm trying to get to Ballarat and make my fortune." He looked forlorn and harmless so she relaxed and picked up another plate.

"You're welcome to join me. Tie up your horse and come and have some soup."

Eagerly he did as she said and hurried to her campfire for the plate she was filling. She watched him gulp the food down, and it appeared that he'd told the truth. She watched him closely as she ate. "What's a young boy like you doing out here all alone?" she asked.

"I had some trouble at home. I had to get away."

"Where do you hail from?" Rebecca questioned him as he ate.

"Echuca," he said, sitting back, his hunger satisfied.

"What's your name, son?" asked Rebecca, still probing.

"Wally, Wally er Smith."

She smiled. Funny how the name Smith was used when people were trying to hide their real identity. She let it slide then continued to probe. "What sort of trouble, Wally?"

He looked down, then up again. "My dad died a few years ago, and Mum married another man. He worked on the wharfs. He didn't like me, and I didn't like him."

"I see, and now you want to go and find gold?"

"Yes, they say a fortune can be made."

"How old are you, Wally?"

"Old enough to take care of myself. I'll be seventeen next week."

"Have you thought about what your mother would think of you running off?"

"She wouldn't care. Probably glad to see the back of me."

Rebecca shook her head. Life wasn't just hard for her, it was hard for everyone without money or position.

"You say you came from Echuca. Do you know of a man by the name of Corcoran? A brute of a man, well over six feet tall, shaggy beard, dirty clothes with a young girl of nineteen and a young girl of around seven? He stole my daughter."

"No. We lived on a small farm just outside the town. Never knew hardly anyone." He wiped his nose with the back of his hand and sipped a mug of tea Rebecca handed to him.

"I heard he might be in Echuca. What's the place like?"

"Like any small town. If you have money it's all right. If you don't then you have no chance of a decent life. That's why I'm goin' to Ballarat to find some gold and make some money. When I'm rich I'll come back and kill that prick."

Rebecca had heard those words before. Campbell had the same venom, and she hoped this boy wouldn't turn out like him. "My advice is to forget any revenge. Just try to live a normal life and be happy."

The boy sneered. "And what are you goin' to do when you find this bloke who stole your daughter. Shake his hand and wish him well?"

Touché, thought Rebecca. She was no better than this boy as she, too, was hell bent on revenge.

"You need money if you want to stay in Echuca," he said, staring at her.

"I have ten pounds. That will get me by for a while. I'll get a job and then continue my search."

"I got ten pennies. That's not going to get me far."

"Then I wish you well, Wally."

He eased himself to his feet then stepped towards her. Before she could do anything, he pulled a long knife from his belt, the steel shining in the light of the fire. He grabbed her by the hair and put the knife to her throat. "Ten pounds will get me a long way. I want it."

"Is this how you repay an act of kindness?" gasped Rebecca, feeling the steel against her soft throat.

"I have to survive. Where is it?"

"It's in a purse under my dress. Don't hurt me," she said, her eyes widening.

Wally eased her down to the ground, grabbed a small cord of rope from the side of the wagon and tied her hands behind her back.

"What are you going to do?" she asked with a nervous tone. Hell, he was only a boy, and robbing her.

"Get the money." He lifted her dress above her waist and found the purse. Kneeling on her chest with one knee, he opened the purse. An array of coins fell out and he gathered up some sovereigns and loose change, thrusting them into his pocket in triumph.

"You have the money. Untie me and leave," said Rebecca, angry at what was happening.

Wally still held her with his knee, staring at her. Rebecca had seen that look before and shuddered at what he might be thinking.

"Let me go, Wally. You have the money."

He didn't speak as he held her helpless then pulled her undergarments down and off.

"No, Wally. You can't do this. I'm old enough to be your mother."

"Never had a woman before. It's time I had."

She watched him undo his belt and lower his trousers, still keeping her pinned down. She could see his erection standing firm.

"You could be hung for this," she said, still afraid he would kill her after the event.

"No one will know. Open your legs."

Rebecca kept them closed until she felt the knife pricking her throat.

"Open them I said!" he shouted, and she sighed, knowing he was not going to stop. Giving herself willingly for a price was one thing, but this was something else entirely. And a young boy doing it? It only reinforced her idea about men. None could be trusted, no matter how old they were.

"Please, Wally. You don't want to do this," she pleaded with him.

"That's what you think."

Rebecca felt him slip into her, and she lay there motionless as he thrust into her with fast steady strokes. It was over quickly, and she heard him gasp as he climaxed, then lay on her for several seconds.

"It was better than I thought it would be. I'm goin' now. Thanks for that."

"You can't leave me tied up here. I'll die."

"Don't want to kill you, lady. I've got your money, and I'm no longer a virgin. Turn over."

She rolled over and felt him undo the rope. She pulled down her dress, feeling the stickiness between her thighs.

Wally shoved his knife into his belt and walked towards his horse, confident she could do him no harm. Rebecca reached under the blanket for her pistol, found it and aimed at his retreating figure. She pulled the trigger. He screamed and fell, clutching his leg.

"You shot me, you bitch! You shot me!" he said. Blood oozed from the wound in his leg and ran through his fingers.

Rebecca felt ashamed she'd had to shoot a young boy and walked slowly towards him. "When you rob and rape women what else can you expect?"

"I didn't want to hurt you. I've never had a woman before. I wanted to try it out."

"Then earn some money and buy it from some of the whores in the gold fields. Turn over."

"What?" he gasped, still holding his leg.

"I said turn over, or do you want me to put another bullet into you?"

Quickly he turned, and Rebecca tied his hands with the same rope he had used on her. She rolled him back, and he looked dumbfounded when she undid his belt and pulled his trousers down.

"You want to rape me?" he howled.

She looked at him with contempt and inspected the wound. "You're lucky. The bullet has gone right through and missed any bone."

He sat with his hands behind him as she reached for the billy and boiled some more water. Leaving him on the ground, Rebecca climbed into the wagon and returned with cloth she had ripped into bandages. She bathed the wound and wrapped it tightly, making the bleeding stop. Wally sat staring at her as though he expected her to kill him.

"Go ahead and shoot me. I don't care," he said sullenly.

"Shut up." She went through his trouser pocket and retrieved her money, then untied his hands, stood back still holding the gun and scowled at him.

"Get dressed and put your trousers back on. Dress the wound every day unless you want it to be infected."

"You're not going to kill me?" There was a sound of amazement in his tone.

"No, I'm going to give you some advice, but whether you follow it or not is up to you."

He said nothing and stared at her.

"You are only a few years younger than my daughter. If you continue to rob and rape then you will be imprisoned or hung. I don't like to see young people with no future. Go to Ballarat and try to find gold. If you can't, then get an honest job. Some day you will meet a girl and want to raise a family. A family is everything. Heed my words for you have no future at all unless you do. Take it or leave it, that's up to you. Now get on your way. If you come back, I will shoot you, and this time it won't be in the leg."

"Yes, ma'am. Can I go now?"

"Yes. Wait a minute," she said, frowning deeply then sighing. Rebecca threw two sovereigns to the ground, and Wally stared at them, not believing his eyes.

"Take them. It will at least get you something to eat on your trip to Ballarat."

"Are you goin' to tell the troopers what I did?"

"No, but if you do it again then you won't be as lucky as this. Now go."

He gathered the coins and quickly mounted up. Rebecca watched him disappear into the gloom then attended to her needs. The last thing she wanted was to be pregnant from a rape. All men were bastards, even young ones like Wally. She hoped she had done the right thing in letting him go. One more man between her thighs was something she could bear. But woe betides him if he ever put a young girl to the same trauma. She prayed he had learned his lesson.

The day she arrived in Echuca the temperature seemed to be climbing through the roof. It was a dry heat that made her feel listless as sweat formed on her forehead. However, grateful she had the shade of the wagon cover to protect her from the sun's rays. Dust rising into the air from the passing wagons formed a cake on her skin. Rebecca wiped her face clean before getting off the wagon. She checked herself in a hand mirror and felt satisfied with what she saw. Her face was still pretty with few wrinkles. Even her hair was void of streaks of grey.

Nothing had changed much since her first visit with Campbell. People hurried down the streets, wagons rolled past with goods heading towards the wharf to send the precious cargo to its destination. She needed some rest to regain her strength so she selected a site along the river to set up camp. It was unusual for a woman to be driving such a wagon alone, and she collected many stares on her entry to the town.

She changed her clothes and walked around town, getting a feel for the place before she made any enquiries. The wharf attracted her as a place where men worked to load and unload the many riverboats tied up. Maybe it would be a good place to start.

Apart from Ballarat, it was by far the busiest place she had seen. Even Bathurst did not have the atmosphere of this town. She inspected the shops down the main street and watched a coach depart on its trip to Melbourne, people waving teary farewells to the passengers.

Rebecca asked in many of the shops about a man with a young girl who might have passed through the area now over twelve months ago, but received no positive sightings.

"Sorry, lady, who can remember someone like that?" was the usual reply.

Disappointed, she entered a clothing store, the one she had gone into when she first came to Echuca, and asked the man there.

He scratched his head. "A man with a young girl you say? It's hard to remember everyone who's come and gone in the past twelve months."

"He was a brute of a man. Big and hairy with a scar on his cheek. Went by the name of Corcoran. They say he fights with his bare fists."

"Corcoran? Did you say Corcoran? That description doesn't fit the Corcoran I know. As a matter of fact, there was a man named Corcoran who just left here a few minutes ago. He came to order a dress for his wife."

"Do you know his wife's name?"

"Of course. Her name is Mary. A very pretty young woman."

Rebecca's heart soared. "They're still living here?"

"Yes, as a matter of fact I saw him talking to a gentleman only a few minutes ago by the coach departure station.

Rebecca raced from the store and saw two men still chatting by the rail. One was a well-dressed man in fine clothes; someone who Rebecca ignored for it was the other who took her interest. He was big, wearing dusty clothes and sported a huge beard that covered his face. It was hard to remember Corcoran from so long ago as she'd had only a glimpse of him as she lay in her bed.

She had encountered many rogues in her travels, and he was no different. The miners of Bathurst were of the same breed as were the timber cutters she'd had to entertain to gain funds for her search. The man was repugnant, and her heart went out to poor Mary having to submit to such a creature. She walked to them quickly and even as she approached, she could smell the man. He must not have bathed in months.

"What have you done with her?" she screamed loudly.

Both men turned with surprised looks on their faces. "What?" the bearded man said, a look of astonishment on his face. "Are you talking to me, lady?"

"Yes, I'm talking to you," shouted Rebecca, her face masked with fury. "My daughter. What have you done with her?"

"I haven't got your bloody daughter, you old crow," he snarled. "The bloody woman's mad."

"You stole her four years ago. You took my Mary from me in Parramatta."

"Ain't ever been to Parramatta, you old bat," he said.

"I'll go to the police, Corcoran. They'll make you tell."

"You've made a mistake missus. My name ain't Corcoran. It's Turner."

Rebecca's face went white.

"It's true, madam, this man is named Turner," the gentleman said. "I was just discussing some business with him."

Rebecca was lost for words.

Turner left, muttering.

"You appear distressed, madam. Perhaps I could escort you to the tea room. Maybe I could help."

"Thank you, sir. My name is Rebecca McBride, and I'm seeking my daughter. She was stolen from me by a thug named Corcoran."

"Corcoran, I know a man named Corcoran. Perhaps I can be of assistance."

They sat in the tea-room, and Rebecca composed her now tattered nerves as the man poured the tea. She watched the steam rise from the cup and then took a scone, realizing it had been hours since she had eaten. She looked around, noticing the tearoom for the first time. Well-dressed women sat with friends, eating pastries and exchanging gossip. It must be one of the higher establishments in the working town. The crockery was first class, the tablecloths of the finest linen and tasteful decorations. The surroundings eased her jagged nerves, and she studied the gentleman who was taking care of her.

"I didn't catch your name, sir," she said, blowing her nose.

"Smith, Brian Smith," he lied as he looked into her eyes.

"That's a coincidence. Smith was my name before I married."

"It is a very common name, unfortunately," said Brian offering her another scone.

"This Corcoran you spoke about. Does he have a girl with him named Mary?"

Brian smiled sympathetically at her. "I believe he does, and a daughter named Bridget. I think his wife also has a young son, no more than three years old. There is another lad living with them. I think they have adopted him, for it seems he was an orphan."

"Do you know where they live?" asked Rebecca, excited.

"I believe it's on a property some fifteen miles from here."

"Can you point me in the right direction?"

Brian touched his chin with his finger and smiled broadly at her. "I can do more than that. My own property is in the same direction. I'm about to leave for home now, and I can escort you."

Rebecca's blood surged at the thought of seeing Mary once again.

"I have my wagon by the river. I'll need to take it if I'm going to leave with my Mary. Do you know this Corcoran personally?"

Brian nodded his head. "I have had some contact with him. He's a brute of a man who doesn't step back easily."

"I have a weapon with me. If he tries to stop me from getting Mary, I'll shoot him."

"Then he'd better be wary. You go and fetch your wagon, and we'll be on our way." Brian smiled to himself at his play-acting. "I'll mount my horse and meet you here in five minutes."

Rebecca thanked the man and left her tea half finished. She raced back to her wagon and broke camp. She slipped her pistol under her dress. If Corcoran was going to make trouble then she was going to be prepared. It was lucky she had this gentleman with her for protection. At least she had some help if Corcoran became nasty.

CHAPTER TWENTY

Brian tied his horse behind the wagon and took over the reins as they headed towards his property.

"You have no Mister. McBride with you, Mrs. McBride."

"Call me Rebecca. No. My husband is dead."

"I'm sorry to hear that," said Brian, feigning sympathy.

Rebecca frowned deeply as just the thought of McBride made her stomach turn. "Don't be. He was scum and treated Mary and me like dirt. He was much the same as this Corcoran who stole Mary."

Brian threw her a glance. "Then how did a handsome looking woman like you come to marry him?"

"Not that it's any of your business, Mister. Smith but…"

"Call me Brian. And I'm sorry for prying."

She nodded. "Sometimes a woman has no choice."

"I understand."

A look of relief flashed over her face. "My husband nearly beat me to death, and it took months for me to recover. When he died, I began to look for Mary. She's all I've got in the world."

Brian flicked the reins to hurry up the horse. "And this Corcoran just took her?"

"My husband sold her for fifty pounds. He told Mary to marry him, or he would kill me."

Brian feigned more sympathy. "And you've not seen her since—or Corcoran?"

"All I know was that Campbell and I began searching together and heard about a fist fight between Corcoran and a man named Bone Crusher Molloy."

"Campbell?" Brian frowned.

"Campbell McGregor. He was Mary's sweetheart when she was sold. He came with me to look for her."

Brian raised an eyebrow at this news. "Really? Where is he now?"

"Digging for gold in Ballarat. He's just as big a scoundrel as Corcoran. He killed his partner to get a fortune in gold. I took back the money he stole from me and came looking for Mary."

"And what will you do if this Corcoran refuses to let Mary go?"

"I have a gun. I'll kill him if I have to."

"You sound like a dangerous woman, Rebecca. This man had better be wary."

"Anyone who comes between Mary and me had better be wary."

"Corcoran has a daughter with him, a young girl about six or seven and another young child. I believe it's a boy no more than two."

"That will be a problem. It has to be Mary's child. The scoundrel made her pregnant, and the baby is the result."

"Do you expect him to just give up his child?" Brian kept his eyes on the trail as he thought about Campbell and what might happen if he arrived.

"He probably won't care. I said he was a monster."

Brian defended himself, just in case she did want to shoot him. "Corcoran never struck me like that, but I suppose other people might judge him differently. I know he hasn't hurt your daughter. She seems contented."

"I hate the man for what he has done to me and to Mary." Rebecca's fist turned white as she gripped the side of the wagon while Brian drove.

"Then we must face the man together and demand justice."

Mary sat back, happy this man would back her up.

They drove on until they passed the shack by the river that Brian had erected when they arrived in Echuca. It now stood in ruin.

"That used to be their house," he said, pointing out the shack.

Rebecca stared at it. "It's the sort of place I would expect him to provide."

They drove up the long drive leading to the house, and Rebecca frowned.

"Is this where they live?"

"I believe so," said Brian casually.

"Are they employed by the owner? It's certainly a grand house."

"Probably live in a shack at the back." Brian grinned as he pulled the horses to a halt.

"We'd best go around the back," said Rebecca. "I wouldn't want to disturb the owners."

Brian nodded and led her around the back to the kitchen. Rebecca could hear Mary humming a ditty to herself as she rolled out some scone dough. She looked up, expecting to see Brian when her eyes fell on Rebecca.

"Mother," she screamed throwing flour into the air and ran to her with her arms outstretched, still covered with flour. The two women embraced, tears running down both of their faces as they clung to each other.

"How did you find me? How did you get away from Poppa? When did you arrive?"

Rebecca looked around fearfully. "Hush child. We must get away before that monster of a husband of yours comes back."

Mary looked at Brian, not understanding. "Brian, you found her?"

"You must thank Mister. Smith for helping me, Mary. If it wasn't for him I'd still be looking."

"But mother…"

Rebecca became agitated and gripped Mary's hands tightly. "Hush, Mary. We must ask your employer for protection before this beast comes back."

"Mother, you don't understand. I'm quite safe here. My husband wouldn't hurt you or me. He's a good man."

Rebecca threw her hands in the air. "That hairy brute is a good man after what he's done? He's turned your brain, girl. I have a wagon outside. Get your things and we'll escape before he comes back."

Mary looked at Brian's smiling face, finally understanding his joke. "Mother, I'd like you to meet my husband, Brian Corcoran."

Brian bowed and held out his hand.

"This is your husband?" Rebecca couldn't believe it.

"And what's more, this is our house."

Rebecca staggered, and Brian pulled out a chair for her to sit.

He took her hand, which she snatched away quickly. "Would you like a drink, Rebecca? I'm sorry I fooled you, but you might have shot me."

Rebecca's eyes widened as she looked first at Brian, then at Mary. "But this can't be the man who took you. He was so ugly and repugnant."

"She made me shave and clean myself up. She's a hard woman."

Confused, Rebecca pulled the revolver from beneath her dress and pointed it at Brian.

He grinned at her, not concerned by the gun. "Before you blow my head off, Rebecca, there's three things I'd like you to do. Hold your grandson, as I'm sure he'd like to meet his grandmother, have some supper as it's getting late, and pick out one of the bedrooms. If you're going to live permanently with us then it's best that you're comfortable."

Rebecca slowly lowered the gun, her face still confused. She could see Mary wasn't distressed at all. She was further confused when Mary walked to Brian and slipped her arm around his waist.

"Put that away, mother, I said Brian won't hurt you. Come and see Robert; he's still sleeping."

Rebecca still couldn't believe it. She looked around the room at the decor; the walls made from stained timber and the highly polished furniture. A gun rack by the door held a shotgun and two rifles. The windows were huge and gave a nice view of the Murray some hundred yards away, and the ceilings were high, giving the house a spacious look, a home only the rich could afford.

"How did you get all this? Is the man a bushranger?" Rebecca asked when they were in the nursery alone.

"Through sheer hard work and a little luck," said Mary.

"Has this man really been kind to you, Mary?" she asked.

"Yes, mother. He knows he did wrong in taking me, but swore he would take care of me and help find you one day. How did you get away from Poppa?"

"I poisoned him with toadstools, nine months after you left."

"And you came after me alone?"

"No. Campbell came with me when I started to hunt for you."

"Campbell? He's here?" Mary's eyes lit up at the mention of his name.

"No. He's in Ballarat digging for gold. He said he wanted to get rich before he came to claim you."

"What do you mean? He's not a digger."

"It seems money is more important to him than you."

"But he's coming for me. I just knew he would."

"Don't get too excited. He's not the man you thought he was.

"Do you mean he's changed? He must have, he's older now."

Rebecca shook her head. "He's changed all right, but not for the better. He's selfish and cruel."

"Campbell's not like that, he's not like that at all."

Rebecca stared at her daughter. "Be wary of him, Mary. He says he loves you, but he only wants you to give him a good standing in the community once he's rich. He says he needs a pretty wife who will give him many children."

"Does he know about Robert?" Mary asked nervously.

Rebecca nodded. "Yes. He said he wouldn't be looking after another man's child and that he would kill Corcoran when he saw him."

Mary gasped at this news "Brian has been very good to me. He's taken care of Robert, Bridget, and Sean."

"Who's Sean?" said Rebecca.

"He's a boy we found on the trail. His parents were murdered, and Brian took him in. He's a nice boy."

"Your husband took him in?" Rebecca was learning more and more about Brian every minute.

"I know you're surprised, but he really is a good man."

Rebecca took her hands again and faced her, staring into her eyes. "He's twice your age, Mary. He has used you, hasn't he?"

She nodded knowing she could not hide the truth. Robert was proof. "Yes, I am his wife. But he is always very gentle."

"Then this child really is his?"

"I wasn't sure whether it was Campbell's, Poppa's, or Brian's. But now it's_clear he's Brian's as he has his coloring and features."

Rebecca sighed at the thought of the oncoming problem. "Then what are you going to do when Campbell comes?"

"I don't know. I still love Campbell, but I have Robert, Bridget, and Sean to care for. I'd find it difficult to leave any of them, and I certainly won't leave Robert behind."

"You don't know what Campbell is like now. Campbell is going to come and try to kill Brian. Brian might be the better husband."

"Brian has taken a terrible beating for me. He's been generous and protected me when I had Robert, and he's worked hard. It's true it will be hard to leave him, but he did take me from you. When do you think Campbell might come?"

Rebecca gave a snigger. "He won't come until he's cleaned out his claim. I suspect he killed his partner to get control of it."

Mary had a disbelieving look on her face. "Campbell killed a man?"

Rebecca nodded. "I can't prove it, but I think it's true. Perhaps you had better warn Brian."

"Brian already knows he'll come one day. He tries to change the subject when I speak about it."

"He'll have a lot to lose if you go. You had better think seriously about the problem."

"Let's put this problem behind us. This is more important." Mary picked up the child and placed him in Rebecca's arms. "Meet your grandson. I named him after my true father."

Rebecca gave a stifled cry as she picked the infant up in her arms. Corcoran may be a brute, but he had given her a grandchild to be proud of.

For a month, Rebecca observed Brian, trying to make up her mind as to whether he was a saint or a sinner. She noted how he treated Sean as a son of his own, he seemed a loving, caring father around Bridget and Robert and showed no aggression or hostility about her presence. He did his best to make her feel at home, and her attitude softened the more she observed him.

She came outside one day when he had taken off his shirt and was chopping wood for the fire. She noticed the scarring on his back. He didn't have to tell her what caused them.

"You've been flogged at some time," she said.

"How did you know?"

She frowned heavily. "Because I've seen it happen many times. I was flogged myself on the trip out here."

"Then you know what the English are like," he said without stopping. The sound of the axe hitting the wood echoed loudly.

"You came here as a convict?" Rebecca had to know more about him.

"As a fifteen year old boy from Ireland, transported for ten years."

"Why didn't you go back?"

"To what? All my family is dead, and this country is hard but better than Ireland. I have no wish to return."

"I have to ask this, Brian. Do you love Mary?"

He dropped the axe and turned to her. "You ask because I bought her from your husband?"

She nodded. "I was forced into a marriage to a brute. I hated every day of it, having to submit and be his slave. I didn't want that to happen to Mary."

He posed an interesting question. "Do you think Mary is unhappy?"

Rebecca shook her head. "I admit I'm surprised. I had visions of you doing terrible things to her in these last four years, but she does appear happy. I thank you for looking after her."

He sighed and wiped his brow with the back of his hand. "Look, Rebecca, I did have selfish motives for taking her. I had a baby daughter who needed a mother, and I couldn't work a property and look after Bridget at the same time. Yes, I know I'm almost twice Mary's age. I'm probably your age, and yes, I have used her for my gratification. I have tried to be gentle and only bothered her when I could stand it no longer." He picked up the axe once again and gave his attention to the wood.

"I must admit she could have done a lot worse than be married to you, but do you love her?"

Brian looked at her. "I was attracted to her from the moment I saw her. You're right. I was disgusting looking, and there was no way she would ever have even considered me. It was the only way I could get her, and of that I'm not proud." He now had a sober look as he thought about his sin of taking her.

"Once I had her I was determined to make her life as pleasant as I could. She cared for Bridget, and for that I'm grateful. Do I love her? Hopelessly, but I have never told her for I know one day she will leave. When that day comes then I want her to have no conscience about going. If by some miracle she wants to stay, then that day will be the happiest day of my life, but I hold out no such hopes."

Rebecca seemed satisfied with his reply. "You know Campbell will come."

"Sooner than I hoped, but if he does then she will have to make a decision."

"And what of Robert?"

"I love him dearly, but I wouldn't break Mary's heart by keeping him from her."

This surprised Rebecca. "But it would break yours."

He nodded sadly. "I'll still have Bridget and Sean as my family. I've lost a child before. I'd hoped you would stay here with us to complete Mary's happiness, but I suppose if she goes then you'll go with her."

Rebecca began to feel sorry for him. "As you say, it's a decision she will have to make, but Campbell is not the sort of person Mary should end up with."

"I'd thought about fighting this Campbell, but it would achieve nothing. If I killed him Mary would never speak to me again, and we could never achieve any happiness. At least it will be her decision if she leaves, and that makes her luckier than you or my first wife."

"You're a strange man, Brian Corcoran, if we had met twenty years ago then maybe my life would have been different."

"You can be sure I wouldn't have hesitated to select you then, but that's a different story."

She smiled and returned to the house thinking Mary had a very important decision to make.

Chapter Twenty-One

Campbell waited for the geologists to speak. They had been inspecting the mine for over an hour, and the signs weren't good. The fabulous seam had suddenly petered out, and the ten thousand pounds Campbell had expected to make had suddenly shrunk to six thousand. It had been sudden and unexpected, and Campbell had been as surprised as anyone when it ceased to pay.

"That's the uncertainty of gold, Mr. McGregor," said the man. "One minute you're rich, and the next it's gone."

"But it looked so promising," said a disappointed Campbell. "Everyone said it was going to be a huge strike."

"Well you have done well out of it, after all, six thousand pounds is a fortune in any man's language."

"But not enough to gain the position I want," he scowled. "Is there nothing to be done?"

The man scratched his head and frowned. "Well, you can't go any further west," he said, pointing in that direction. "You would be in the next man's claim. The only other alternative would be to dig down, but that would require a large amount of labor."

"How much?" asked Campbell.

"You would have to spend most of what you have already gained to buy better equipment. Then there's the wages of diggers, who are now getting two pounds seven and six a week from other mine owners. Of course there's no guarantee that you'll find more gold."

Campbell did a quick calculation in his head. He would need at least ten diggers, which would mean that he would have to fork out over twenty pounds a week just in wages. It was hopeless, and he knew he was beaten. He would have no alternative but to close the mine.

"It seems I have no choice but to take my money and run."

"I think that's the best way to go," said the man. "It's only the big mining companies who have the resources to do such work."

Campbell paid the man and returned to his miner's hut to think about the problem. The hut was crude and uncomfortable but necessary to safeguard his claim. Of course he had enough to live comfortably in Ballarat, but only visited the place when he was in search of clean women. His money allowed him to move up-market as far as the whores were concerned.

Six thousand pounds would allow him to buy a reasonable holding of land, but he badly wanted to be looked upon as one of the gentry, a position only money could bring. In England one was born into such a position, but in Australia it was only wealth that counted. He would need a wife, a pretty one who would be acceptable to the society, someone like Mary who would give him the appearance of respectability.

Rebecca would be a problem, as having a mother- in- law who was a whore would not be looked upon favorably, but he could ship her away to some corner where she wouldn't be noticed. Maybe he would be lucky enough to have her die, or maybe he could arrange some sort of accident. Yes, he had no choice now but to continue his search for Mary. But where to start? It had been twelve months since Rebecca had left with his four hundred pounds. Then he remembered.

She had said something about some fight between Corcoran and a champion fighter at Echuca. That was where Rebecca had gone, and that was where he would start.

It didn't take him long to sell everything he could and make arrangements with his bank to give him credit. He was going to take no chances with bushrangers by carrying large sums of money with him. Setting off on horseback, he stopped at the various towns he met on his journey to Echuca. The first stop was Bendigo, another gold town where people seemed just as busy as at Ballarat. Here he bought a good quality handgun, something he would need when he met up with Corcoran.

Staying at the best inn he could find, he was reading the Bendigo and District news at dinner when he saw it, the item on the third page. 'First ex-convict elected to council.' His eyes opened wide as he read on. "Mr. Brian Corcoran was elected today as the fourth member of the Echuca Council. Mr. Corcoran came to Australia as a fifteen-year-old convict and has forged the wilderness to establish a fine property named after his pretty young wife. The Mary McBride is a property of over five thousand acres stocked with the finest Merino sheep. Mr. Corcoran is remembered as the man who fought a bruising battle against the heavy weight bare-knuckled champion of Victoria, Bone Crusher Molloy. Molloy won the fight, but Mr. Corcoran won a huge bet that enabled him to buy the property he now owns. He was sworn in with his wife Mary, his mother-in- law Mrs. Rebecca McBride and his three children present. Mr. Corcoran has pledged to continue to make Echuca the thriving city of the Murray."

Campbell smiled when he read it. Perfect. With Corcoran dead, Mary would own the farm. He would use his considerable charm to woo her again, and when they married he would be the respected landholder he sought to be.

Mary would have to do as she was told just as any wife was compelled to do. There could be some trouble with the law, but when it was exposed Corcoran had bought Mary and forced her into marriage then there would be no sympathy for the man.

They would make up a tale of continual rape and virtual slavery. He would say that Corcoran died attacking him when he threatened to expose him to the council. Of course Mary would back him, but he wasn't so sure about Rebecca. She could pose a problem. He would work on it and come up with a solution. Maybe he could say he caught Corcoran raping Rebecca and when he killed her, Campbell was forced to shoot him dead. It was complicated, but he would think about it on the way to Echuca.

* * * * *

Now content, Rebecca enjoyed the quiet and peaceful life on the property. It seemed Brian expected nothing from her in the way of work and that amazed her. She had never been one to lie around and joined in to help Mary in whatever way she could. The only thing that disturbed her was that Mary made mention of Campbell coming for her every three or four days. It seemed obvious she couldn't get the thought of her first true love out of her mind. She also noticed how Brian would stare at his wife whenever he thought she wasn't looking. This man really did love her daughter.

One nice day they drove into Echuca to shop. Men raised their hats as they passed and women smiled and stopped for a chat.

"Good morning, Mary," said one woman holding a small child.

"Good morning, Erica," replied Mary as they walked past.

"Who was that?" Rebecca asked.

"Erica is the wife of one of the counselors. The people here are always friendly."

Rebecca laughed. "Back home you wondered if the men were going to rape you, and the women hardly ever acknowledged you."

"I think Poppa might have caused that," she said, smiling at her mother.

"Everyone seems to respect you."

Mary agreed. "It's because Brian has done such a good job on the council. He's rich and famous."

Rebecca wondered if Brian would react violently if Campbell appeared, or would he do as he said and just let Mary go if she wanted to leave. The man she hated had turned out to be her friend, making her grateful for the life she now led. Brian had accepted her into his family as if she had always been part of it, and for the first time in her life she felt needed.

While sitting in the parlor one morning they could see Brian playing with the children outside. Their laughter was infectious and both women smiled at each other.

"Brian is a good father. The children seem to love him dearly."

Mary nodded. "It's always like this every Sunday. He chases them around the garden, and even Wolf joins in.

"I have to tell you Mary, not for one minute did I ever expect you to be this happy and have such a loving husband."

"Yes, I wonder if Campbell will show the same free spirit with children as Brian does."

"I doubt it." She resumed the knitting she had started, a jumper for her grandchild.

On a bright spring morning, Brian worked felling a tree in the paddock. He had been at it for over two hours, and the ringing of the axe against timber reached the house as the axe bounced off the hard Red

Gum trunk. Mary gathered up a basket with food in the form of scones and a billy of tea.

"Come on Mother. Brian will want some refreshment after all that work."

Rebecca smiled. No way would she ever have taken McBride tea and food without being ordered, but here was Mary thinking about her husband's welfare. Together they walked the hundred yards down the paddock to where Brian chopped into the stout trunk. He held his back, wiped his brow and looked with satisfaction at the tree almost ready to fall.

"We thought we'd bring you something to eat and drink," Mary said as Rebecca placed the basket on the ground.

"Thank you, ladies, it's sorely needed." Brian sat down, the sweat pouring from his back.

"You've been working hard on this old tree, Brian," said Rebecca, looking at his progress.

"It's not going to beat me. This is grand land, and I regard it as paradise. It makes all the sweat and tears over the years worth it."

"Rose would have been proud," said Mary, quietly.

"That she would, lass, but she's gone, and I'm sure she would be smiling down on all of us now. I hope you're proud of what we've done."

Mary looked at Rebecca before she replied. "I never expected things would turn out like they have when you took me. You've shown me a side of life that has only been one of kindness and consideration. I am proud of what we've done."

"And there's good times ahead of us," he said. "It's a good place to raise children."

"Well, we'll let you get back to work," Mary said, springing to her feet.

As Mary and Rebecca stood up, a creaking sound alerted them, and they looked up in alarm. The big tree began to slowly fall towards them, and they stood mesmerized as it began its descent to the ground.

Without hesitation Brian rose and hurled himself at the two women, knocking them backward from its path. The tree crashed, and Mary heard Brian gasp as he lay on his stomach beside them.

As she jumped to her feet she could see one of the heavy limbs across Brian's foot, pinning him to the ground.

"Brian! Are you hurt?" she said, alarmed at the expression on his face.

"My foot, it's caught. I think it's broken."

Both Rebecca and Mary struggled to lift the heavy limb but found it impossible to move.

"I'll get the axe," said Mary, voice trembling.

"No, get the bow saw. The timber is too hard." The sweat poured from his brow from the unbearable pain.

Both Rebecca and Mary cut as quickly as they could, and when the branch finally parted they were alarmed to see Brian unconscious from the pain. It had been separated from the main trunk, but the weight of it still defeated them, so together they used another branch to lever the timber away from his body and quickly pulled him clear. Mary, her face pale, stroked his face until his eyes opened while Rebecca removed his boot and inspected his foot.

"You're right. I think it's broken. I'll make a splint while Mary goes for the wagon. We'll have to get you to the doctor."

"You always were careless," said Mary, tears running down her face. "You saved our lives."

"I should have been more careful in felling the tree." He grimaced as Rebecca tied the splint with his bootlace around his ankle.

"Look at it this way, Brian," said Rebecca. "Now you'll be forced to have a rest."

"With two pretty nurses, then maybe it won't be so bad."

"The man expects us to slave over him, Mary. Do we have news for him?"

The three of them laughed shakily. It was over five hours before they could reach Echuca where the doctor attended to Brian. Another week passed before Mary allowed him to get out of bed and hobble around on crutches.

CHAPTER TWENTY-TWO

Campbell rode into Echuca and noted its change from the time he had been there before. More buildings erected, and the population appeared to have grown even larger. He tethered his horse outside an inn and took a room for the night. A young pretty girl attended him, giving him a sly smile as she handed him his key. Campbell noted her interest and invited her for a drink.

"I have to work until six, Mr. McGregor, but I'd be pleased to accept your invitation then."

"Please, call me Campbell. Your name is…?"

"Ellen, Ellen Preston," she added seductively

"Then I'll see you at six, Ellen."

This was a chance to find out all he could about Corcoran, Campbell thought, and maybe enjoy himself at the same time. Ellen nodded coyly as he let his hand fall on hers for several seconds before pulling away.

He met her as arranged and surprised to see she had on what must have been her best dress. Her dark hair hung around her shoulders, and her slim figure appealed to Campbell. He hadn't had a woman in over two weeks.

After drinks, he invited her to dine with him, and she talked feverishly about all sorts of things, things he had no interest in at all. Still, he put up with her constant chatter in his bid to find out all he could about Corcoran.

"It's so public here, Ellen, perhaps we could go to my room and discuss more personal things."

"That would be nice."

As soon as they entered his room Campbell pulled her close and kissed her. When she returned his kiss his fingers went to her dress, and he pulled it down to expose her pert breasts.

"Oh, Campbell," she sighed as he lowered the rest of her clothing. "Please be gentle." He smirked. Her pretense of virginity was almost laughable.

He smiled confidently. "You are going to have the best time of your life," he said, his hands exploring her body. They were both naked, and it was plain she wasn't a virgin as she took him in what appeared to her experienced hand. In no time at all, they were in bed. The thrusting of their bodies revealed a lost passion he enjoyed. Her tongue delighted him, and he wondered if she had ever been a whore. She certainly knew how to make a man happy. After he took his pleasure he began to question her.

"I'm actually here in Echuca to find an old friend of mine. Perhaps you know him. His name is Brian Corcoran."

Ellen's eyebrows lifted. "Mr Corcoran? Why he's one of the councilors!"

"Then you know him?" Campbell acted casual as he lay back, still naked, her hand resting on his crotch.

"Not personally, but I have seen him. He has a big property out of town. He broke his foot some weeks ago, so he doesn't come to Echuca much now."

Broke his foot, thought Campbell. This could be easy. "Then who does all his business?"

"His wife, Mary."

Campbell grinned to himself. If Mary handled the business then it made things even easier. She would know what all the assets were.

"Then she must have a good knowledge of the business."

"I suppose so. She often comes in with her mother and children."

"Children?" He thought she had only one.

"Yes, she has three. I don't know much about them."

He leaned up on his elbows. "Why this is splendid news! Perhaps you could direct me to their property in the morning."

"All right. It's not hard to find," she said, resting on her elbow, her hand still holding him.

"But enough of old friends," he said and fondled her breasts once again. "We have hours before morning comes. Perhaps you can show me your talents once again. You have a very sensuous mouth."

She smiled and dropped her mouth to his groin. "You know how to make a girl happy, Campbell, I'm enjoying myself immensely."

"So am I," he said, lifting her head. He entered her again and slowly thrust deep inside her.

* * * * *

Sean saw him first. "There's a man coming on a horse," he said, and Rebecca looked out of the window. At first she didn't recognize him, but then froze. "Oh my God," she said softly as Campbell pulled up and alighted from his horse.

"Who is it, Mother?" asked Mary as Brian struggled to his feet, supporting himself on his crutches.

Rebecca's face went white. It was decision time for Mary. "I think you had better come and see."

Mary also looked out of the window and cried with delight when she laid eyes on him. He looked just as handsome as ever, dressed in smart clothes. Her heart raced.

"I'll let him in," said Rebecca soberly, and opened the door. She threw a glance at Brian who stood motionless on his crutches.

"Rebecca, how nice to see you again," smiled Campbell, but she knew it was a false greeting.

"Campbell," yelled Mary, rushing to him grasping his hands. "I just knew you'd come one day. I'm so glad to see you again." She stood back to admire him.

"You haven't changed a bit, Mary, just as beautiful as ever."

"Mother said you were in the gold fields and struck it rich."

Campbell looked at Rebecca and scowled, expecting to hear how he had murdered old Blaster Harry, but if Mary knew of the deed, she gave no indication.

He turned his attention back to Mary. "I did have some luck, but the claim petered out. I do have enough to support you, however."

Rebecca and Brian stood in the background, waiting to hear Mary's reply.

"This is my husband, Brian Corcoran," she said, ignoring his statement.

He gave Brian a sneer. "So I see, the man who stole you from me." He made no effort to greet Brian.

"Yes, but that was a long time ago now. Lots of things have happened since then."

Campbell took her hands in his. "So I hear. I understand this rogue raped you and gave you a child. He deserves to pay for that."

"It's true I have a child, but Brian has treated me fairly and has saved my life on at least two occasions. He's a good man."

He gave another sneer. "Don't make excuses for him, Mary. He bought you like a slave for a miserable fifty pounds."

She glanced across at Brian and Rebecca. "He had his reasons, even though I don't agree with them, but he has treated me kindly."

"But now that's ended. You must come away with me now, Mary, and be my wife."

"But I'm already married, and there's the children to care for."

Brian tottered on his crutch as he listened, his face dark and filled with despair. "You don't have to stay with me because of the children, Mary. I don't want you to go, but I'll not force you to stay against your will."

Campbell gave a small laugh. "There you are. Come with me, Mary, and leave him with his brats. We'll build another house bigger than this one and live far away from here." He looked in Brian's direction with a sneer on his face. This was going to work out well.

"They are not brats. They are good children." Then another question came to her. "And what about Mother?" She still held his hands, but her face filled with dismay.

"Rebecca can come and visit whenever she feels like it, provided she doesn't interfere with our lives."

"She's waited years to catch up with me. I'll not leave her."

He gave Rebecca an insolent look. "I can see she's poisoned your mind about me, just like she poisoned her husband. It would be better if she lived apart from us."

Mary looked stunned. Could this be her Campbell? This man who had no feelings for her children or her mother? "Campbell, how can you say that? She's part of me."

He lifted his lip in another sneer. "You know, of course, she stole four hundred pounds from me."

"It was the money you stole from me," snapped Rebecca.

"I earned it looking after you when you entertained all those timber cutters. They paid well for a whore."

Rebecca's face went blank as she looked sharply at Mary.

Mary slowly turned to her mother. "What does he mean, Mother?"

Rebecca's face told of her fear. "It was the only way I could find you. We were starving, and we needed money. I had no choice."

"She made a bloody fortune. Must have taken on one hundred and fifty of them over a week. They all said they were satisfied, too."

Campbell grinned as he looked at Rebecca. "She spent a few days on her back as they pumped her up. I can still hear the cries of pleasure from them."

Mary stared blankly at her not believing what he was saying. "Is this true, mother?"

"I had to, Mary. I had no other choice," Rebecca stammered.

"Don't judge your mother," said Brian calmly. "She's had a hard life and deserves your respect in the way she's cared for you. If she had to do that then it was only because she loved you."

Campbell put his hands on his hips and grinned at Rebecca again. "Then there was the brothel she opened in Bathurst."

"Brothel?" Mary's mouth dropped open.

Rebecca looked down, unable to meet Mary's eyes.

Campbell continued. "It was a mining town. The business was going well, but I insisted we go to look for you."

"Liar, you wanted to stay, but I had to find Mary," shouted Rebecca.

Campbell turned back to Mary. "Then she heard about the gold strike in Ballarat and made me go there and dig for gold. The moment we made a small strike, she robbed me of the money and left. Fortunately I found a seam and now have a small fortune, no thanks to her."

Rebecca stared in disbelief. "Don't listen to him, Mary. He lies. He tried to keep me from looking for you. He even wanted to have sex with me."

"Now why would I want to have sex with an old woman?"

he said with a smirk on his face.

Mary's face was ashen. She looked back and forth between her mother and the man she thought she had loved, unsure of who to believe.

Brian spoke once more. "This man would do or say anything to get you, Mary. Your mother would move heaven and earth to find you. I don't believe one word he says."

Campbell turned to Brian with a snarl on his face. "Shut your mouth, Corcoran. Mary's coming with me, and there's nothing you can do about it."

"That choice is hers," said Brian, still standing on one foot and resting on his crutch.

Campbell looked around the room and then smiled at Mary. "I must admit, it's a fine house and property you have, Mary."

"It's my husband's property, Campbell, not mine."

"But it would be yours if he died."

"He's not ill. He just has a broken foot, which will mend quickly."

Campbell touched his chin as if in deep thought. "But just suppose he did die. Then you would become the owner, free to marry me. We could work this property together."

Doubt swept over her. She didn't like the way this was going at all. If Brian died it would hurt her badly. What was Campbell talking about? "Brian deserves what he's got, and he is my husband."

"I think I can fix that," he said and pulled his revolver from his coat.

"Campbell! What are you doing?" Mary gasped.

He kept the gun trained on Brian who stood grim faced. "It's simple. He stole you and forced you to marry him after paying your stepfather good money. He's continually raped and beaten you. As a member of the Echuca Council, he was terrified this would get out and tried to kill me. I shot him dead. He'll get no sympathy from the good citizens of Echuca."

"You're going to kill him?" she said, not believing what he was saying.

"And what about me, Campbell?" asked Rebecca. "Are you going to kill me, too?"

He took a sideways glance at her. "I'm sure you wouldn't want people to know you've been a whore, and Mary certainly wouldn't want it to get out."

"No, Campbell. You can't do this." The truth about Campbell was beginning to dawn in Mary's mind.

"Can't I?" he said and fired straight at Brian. The bullet struck the older man in the shoulder, and he staggered back and fell against the wall, striking his head.

Mary screamed and threw herself across Brian's body. "You've killed him! You've killed him!" Her voice rang a high shrill.

"Step aside, Mary, and I'll finish him if he's not already dead." He raised his gun again.

"I can't marry you, Campbell, I just can't," she cried, not moving away from Brian's fallen figure.

"For heaven's sake, why not?" he said, scowling.

"I'm having another baby and—" She hesitated for a few seconds. "And I love him."

There was silence for a moment as Campbell took in her words. "You love this scum? You can't be serious."

"I am. Now get out! I never want to see you again." She stroked Brian's face gently with her hand, her tears gushing down her cheeks.

"You think I did all this for you to tell me to go? You'll marry me, and we'll work this property together."

"Never. I have a new baby coming, and I won't live with the man who killed its father." The anguish on her face enraged him.

"You're coming with me. I'll soon knock sense into you." Rebecca moved towards him, and he spun around, pointing the still smoking gun at her. "Another step and you'll be dead, too. Now out of our way." He grabbed Mary's hand and dragged her outside to where his horse stood tethered. Brian's horse stood alongside his as Sean had been riding it.

"Mount up," he snarled, pointing the gun at her.

Still sobbing Mary mounted Brian's horse. Campbell urged the horse forward leaving Rebecca, Sean and the children staring at them in shock.

"Where are you taking me?" Mary managed to ask.

"Down the road a bit. You are going to give me the favors you gave Corcoran. Then I might kill you like I killed him if you resist."

Her heart thumped against her chest. Campbell was going to rape her. This man she thought she loved was going to rape her. Her mother had been right. He was a man of evil.

* * * * *

As soon as they left, Rebecca ran to Brian. Blood was seeping from his shoulder and staining his shirt. She was afraid he was dead, but then noticed he breathed.

"Sean, get some cold water," she ordered the boy. Sean ran to the kitchen and returned with a bowl of water and a soft rag. Rebecca had placed a pillow under Brian's head, and gently dabbed his brow with the cold fluid.

He gave a groan and opened his eyes. He tried to sit up, but Rebecca pushed him back.

"Mary, where is she?" His voice stammered.

"Campbell took her only a few minutes ago. She thinks you're dead."

"I have to go to her." He tried to sit up again but fell back with a groan.

"You can't even sit up. I'll go and get her. You stay here with the children." If Campbell thought he was going to get away with this then he was mistaken.

"Sean, stay with your father," she ordered.

"No. I'm coming, too," he said. "I have to help save Mary."

Rebecca nodded. Sean had every right to help his mother. "Okay, let's go."

Sean stopped at the gun rack and took down the shotgun. Rebecca nodded her approval and both hurried to the barn to find the horses. There was no time for saddles and so they both rode bareback. They were soon on their way with Wolf running alongside them. He sniffed at the ground and leading them in the direction Campbell had taken Mary.

* * * * *

Campbell pulled up the horses in thick bush only a mile from the homestead.

"This will do," he said and pulled Mary from the horse. He threw her to the ground and stood over her, his gun in his holster and his hands on his hips.

"Last chance. Marry me or suffer the consequences."

She looked up at him with venom in her eyes. "Never. You can kill me, but I'll never marry you."

"Your choice. Lift your dress."

"No."

He reached down and placed his hand in her bodice and ripped it open revealing her breast. Then he held his hand on her throat and began squeezing.

"Looks like it has come to this, bitch." His other hand went up her dress, and he ripped her underwear from her body. She struggled, but his hand was squeezing the life from her.

"Shit," said Campbell, as Mary slumped forward. He wanted her awake when he did it. He wanted to look into her eyes and watch her squirm as he plunged into her. He released the pressure on her throat and waited until she woke up again. She still breathed so he knew she wasn't dead.

Mary opened her eyes, looked up at Campbell and struggled. He placed his foot on her throat and held her down, drawing his gun above her head.

"Now you're going to open your legs. Or I will kill you now."

"My baby. I'm going to have a baby," she cried out in anguish.

He took his foot from her throat and stood over her, holding the gun while he undid his breeches with his other hand. When he was exposed he sneered at her. "You've seen and felt it before. Enjoy."

Suddenly, his hand seemed to explode as the gun went flying away a millisecond before he heard the shot. Blood flew everywhere, and he stood looking at what was left of his hand. He turned and saw Sean pointing the shotgun at him.

Rebecca calmly walked over, picked up his weapon, and pointed it at him. She kept her eyes on him but spoke calmly to Mary.

"Did he rape you?"

Mary struggled to her feet and pulled her dress down. "He was about to."

"Then his hesitancy saved his life for I would have killed him if he had." She looked with contempt at Campbell.

Mary grabbed the shotgun from Sean's hand and pointed it at Campbell. "But he killed Brian! I'll kill him for that!"

Fear spread over Campbell's face as he looked at the barrel pointed at his head.

Rebecca's gaze softened. "Brian is not dead."

Mary's eyes brightened up. "He's alive?"

"Yes. Now, Campbell, get on your horse and never come back here. If you do then we will kill you. Is that clear?"

Still holding his shattered hand, Campbell whimpered and nodded. He awkwardly climbed onto his horse and rode off without looking back.

Rebecca dropped the handgun and took Mary in her arms. "Wipe those tears, child. Your husband is waiting for you."

They hurried to Brian's horse where Mary mounted, and they rode back at top pace with Wolf barking in the rear. Mary rushed inside to find Brian sitting in a chair, the children at his feet.

"Mary," he said, almost choking. "I thought I'd lost you. Are you all right?"

"Yes, but I'm afraid Campbell's not. Sean shot him in the hand before he could rape me. He may go to the police."

Brian smirked. "I don't think so. He'd have to explain how he got shot. He'll go to a doctor and tell them he accidentally shot himself."

"I love you, Brian. I never thought I'd say that, but it's true. When he shot you I thought my life had ended." She gave another sob and threw her arms around his neck, kissing him passionately.

He eased her away and looked into her eyes. "I love you, too, Mary. I have from the moment I met you." He savored the feel of her in his arm. "I love you dearly, but you're a very dangerous woman."

"Me? Dangerous?"

"Since I've met you, I've been nearly drowned, I've been speared, I've been beaten to a pulp, I've broken my foot, and now I've been shot. Do you have any more punishment in store?"

She gave a giggle. "Yes. I want to have at least three more children, and I want more loving attention than once a fortnight." She touched the end of his nose with a finger.

"You could be sorry you said that," he said, grinning through his pain. "But I'll do my best. I think I can manage that provided your mother is here to protect me."

"She's not going anywhere without me, and I'm definitely staying. I have three children to look after," she said, putting her other arm around Sean. "And another one to come."

"I love you, Mary McBride," he said, tears forming in his eyes.

"I don't know this Mary McBride. My name is Mary Corcoran," she replied, kissing him softly on the lips.

The End

About Bruce Cooke

I was born in Melbourne Australia but now live in country town Shepparton.

When I met my beautiful wife it was love at first sight, and we now have three wonderful kids who are grown up and have left the nest. In my youth I worked as a plumber, but after ten years I changed vocation to become a trade teacher in the Technical Division and TAFE. (Technical and Further Education). When promotion came we moved to country Victoria, and I wondered why anyone would want to live in a big city.

At first I had no passion for writing as my time was taken up with my family, career and sport, but when I took an early retirement after 29 years of teaching, the writing bug hit me. I always had an interest in Colonial Australia, particularly the gold rush days so I decided I would write a story about this time involving the outback. The saga of the era was like a narcotic because very little of the times are taught in the education department schools. I undertook several creative writing courses and developed a passion I couldn't control.

Stories and characters kept jumping into my head, and I began playing "what if". As soon as I finished one book I started another, hardly bothering to present it to publishers. I now have fifteen lying in the drawer. My thirst for writing was so strong, I also did a script writing course. An opportunity arose when I was asked to write the initial script for a musical based on the C.S. Lewis children's classic, *The Lion, The Witch and The Wardrobe.* The million-dollar production ran successfully in all the State Capital cities of Australia in 2004.

Printed in the United States
by Baker & Taylor Publisher Services